Dear Reader:

Thank you for picking up this copy of *Party Girl* by Pat Tucker. Pat is a phenomenal storyteller and she returns with a controversial topic within her home state of Texas—its Law of Parties. Under this law, a person can end up on Death Row simply by the company they keep.

We always hear about the consequences of guilt by association; many can relate to this experience. However, in Texas, it can be a deadly outcome for someone who is "innocent." Pat takes a look at Hope Donovan who accepts a ride from two thugs, and all are later pulled over following a deadly convenience store robbery. Hope has a lot at risk as she is married with children. Discover what transpires while she is incarcerated for the crime and how it affects her relationships with her husband, Brendon; and her family.

Pat offers another thought-provoking title, *Daddy by Default*, her Strebor Books debut novel, that examines the issue of paternity. Check out Pat's *Football Widows* about the activities of football coaches' wives while their husbands are hard at work and traveling to away games. No matter what the subject matter, Pat Tucker is a compelling writer and I am sure you will enjoy her work.

As always, thanks for supporting the authors that I publish under my imprint, Strebor Books. All of us truly appreciate your support. If you would like to contact me, please email me at Zane@eroticanoir.com.

Blessings,

Zane

Zane
Publisher
Strebor Books International
www.simonandschuster.com/streborbooks

PARTY GIRL

ALSO BY PAT TUCKER

Football Widows
Daddy by Default

Z ANE PRESENTS

PARTY
GIRL

A Novel

PAT TUCKER

SBI

STREBOR BOOKS

NEW YORK LONDON TORONTO SYDNEY

Strebor Books
P.O. Box 6505
Largo, MD 20792
http://www.streborbooks.com

ISBN 978-1-59309-402-7
ISBN 978-1-4516-5673-2 (e-book)
LCCN 2011938317

First Strebor Books trade paperback edition February 2012

Cover design: www.mariondesigns.com
Cover photograph: © Keith Saunders/Marion Designs

10 9 8 7 6 5 4 3 2 1

Manufactured in the United States of America

For information regarding special discounts for bulk purchases, please contact Simon & Schuster Special Sales at 1-866-506-1949 or business@simonandschuster.com

The Simon & Schuster Speakers Bureau can bring authors to your live event. For more information or to book an event, contact the Simon & Schuster Speakers Bureau at 1-866-248-3049 or visit our website at www.simonspeakers.com.

ACKNOWLEDGMENTS

Some things will always remain the same for me. I'd like to Thank God Almighty first and foremost. The greatest appreciation goes to my patient and wonderful mother, Deborah Tucker Bodden, my number one cheerleader; and sister, Denise Braxton; my brother-in-law, Tavares. Thanks to my stepfather, Herbert, for keeping my mom happy; and Lydell R. Wilson, thanks for your patience, love, and support.

I'd like to thank my handsome younger brother, Irvin Kelvin Seguro, and his fiancée, Amber; the two best uncles in the world, Robert and Vaughn Belzonie...Aunts Regina and Shelia...my older brother, Carlton Anthony Tucker; my nephews, nieces, and the rest of my entire supportive family.

We don't share the same blood, but I love them like sisters: Monica Hodge, Marilyn Glazier, LaShawanda Moore, Lee Lee Baines, LaKeisha Madison, Tameka Brown, Kevina Brown. My love and thanks to Tiffany A. Flowers, Keywanne Hawkins, Desiree Clement, Yolanda Jones and the rest of the most exquisite ladies of Sigma Gamma Rho Sorority Inc. and especially all of my sisters of Gamma Phi Sigma here in Houston, TX.

I'm blessed to be surrounded by friends who accept me just the way I am. ReShonda Tate Billingsley, thanks for your constant support, listening ear, and faith in my work; Victoria Christopher

Murray for being such a kind and giving person, and Nikki Turner.

Many, many thanks to Alisha Yvonne, Markisha Sampson, Lt. Col. Logan, my KPFT Family, Ron Reynolds, Marlo Blue, John Brewer, Luke Jones—you all make my days easier so that I can focus on writing at night!

Special thanks to my super agent, Sara, and a world of gratitude to my Strebor family; the dynamic duo Zane, and Charmaine, for having faith in my work. Special thanks to the publicity Queens: Adiya Mobley and Yona Deshommes for helping to spread the word about my work.

My deepest gratitude goes out to you, the reader! I'm so honored to have your support. There were so many book clubs that picked up Football Widows, and for that, I'm grateful. A special shout-out to some of them: The Bible of AFAM Lit: Black Expressions book club. Sisters are Reading Too (I think if I wrote an essay, they'd read it & I love them for that! They have been with me from Day One!!) Special thanks to Divas Read2, Happy Hour, Cush City-Girlfriends, Inc., Drama Queens, Mugna Suma, First Wives, Brand Nu Day, Go On Girl, TX 1, As the Page Turns, APOOO, Urban Reviews, Ella Curry and so many more!

Also huge thanks to all of the media outlets that welcomed me on the airwaves to discuss my work: "Inside Her Story" with Jacque Reed on the "Tom Joyner Morning Show," Yahoo Shine, Hello Beautiful, Essence.com, the Huffington Post—Fictiondb, Houston Chronicle—Guest Blog, Junebugg Blog, Onnix Blog, Author Tuesday's presents, Northparan.com, The Book Depository.com, Black Pearls Magazine, S&S Tipsonlifeandlove.com, nextreads.com, The Dallas Morning News.com, Interview—KFDM-CBS Beaumont, TX, 3 Chicks on Lit, Clear Channel Radio News & Comm. Affairs, KIX-96 FM, KARK-TV Little Rock, AR-KPRC NBC, Houston Beyond Headlines, Artist First radio show, The Mother Love Radio Show, It's Well Blog Talk Radio March 7th.

If I forgot anyone, charge it to my head and not my heart. As always, please drop me a line at rekcutp@hotmail.com or sylkkep@yahoo.com. I'd love to hear from you.

Warmly,

Pat

When I heard about Texas' Law of Parties,
I thought there was a mistake...
then I learned of the many people
who were convicted and condemned for crimes
they didn't commit and I was floored!

PROLOGUE
HOPE

When the car fluttered, and seemed to be making a clunking sound, the next thing I knew, I was pulling over. My heart was racing.

"Uh-oh!"

As I steered the car off to the side of the road, I bit down on my bottom lip. I allowed it to decelerate before I brought it to a complete stop. By the time I jumped out, the car had started smoking. I didn't know if the thing was gonna blow or not.

"Dammit! Now what?" I sighed.

I glanced around in both directions and could barely see a few feet in front of me. The hiss from the engine had me completely spooked. It was pitch-black outside and besides the sounds from the engine, the only other sounds I heard for miles were crickets and grasshoppers. What little I could see was only visible because I didn't turn off the headlights.

I shivered from the cool February night air, but trembled at the thought of becoming road kill. Here I was on a deserted, two-lane road out in the middle of nowhere!

Since I had to get Mona there before eight, it was already dark and I didn't feel good about being out here all alone. I wasn't sure if I should try to walk back toward Hempstead, where I thought I remembered a convenience store, or take my chances and walk up toward Prairie View University.

In the hour or so that I'd been trying to make up my mind, only two cars had passed along on Highway 290. During that time, I tried to flag them down with no luck and I was trying to see if the car might cool off. When it didn't, I was more than pissed. Brendon would be fussing by the time I finally made it home. Whenever he was home alone with all three kids, he acted like he forgot how to father.

Suddenly what looked like a familiar car came swooshing past me. I shook thoughts from my mind; no way that was who I thought it was. I had only been stranded for a little more than an hour and I was already getting delusional. Only in my dreams would someone I know be way out here just when I needed them.

I looked back at the car that was still smoking and decided to leave it. Since it hadn't exploded, I walked back over, removed the key from the ignition, and put it near the middle console.

"Oh, well, guess I'll send a wrecker for it when I make it to the university."

I flung my purse over my left shoulder and started walking toward Prairie View University. With my luck, I'd make it before sunup the next day.

Less than twenty minutes later, the candy-apple 1964 Chevy Impala on spinners that first zoomed by going east was now headed west and slowing as it pulled up alongside me.

"Q, that you? What you doing way out here?" I asked, feeling so happy I could kiss him. For the first time since the breakdown, my night didn't seem as bleak.

"Whassup, Ma?" Quenton said.

Quenton Tolland and I went to Yates High School together. He had been up to no good since he could walk and talk, but at this very moment, I was so glad to see him and his sidekick, Trey,

I didn't know what to do. It's not like I was about to marry the guy. I needed a ride, and he had wheels.

"Looks like you need a lift," Q said.

"Do I! Mona's car broke down on me a few miles back. Did you know it was me when you passed the first time?" I asked.

Trey looked uneasy, but I never liked him anyway, and I suspected he didn't care for me too much either. Knowing him, he probably tried to talk Quenton out of turning around and coming back for me.

"Girl, I'd know you anywhere," Q joked.

I really didn't care whether he realized it was me or some chick he was about to try and pick up. I was simply glad he turned around.

"Believe me, playboy…this ain't the business," Trey said with his creepy-looking self.

"Aw, dawg, chill. Hope is the homegirl from the neighborhood," Q said. He turned back to me. "C'mon, hop in; we kinda in a hurry."

"Well, I'm real glad you stopped then. What's the hurry, and what y'all doing way out here anyway?" I asked.

"Whassup with all these damn questions; you working with the Feds or what?" Trey asked. He looked at me like I'd stolen something from him.

Trey, whose last name I didn't care to know, had big, dark eyes that made him look like he was always surprised. Other than that, his face never had any expression. He was chubby with fat cheeks and had a massive scar that ran from his left ear to the edge of his mouth. It looked like he was on the losing end of one too many knife fights.

I ignored Trey and quickly shuffled into the backseat of Q's car. I was glad they'd come along when they did.

"So Q, how's your mom and your sister?"

Quenton was cute. He was small, but growing up he was known for his quick temper and being short on patience; most times if he had trouble, it was because he started it.

"The fam's good." Right when he was about to turn the radio back up, three police cruisers whizzed by with their strobe lights flashing and sirens blaring.

"Dang, where's the fire?" I looked at the cars through the back window. "I'm glad we're going away from the drama; whatever's going on."

I turned my head in time to see Trey exchange an odd look with Quenton, but that was none of my business. I figured Trey was probably still salty about them turning back for me.

"Yo, Hope, what's up with your girl Stacy? Why she act like she all too good and shit?" Trey said.

I started to ignore him, but didn't want to start anything after they'd helped me out with a ride. I wanted to say, "*Really*, Trey, are you serious?"

"Stacy's married," I replied instead.

Two more cruisers swooshed past us. I noticed Q's eyes glance up to the rearview mirror, and it looked like he watched until the cruisers were only taillights and strobe lights in the dark night.

At that moment, my purse toppled over and most of my stuff spilled onto the floor. "Dammit!"

"What?" It was Q.

"No biggie; my stuff spilled out of my purse." I quickly started feeling around on the floor of the car. I found my compact, my tube of lip balm, and the dead cell phone. I tossed them back into my purse, then felt around for the rest of my stuff.

"Oouch! What the hell is that?" I pulled my fingers to my mouth.

"Whassup?" Q asked.

"I don't know. What's under your seat, Trey? Something burned the heck out of my fingers." I tried to examine my fingers, then sucked them again for relief.

Trey looked at Q and Q looked at me in the rearview mirror, but neither one said anything.

I went back to examining my fingers when suddenly Trey's next words snapped my eyes onto the road ahead.

"Damn, dawg, what the fuck!"

My body jerked forward violently when Q unexpectedly stepped on the brakes. The tires screeched and it felt like we skidded to an abrupt stop. I didn't know what was going on, but it didn't look good.

Suddenly, my heart felt like it was also about to stop. I struggled to catch my breath while staring ahead with wide, worried eyes. There were at least three police cruisers blocking the road with their strobe lights on. If that wasn't enough, officers stood behind open doors with their guns drawn and pointed directly at Q's car.

The very car, I was riding in!

"Q, wh-what in the world is going on?"

"Shut the fuck up!" Trey turned and hollered at me. He had a menacing expression on his face. All of a sudden he bent down and started to reach under his seat.

Q held his arm out and stopped him. "Nah, big homie, just chill!"

"I told yo' ass we ain't had no business turning around for this chickenhead; now what?" He was fired up and I was confused.

"Who you calling a chickenhead?"

Now sirens were blaring from behind. One quick turn and the strobe lights were so bright it no longer looked like night outside. That's when I realized how crucial the situation was, and I was petrified.

I swallowed the massive lump in my dry throat. My heart felt like it was about to give out on me, and my body went from dry to drenching wet with sweat in no time.

Suddenly, I got the eerie feeling that maybe I should've taken my chances alone on the side of the dark, rural road. There was no way for me to know how much of a grave mistake accepting that ride would turn out to be.

TWO
FIVE YEARS LATER — HOPE

T he sound of keys dangling at the door startled me. I jumped and started scrambling for cover. I was trying to get dressed, but before I could finish, the door flew open. Well, as much as a massive door of bars could fly. Still, it seemed like it all happened so fast. I already anticipated a messed-up day, considering it was February 12th, the sixth anniversary of Raakin Binnaz Senior's death.

"What the hell?" I looked over my shoulder at the two male guards who were now standing in the doorway.

I wasn't sure what had gone down, but I hadn't done a thing, and I wasn't in the mood for any drama. I was so sick and tired of them pulling rank for every little infraction.

"Donovan, move out!" Captain Eric Johnson's voice was cold and void of any emotion; nasty as usual. He got on my last damn nerve. I rolled my eyes. Here we go!

"Uh, hold up a sec; I'm still trying to get dressed." I always gave him major attitude. Every damn day he was on the job, he acted like he was trying to win employee of the month! He was always putting all kinds of extras on it.

"Donovan, move out now!" he demanded. Captain Johnson was big and burly. I was of no threat to him whatsoever, but you couldn't tell by the way he was yelling and carrying on.

I was confused. Here I was in nothing more than my bra and panties, and this C.O. was telling me to get out? And why the hell were they even in here? Why wasn't a female correctional officer with him anyway?

"You need to move; we not gon' say it again. Drop your things and move out!" Captain Johnson repeated.

This time he had his hand on his baton, like if I didn't follow instructions, he'd be talking with action instead of words. I was pissed, but I didn't need any infractions.

I dropped the shirt I was struggling to put on, and assumed the position. I stood with my face toward the wall and placed my hands on top of my head. I was so vexed.

This is bullshit!

Soon my right arm was grabbed, yanked down hard, and a cold steel cuff was clamped around my wrist; then he did the same with my left arm. I winced in pain, but these bastards didn't care.

"Damn, you ain't gotta be so rough," I said.

As I was led out of the cell with a little shove, I saw the other women, also half-naked, being steered into the multipurpose area.

"From here on forward, y'all will be brought out in your panties and bras to get dressed."

My eyes got wide as Captain Johnson continued yelling. I was confused, but trying to understand what had brought this on. He must've bumped his head on one of those steel doors.

"Once out here, y'all can move over to the right corner of the multipurpose room and put your clothes on over there." He motioned with his head.

The other inmates were snickering and complaining under their breath, but I wasn't about to take this shit quietly.

"Captain Johnson," I said as calmly as I could.

He eyeballed me but didn't say anything.

"What exactly is the reason for all of this?" I struggled to remove the twist from my neck.

"Donovan! That's the new policy and procedure for segregated offenders!" he yelled.

I looked at him like he had to be kidding.

"So we can't get dressed in our cells anymore?"

"Like I said, new policy and procedures for segregated offenders," he repeated.

How could this be? It had to be a constitutional violation. There was no reason in the world why we should have been treated in such an inhumane way; really what was next, organized rapes? That had to be the next step if we were now gonna be paraded around the facility in our panties and bras. Most of the correctional officers were women, but there were a number of men, too. I didn't understand why they didn't have the female C.O.'s handling this so-called new procedure. It was like we were putting on a peepshow.

"If you ask me, this is a sick, sadistic, male fantasy of sado-masochism put into play 'cause administration realizes they got the so-called *power* to do what the hell they want," Pauline Brown said.

She was a handsome woman who was there for killing her ex-husband, his mother, and one of his sisters. Pauline was big and nearly more muscular than the two guards who were harassing us. She sported a very short hairstyle that was always neat.

"Zip it, Brown," Captain Johnson said in her direction. "Ain't nobody asked you nothing!"

He picked his speech back up again.

"Only female officers will be stripping and escorting you; male officers will be asked to step aside so they can't see you," Johnson had the nerve to say like *that* was gonna make all of the nonsense okay.

"You think we any safer with some of these *female* officers? Shoot, they just as perverted as you male officers," Evelyn Philips said.

Evelyn had the face of the stay-at-home mom next door. She was a petite little soccer mom type who was locked up for killing her three kids to be with a man who wanted her but didn't want any kids.

"Umph, I wanna know what man can't look at a woman, knowing she'll be in her panties and bra and handcuffs, too? This has got to be a direct violation of our constitutional rights, not only as prisoners, but as women who are trapped in a system of where male egos and secret exotic power trips are going on," Pauline said.

"This is so uncalled for, and it can't be justified at all," I added.

I stood outside and waited like I was instructed to do. Even though I didn't say anything else, I was pissed. It was bad enough we'd been forced into those small cells in the old decrepit building. The Mountain View was one of the oldest in the Texas Department of Criminal Justice System. As if the old building wasn't bad enough. The rules seemed inconsistent, some inmates got only one hour of recreation a day.

And on the real, they scheduled that so early in the morning that no one wanted to go. We only got one hour of TV five days a week. One way to get around that was to get a job, so most of us worked.

We were also being strip searched six, sometimes ten, times a day, and most of the time we had never left our cells from one search to another. So why all the strip searches; especially if I ain't been nowhere but in that tiny-ass cell?

Then, they went through our property with no care whatsoever. By the time they were done, our property was left all over our cells. Didn't have anything with any kind of sentimental value, 'cause they were gonna trample all over it, trash it, and dare you to say something about it. We were inmates, but damn, they treated us like animals instead of human beings.

Okay, I get it, we were on Death Row. Death Row inmates are separated from general population, supposedly so they can maintain safety, security, and order among general population offenders and correctional personnel.

But how much sense does it make that *we*, who were all death row inmates, had been there together for years, but we couldn't even talk to each other?

It they had their way, we'd sit behind bars, in tiny cells, twenty-four hours a day for years, alone, and not talk to *anyone?* Maybe they hoped we'd go crazy up in the place. And if anybody had a reason to go crazy on the row, please believe, *yours truly* was that person. There were less than a dozen females on death row in Texas, and while I couldn't speak for the rest of them, I could tell you without the least bit of hesitation that I, Hope Dawn Jenay Donovan, was innocent and was wrongly convicted and condemned.

People always say everybody in prison claims innocence, but I can do more than *claim* it. I had done nothing, well, nothing unless you count being in the wrong place at the wrong time. Now because three people lied on me, I was set to get the ultimate punishment for a crime that I didn't even commit.

THREE
ADENA

"*Your* Bible says an eye for an eye!"

I was so angry now. I hated when this day came around each year. The press seemed to never forget. They found me on other days, too, but on this particular day, on February 12th, they seemed to hunt me down, and I couldn't hide even if I wanted to.

"Mrs. Binnaz, but what about those who say putting her to death won't bring your husband back? What about those who say this is nothing but meaningless revenge?"

I didn't know if I should look into the camera or at her. I chose to look at her, this young reporter who I welcomed into my home. I understood how they worked; I had lots of experience with the media. They asked emotionally charged questions on purpose. They knew when they came to me, I would speak my mind with passion. I gave them the sound bites they wanted. I'd learned the importance of saying what was necessary for *must-see* TV.

They understood that my heart was still filled with raw unadulterated hatred, and I wasn't afraid to say so, so, I figured that was why they kept my number in their Rolodex.

"They don't know my pain." I choked back bitter tears and sighed.

"Those people, the ones who judge me because I want to see this woman pay, they don't understand what I've been through. My husband was a hard-working man. We came to this country to flee violence and my husband was gunned down like a rabid animal for a mere two-hundred fifty dollars? My children are fatherless." I leaned back and cleared my throat. "Yes, those people, the ones who judge me, you tell them to explain to my two children why their father will never come home again. You tell them to hear my children's cries late at night when they think I'm sleeping, but I, too, am muffling my own cries."

"But what about rehabilitation?" she asked.

Now I knew for certain she was only trying to get a rise out of me. My record regarding rehabilitation in the Texas Department of Criminal Justice System was well known. Each year they asked the same questions and I gave the same answers, but still they came.

My eyes narrowed and I pursed my lips. I felt the fiery burning in the pit of my belly and my ears started to sizzle with heat.

"The Texas Department of Criminal Justice is a broken system. We pay for the underbelly of society to get a warm meal three times a day; they're housed and treated humanely with rights for *their* protection, but what about their victims? I say you punish these criminals the very way they punished my husband and other innocent victims; it would be a lot cheaper," I said.

"So you will be there, to witness the execution?"

"I will be there if I have to walk through the flames of hell on bare feet. On that glorious day, my husband's death and that of those other two innocent victims will be avenged!"

"You said avenged?" she asked.

"I said and I mean avenged!"

Two years after my husband Raakin Binnaz's senseless murder, I began a group for other crime victims. If it hadn't been for True Justice, I would've crumbled, crawled into my husband's casket and died right alongside him. Sure, I needed to be strong for my children, but I felt weak. I wanted to die, but with the help of others who had known my pain, who thirsted for the same blood I lusted for, I was able to rise from sure and sudden death. Now, my mission was to see that the state of Texas continued to carry out the ultimate punishment for the worst of the worst, and give them a taste of their own medicine.

After the interview the reporter smiled and thanked me for once again welcoming her into my home.

When the cameraman turned off the camera, I expected her to say something more, but what she said made me want to spit in her face.

"I figured you'd have a change of heart by now. She's a mother with three kids," she said matter-of-factly, like that was supposed to make a difference.

I studied her expression in hopes that she would recognize mine. I assumed it must've dawned on her that I was gazing at her in bewilderment, and when it did, she retreated a bit. But her regret was too late.

"My husband, Raakin Senior, was a father of two. He was a proud, hard-working man who came to this country with nothing more than the clothes on his back and a few dollars in his pocket. Together, we worked hard and built a thriving business. We never begged, we never stole, we worked hard for everything and we obeyed all the laws of this land. Now you tell me why should *she* be given any special treatment, simply because she spawned children who were of no concern to her when she committed this crime?"

Little Ms. Barbara Walters wannabe didn't have an answer for that. She stared at me blankly and continued to roll up the cord to her microphone.

I smiled sweetly. "I'll be there on that glorious day, front and center. But in the meantime, while I count down the days, they can hold every vigil, plaster the airwaves with nurturing family pictures of her, and write petitions and appeals until their fingers bleed. But deep down, her supporters, they know like I know, the state of Texas leads the country in carrying out executions and I'm proud to say I wouldn't change a thing about our state's record."

She was still rolling the cord, but much slower now.

"Yes, every day I pray to Allah for strength, that I will remain healthy, and I will be present front and center, with a huge grin across my face when her day of reckoning finally comes to fruition."

FOUR
BRENDON

I was more than a little nervous, sitting there burning up under the warm lights. Dave Atwood, the founder of the Texas Coalition to Abolish the Death Penalty, sat on to the right of me. I'd met this retired oil company engineer turned tireless activist during Hope's trial. By then he had been on a fifteen-year odyssey to end the death penalty here in Texas.

As I listened and waited for my turn to speak, my thoughts were all over the place. I never liked the idea of being on TV, or talking to those newspaper reporters, but it's what I had to do to try and save Hope's life.

"So once again the eyes of the world are focused squarely on Texas," the host said.

I was one of three guests on the TV show *Watching Executions*. The host, Pascal Edwardo, reminded me of that guy Geraldo Rivera, only a younger version. He had the thick mustache, the wavy hair, and he was dressed real sharp. But he was a small man.

"The Texas Law of Parties gained national prominence in 2007 during the high-profile case of Kenneth Foster, Junior, whose death sentence was eventually commuted by Governor Rick Perry following a national grassroots movement to halt his execution. That's the same kind of movement supporters of twenty-nine-year-old Hope Donovan are trying to once again ignite."

I watched as he suddenly stopped talking, and gave the camera a hardened look. Oh, these TV people! Pascal angled his petite body a little to the left, looked into the camera dramatically, then suddenly turned to look at me.

"Joining us live in the studio is Brendon Donovan, Hope's husband. Mister Donovan, thanks for joining us."

He did another dramatic pause, and I wasn't sure whether to say something or wait. So I waited for him to ask a question. When his eyes bugged a bit, I realized I needed to say something. "Ah, yes, thank you for having me."

"Your wife, Hope Donovan, a mother of three children, is scheduled to die by lethal execution for a crime you both say she did not commit. How is the family coping?"

I shifted in my seat and tried to remember that speaking out helped Hope's case. Keeping it in the media was the best way to make sure people didn't forget about her and what we were trying to do. I had already organized my thoughts. Mona was sitting off to the side, eyeing me like she was ready to jump in if I needed help.

"Well, Pascal, it ain't been easy; it's been a real challenge, but this is nothing new for us. We've been dealing with this nightmare for more than five years now. We're broke, and despite what you hear, there's no real justice for the poor. I guess I want people to know that just like this happened to Hope, it can happen to you, too! The bottom line is, Hope ain't no killer, she didn't commit this crime and we've been fighting to change this very unfair and controversial law that's got her on death row. During the trial, we were up against a DA who built a case on lies. He even found so-called witnesses and got Trey to lie on Hope. We've been trying to bring the truth out but we ain't had no success."

"Yes, Hope's case is one of those that really brings this unfair and unjust law into view. She sits on death row while her two co-conspirators, including the trigger man, received life without parole. We've been following it from the very beginning; her arrest, the stunning trial, and the unconscionable death sentence. All of it certainly has brought the Law of Parties under the microscope once again."

"Yeah, it has Pascal, but ain't nothing being done about it! During Hope's trial, we had one character witness after another, all talking about how Hope wasn't part of this gang of bandits like the DA said. Sure, she made some mistakes in her past, we all have, but linking petty arrests for shoplifting and traffic tickets to murder is a complete out-of-this-world jump." I swallowed back the bile that always threatened to come up when I talked about this, and took a deep breath. The last thing I wanted to do was crumble right there on TV.

"I hate that those people lost their lives, but how do you condemn a woman when all she did was accept a ride from someone she *thought* she knew? She didn't have no idea they'd killed those people when she got into that car. She didn't pull the trigger. How is it that the two robbers get away with their lives and she's the only one facing the death penalty?"

Suddenly Pascal turned to the camera, paused again, then said, "That and so much is what's wrong with this law. In Hope's case, the first to wheel and deal with the DA walked away literally with life." He shook his head solemnly, then stopped, and spoke into the camera. "We'll be right back, for more with Brendon Donovan. His wife, Hope, sits on death row, they say, for a crime she did not commit. We'll tell you how you can help!"

The red light on the cameras and above the massive door went out.

Pascal sighed, then turned to me and the other guests. Dave

Atwood patted my shoulder a couple of times. To my left were Kathryn Kase and Carrie Jones from the Defender's Services, another agency that had been real helpful with Hope's case. Both Dave's and the other group were advocates for inmates and abolitionists leading the charge to get rid of the death penalty.

"We'll talk about the upcoming rally next, but we also want to talk to John Brewer; he's the reporter who talked with Hope and a few others about this law."

A few minutes later we were back on. I never knew whether these things helped. In the beginning we thought for sure once people found out about the Law of Parties and how innocent people could get the death penalty simply by association, there would be sheer pandemonium in the streets.

But that never happened. It seemed as if people were only concerned about the death penalty if it hit close to home. Otherwise, they went about their daily lives while those of us in the struggle, continued to struggle.

I sat quietly as Dave talked more about Hope's case and a few others like hers. He also talked about the upcoming rally against the Law of Parties and extended an invitation for the public to join us. We were going to march to one of our state lawmaker's offices and hold a peaceful sit-in until he came to talk to us.

These appearances made me feel like a real loser. Yeah, it kept Hope's case out there in the public and afterward, we always saw a spike in traffic on the website, but in the end, nothing ever really changed. She was still there and we were still living without her.

The show wrapped up and Mona and I stood around talking to Dave, Carrie, and Kathryn for a few minutes.

"You did real good," Mona said to me.

I shrugged it off. Who knew if these interviews helped at all? When we walked out to the parking lot, I couldn't believe my eyes!

FIVE
CHASTITY

"I don't understand. You spend more time raising his damn kids! Umph, it's a good thing you ain't got none of your own; the shit don't make no sense!"

Trevor Oliver stood over me like a raging bull ready to charge. His chiseled chest was heaving, his nostrils were flaring and he looked like he was about to explode. When he was mad, his yellow complexion turned to a bright crimson color quicker than the speed of light.

Trevor was an average-looking man, but he had a really nice body and he was really charismatic, when he wasn't flying off the handle over something or another.

"You're putting all kinds of extra on it," I said.

But it was true to a certain extent. Hope's kids needed my love more than Trevor. They'd been through so much, but Trevor wasn't trying to hear it.

Trevor and I had had a turbulent on-again, off-again relationship since our high school years. You could say he was my first true love. We didn't get along well, but couldn't stay away from each other, no matter how hard we tried.

After high school, he went away to Baylor University on a football scholarship, blew out his knee, then came back home with his college girlfriend and a kid. I never fully got over that.

To me, it was the ultimate betrayal. But despite that, somehow we managed to squeeze two pregnancies in before he actually married Felicia. I lost both babies, but Trevor kept dangling the carrot of us being a family because he knew it was the one thing that had eluded me. I recognized the game he was playing.

But still to this day, I had trouble saying no to him, which always got me in trouble. Hope used to always throw it in my face that, when it came to Trevor, I was wasting my time chasing after a man who clearly didn't want me. And then there were the rumors, but I didn't know what to believe; all I knew was she despised him. Needless to say, he wasn't a fan of hers either and I suspected that's why he really had an issue with me taking care of her kids. That and the fact that it meant less of my attention was focused solely on him.

Trevor's name was added to the list of neighborhood friends who seemed to dip in and out of our lives over the years. He and Felicia divorced not even two years after they were married, and once he turned on his charm, I was pulled right back in.

"I made a promise to my mother and I'll never go back on my word."

"So, my woman goes running every time this fool calls? How's that supposed to make me feel?" he asked.

I wondered when did I become *his* woman again, but didn't ask because I didn't want to ruin the mood. And I also couldn't remember when he'd grown to dislike Brendon so much. They weren't exactly buddies back in the day, but I always thought there was a mutual respect between the two.

"You know it's not like that," I said softly. Anytime Trevor got heated, I would talk to him in a real calm and low voice. It never did much to stop his tirade, but sometimes he'd lower his voice a little.

"Coulda' fooled me. Why did you have to be the one to handle her kids; where's Mona's ass? And what about Jackie, Stacy, or even Betty Jean? Weren't all of them her so-called homegirls, too? I don't see why everything has to fall on your shoulders," he said.

Just the mention of their names took me back. Out of all of Hope's friends, Betty Jean Watson was something else. She was certainly everything we were not. She was confident, outspoken and driven. From the moment Hope was convicted, Betty Jean made it very clear that she wanted Brendon and would do whatever it took to win him over. For a moment there, it looked like she was right on target.

"So what's she gonna do now? I hate what happened to her, even though we were never the best of friends," Betty Jean had said. "I told Brendon long ago, that he was wasting his time with her." That was days after Hope was sentenced to the death penalty.

Betty Jean could've fooled me, since when were she and Hope not the best of friends? I thought she, Hope, and Stacy were as thick as thieves, but whatever.

"I'm gonna give him time to get over her," Betty Jean had joked, "but I won't wait forever before I make my move."

But like many others who swore they'd hang around, Betty Jean was gone a year after Hope was sentenced to death. I figured the competition looked too tough for her; there were so many others. There was Jackie Smith from church who wanted to do whatever she could to *help* with the kids. It was downright strange what happened to her.

Then, there was Tamera Bradshaw who owned a neighborhood beauty shop and thought she was exactly what Brendon needed to help him get over Hope.

But the one who surprised me the most had to be Stacy Howard. In the beginning, she was nice enough, bringing a bunch of dishes over to the house. Her daughter and Breanna went to the same school and were best friends so it was only natural that she was a close family friend.

Stacy and her husband lived across the street from Hope and Brendon, but being married didn't stop her from giving him the eye when she thought no one else was watching. I noticed, but figured there was no harm because she was married.

When her marriage broke up a year or so ago, Stacy knew no shame. She was pretty enough, her auburn-and-blonde-streaked hair really set off her pretty features. She had a nice shape and seemed to take good care of herself. I'd come over at times to find her lounging in some skanky outfit, or she'd pop up and invite herself into whatever was going on.

Imagine my surprise when the doorbell rang one afternoon and I pulled the door open to find her standing there. I hated when Stacy popped up at the house, but what could I say? I was simply the hired help who was volunteering. I was trying to make dinner before the kids got out of school and before Brendon made it home.

"Hey, Chastity, you still around? Uh, I mean, is Brendon here? I saw his car in the driveway and wanted to bring this cake I baked over for him and the kids."

All the while she's talking to me, her eyes were searching beyond me and into the house. I was tripping because there was a big price tag that said the cake came from Kroger's bakery and not her oven. But I didn't say a word.

"He's not here," I said, my eyes moving from the cake to hers. "He left his car here; something's wrong with it."

I may as well have said, "He'll be right back." Stacy gently eased herself past me and strolled into the house like she was invited to come in and wait.

"You know when his shift is over?" she asked.

"No, not sure; he's been working overtime lately."

"Oh, well, I'll put this in the kitchen…mmmm, what's that you making? Sure smells good."

I sighed, closed the door, then turned to follow her into the kitchen. I was fixing catfish, red beans and rice, and green beans.

Before I realized what was happening, Stacy and I were sitting across from each other at the dinner table, like old friends playing catch-up. The small talk didn't last long before Stacy jumped into what she really had come to drill me about.

"So Chastity, who's been over here kicking it with Brendon? I ain't gotta worry about you 'cause of Trevor and all, but I kinda wanna know what I'm really up against."

She was smiling like we were close girlfriends sharing some good gossip; only we weren't.

"Uh, I don't get in his business like that; his wife is on death row, for God's sake, Stacy!"

"Yeah, yeah, but come on, Chastity; it's not like Hope just up and left. She's been gone for years now, and I'm wondering 'cause ain't no way in hell a man as fine as Brendon is sleeping alone at night," Stacy said. Suddenly, she looked at me skeptically, then frowned. "Wait a sec, don't tell me it's been you," she balked. Her eyes widened.

"No!" I said. "You know I take care of the kids but why are you going there?" I asked, irritated.

"I know, I know, and yeah, you and Hope ain't never been able to stand each other, but you probably telling the truth. We all know Trevor would kill both you and Brendon if some shit like that went down," she stated casually.

"Seriously!"

I hated that everyone knew my truth. But, mainly, the last thing I wanted was for Stacy to go running her mouth, spreading rumors about me sleeping with Hope's husband. She was right about one thing; Trevor would completely lose it, so I needed to cut her off before she got that started.

I looked into her light brown eyes. As quickly as they appeared, all thoughts about me and Brendon seemed to have vanished. Stacy leaned in closer, her full breasts all but jumping out of the small tank top she was wearing.

"So, Chastity, tell me, what does he like? You've been taking care of him and the kids for years now. What kind of woman does he want?"

"I don't know!" I frowned like she had offended me.

"C'mon! If anybody knows, it would be you. Do you even still have your apartment? You're over here so much; you still do that billing and coding stuff from home, right? I thought you had moved in. You can't tell me you haven't seen or heard anything." She jumped up. "Oooh wee, girl, I need to pee." She wiggled her hips doing the bathroom dance just as the phone rang.

"You know where it is," I said.

Stacy nodded, then took off down the hall.

I was searching for a pen to take information from the caller for Mona when I realized Stacy was still in the bathroom. I rushed the call so I could see what she was doing.

As I suspected, she didn't use the guest bathroom in the hall, but had snuck into the bathroom in Brendon's bedroom. I crept up on her and watched from the bedroom.

My mouth was hanging open when I watched her carefully pick hairs from Brendon's brush. She sprinkled a few into a snack-sized plastic baggie. Then she opened the medicine cabinet and removed his toothbrush. Stacy opened his hamper and took out a pair of his briefs.

Eeeww, I thought. What the hell did she want with the man's dirty drawers?

She looked around a bit longer, opening drawers, and rummaging through them. I watched as she leaned over and flushed the toilet.

That's when I ran back into the kitchen and grabbed the receiver from the wall.

"Okay, thank you, I'll make sure she gets the message," I said.

Stacy eased back into her chair and put her purse down.

"So, where were we?" she asked.

"Actually we were done," I said.

She smiled.

My beans were boiling and the rice was simmering, so there was really nothing else that needed my attention at the moment, but still, I didn't want to have this conversation with Stacy.

I was about to excuse myself from her and the conversation until she dramatically reached across the table and grabbed my hands. Stacy closed her eyes, and took a deep breath. She exhaled. "Giirrrl, there's something I've been wanting to share with you for a while now."

If I wasn't mistaken, I thought I noticed her eyes misting a bit. It was nothing less than shocking to see the way these women threw themselves at Brendon. The real sad part was that many of them were women both Hope and I had known most of our lives.

"Are you…is everything okay?" I asked.

"Well, I didn't want to say anything and I shouldn't be telling you this, but Brendon and I have been…"

My eyes locked with hers. Instinctively, I pulled my hands back, even though I didn't intend to.

She released another dramatic sigh.

"Are you telling me what I think—"

Stacy shushed me, even trying to place a finger over my lips.

I pulled beyond her reach and frowned. I didn't want her nasty hands on my face. My mind couldn't stop wondering why she had been collecting Brendon's personal things, but I didn't say anything.

"See, that's why I didn't want to say anything. Deep down inside, there's still a part of you that cares about Hope, even after what she did to you, but I also thought it was about time I start trying to bond with you."

"Really? And why's that?"

What hadn't *Hope done to me?*

"Well, you're so good with the kids, Brendon and I felt like there was no point in ripping yet another person from them so, naturally, when we do make it official and get together, publicly we'd have to work something out where you can still be a major influence in their lives. You know how close Breanna and McKenzie are anyway," she said.

My heart slammed against my ribcage and I could barely fight the overwhelming urge to reach across the table and strangle Stacy.

She and Brendon? Could it be?

Could she and Brendon really have been together all this time? Here I thought he was suffering in silence. A man has needs, but when I thought about him, and his loyalty to Hope, it never crossed my mind that he'd be getting it on with one of her best friends.

We never talked about our personal lives, except for little comments he'd make here and there, but was it possible he'd been with her and I didn't know?

"...so again, please don't say anything because Brendon would kill me if he knew I let our little secret out. With all that's going on with Hope, we all know it's just a matter of time, so of course I'm respecting his wishes for now. But whew!" She sighed dramatically again and wiped invisible sweat from her forehead. "It feels so good to finally be able to share with someone. I'm sure you understand what a huge burden this has been for me."

I was dumbfounded.

SIX
HOPE

Finally, I was at peace with my decision. No one was going to be happy, but I was sick and tired of the crap. I was tired of being treated like I was a friggin' wild animal. If people didn't care about those stupid laws in Texas, then I wasn't about to be anybody's poster child for what was wrong in that backward-ass state.

When you're young, black and poor, the system doesn't work for you and I now accepted that. I'd been there for years and no one cared that I was innocent. Only the rich could afford to pay for top-notch attorneys in a capital case, but there were no rich people on death row!

I sat in my cell writing yet another letter to Chastity. I didn't understand what was going on between us. I thought we had finally buried the hatchet, but it really didn't matter now. She never visited me once. Then the letters I used to send were returned unopened until finally, I stopped writing her. Truth be told, this wasn't all that surprising to me at all. Life had a way of going on without you while you were sitting up in a cell.

Even my own mama couldn't stay consistent when it came to visiting me or staying in touch. But that was no surprise, because Mona Clarke couldn't sit still long enough for grass to grow under her feet. But I didn't blame her or Chastity. I wished Chastity would've been able to really forget and move on.

The kids still talk about her, and so does Brendon, but I stopped asking him to give her my messages a while ago. What was the point? She obviously didn't want to be bothered, so I wasn't about to force her. But it didn't stop me from writing. Right now though, I wanted to mainly thank her for all she'd been doing to look after my family and, of course, to say goodbye.

I missed so much about being home. My family was from the Rosenberg Richmond area, a small city right outside of Houston. It was small, but big enough to make you feel like you had the best of both worlds.

In my mind, I still remember driving down Highway 90 and having access to most of the neighborhoods through that main street that ran through the heart of town. We lived in a house off Yoakum Street on the other side of the tracks, and everyone we knew lived within a five-mile radius. It was nothing for us to hop from one house to the next between Betty Jean, Stacy, and me, with Chastity tagging along.

"Let's go to the mall," Betty Jean had said.

Back in the day, the best mall for us to go to was Sharpstown off Highway 59 in Houston. If we were lucky, Betty Jean's older brother would give us a ride and pick us back up on his way back to Richmond.

"I already asked David, but you gotta hurry," she'd said as she stood looking through the screen door.

From the beginning of time, Betty Jean's body had developed faster than any of ours. She had more boobs and booty than some women twice her age, so she was an immediate hit with the boys. I was always thin, never had much of a figure to mention, and was always envious of girls whose bodies already made them look like grown women.

A trip to the mall was a big deal back then. With five dollars, you could survive the entire day of walking around from store to store hoping to be seen. I used to wear braids, and once I got my first basket weave, you couldn't tell me a thing! I remember that particular trip to the mall because that's when we met Brendon.

It was right outside Foley's; before Macy's bought out the chain. Betty Jean was talking to a lady at the makeup counter as the three of us waited.

I noticed a pack of guys coming our way and I immediately focused in on Brendon. It was his eyes that held me.

"Don't look now, but two-o-clock coming your way," Stacy had said.

Stacy was thick, but she was shapely, too. She had pretty, smooth, cinnamon-colored skin with hair that naturally matched her skin. But she couldn't be conspicuous if she tried.

"That's those Fifth Ward boys," she'd tried to whisper unsuccessfully.

Girls from the smaller cities outside of Houston had a thing for and about boys from the Fifth Ward. It didn't matter if it was Third Ward, Fifth Ward or anywhere in between. They were everything our boys were not. They were more edgy. We didn't know if they were really in gangs, or even true bad boys, but they were new and new was always better.

When Brendon strode by with his friends and never gave me a second glance, I suddenly wished Betty Jean was nearby. It never failed; she was a magnet to the opposite sex. I stood there looking like I'd fallen into puppy love until they walked by giggling and kept it moving.

"Dang, girl, why didn't you say nothing?" Stacy had asked, once they'd passed.

"What was I gonna say, and what's wrong with your mouth? How come you didn't say nothing?" I had asked.

As we stood there going back and forth, Betty Jean walked up and had asked, "Who's Chastity over there macking to?"

Our heads snapped in Chastity's direction and sure enough, there she stood near the escalators talking with one of the Fifth Ward boys!

"Who?" Stacy was speechless.

I was suddenly hopeful again, and Betty Jean wanted to go and investigate.

"C'mon, let's go over there." Betty Jean led the way.

I thought Brendon and the rest of the guys were long gone, but the minute Betty Jean stepped to Chastity and the stranger, the others appeared like roaches when the lights flicked on.

"Say, what's your name?" Those were the first words Brendon ever said to me. And he asked, then tilted his head ever so slightly. I was in love. Back then he was skinny with a Gumby haircut, All-Stars and Levis; the epitome of fresh.

We exchanged numbers and, for the rest of the day, the four of us walked the mall with the Fifth Ward boys. Later, I learned he wasn't even from the Fifth Ward. Brendon and his family lived on the Southwest side right near Sharpstown mall. They used to do exactly what we were doing; walking the mall in hopes of meeting girls other than those they knew from around the way. But by then it was too late; it didn't even matter to me.

I knew that day that we'd have a future together. I couldn't have imagined it would turn out like this, but from the very start, we were good together.

"Donovan, visit!" the C.O. yelled.

I swallowed the lump in my throat. This was a visit I wasn't really prepared for, but it had to be done. I hated the visiting room at the Mountain View Unit, where we were forced to talk from behind a wall of Plexiglas. I didn't understand why we couldn't visit in person, since we were in one big room, but it was what it was.

I was dressed in my prison whites; the inmate uniform that basically consisted of cotton pants and a V-necked shirt. I also put on my gold earrings to try and dress things up a bit. I had something very important to tell Brendon and I wanted to look my best.

C.O. Ramirez came to the door to cuff me. I hated the fact that we needed to be cuffed to move around the place.

By the time I was shuffled into the visiting area, Brendon was already there waiting.

Our eyes met and his huge grin turned radiant; his eyes still had a way of holding on to me. Even though a glass separated us, we didn't need a phone because we could hear each other. Beneath the glass was a mesh area. It wasn't big enough for us to slip anything back and forth, but we could talk without using a phone.

"Hey, baby," he said. He put his palm against the Plexiglas and I did the same.

"Hey, yourself."

I wanted the glass to melt so I could once again feel the touch of his skin next to mine. I was always so happy to see him. Of course I had regular nightmares that, like Chastity, he'd one day stop talking to me, stop writing, and stop visiting, but I didn't dare speak that into existence.

"You look good, Hope; I mean really, really good," he said.

I realized my man was hurting. I wished there was something I could do to take away his pain, but what to do?

"Hope, I wanna talk more about this new lawyer," he said.

I could actually see some excitement in his eyes. Didn't he understand that nothing was going to change? Who had time to keep going through the motions?

"Before we talk about yet another lawyer who we both know

ain't gonna do shit, 'cause he ain't getting paid, I wanna tell you something."

Brendon's demeanor changed instantly. The sparkle in his eyes suddenly dulled. I saw his eyebrows bunch together as he tried to study my face.

My heart started racing a bit, too, but this was the right thing to do. I was glad they only allowed one visit at a time for death row inmates at the Mountain View unit.

"I've written a letter to the courts asking that my appeals be stopped immediately," I said. "I mailed it around March 21st."

At first Brendon didn't say anything. His eyebrows nearly went up to his hairline. He looked at me like he was studying me for the first time. I was kind of scared. I didn't know what to expect.

"So, I wanted to tell you because I'm hoping to keep it quiet."

"Why would you do a thing like that, Hope?" he asked.

"I'm tired, baby. I'm tired of fighting. I'm tired of being in here. I want it to be over."

"Baby, do you hear yourself?"

The disgust on his face reminded me of the hatred I used to see in the eyes of strangers who packed the courtroom during my trial.

"I do; that's why I wanted to talk to you about this. I talked to that lawyer and he's saying the likelihood of a higher court overturning this is slim."

"Slim, baby, slim, that's not impossible! Slim means there's still a sliver of hope! What about the kids? You want me to go home and tell them that their mama is throwing in the towel? You had this planned all along, didn't you?" Brendon stopped talking and looked at me. His eyes narrowed, then he frowned.

"There's no point in me begging, huh?" He blew out a breath and shook his head.

"You knew all along," he repeated as if he was talking to himself.

I didn't say anything. He understood my mind was made up, and it was. After my second letter begging for another attorney was ignored, I became more hopeless. Then the last execution shook us all here on the row. Those people wanted blood; they wouldn't rest until every last one of us was put down. I didn't like the state, Adena, or anyone else having that kind of power over me, so this was my way of taking it back.

I wrote another letter. This one was to the appellate court and in it, I asked that my appeal be stopped immediately and my execution date be carried out as promptly as possible.

"It's time. It's been more than five years, my kids are growing up without me, and you guys are used to not having me around. Why prolong this?"

His eyes told me that he was heartbroken, but what could I do? I'd rather be dead than live in a small cage, like an animal. Every day things seemed to get worse around there and I was tired.

"But what about *us*?"

His voice cracked like he was struggling to hold it together.

"I'll always love you. I regret not listening to you every single day. I was wrong but now, I'm simply tired and I want this to be over. I want you to move on. You're young; you deserve someone who's gonna take care of you and the kids."

"That's why you made me stop bringing them…"

"I don't want you hanging on to this. I wanted to let you know before things get crazy. I'm trying to keep it out of the news for as long as possible. I don't want that freak Adena making her rounds with the TV and radio stations. What about Desmond and Jemar?"

Adena's husband was killed during a robbery, and she held me personally responsible for his murder. Every chance she got, she was reminding the good people of Texas that I needed to pay for what I did. Only I didn't do anything! I never even laid eyes on her husband. But somehow DA Conley was able to place me at the scene of the crime and put the gun in my hand. He even got Trey to lie on me. Quenton died after a fight in jail, so he couldn't even vouch for me. Each year around the anniversary of her husband's death, it seemed like Adena went extra hard; all but demanding they put me out in front of a firing squad.

"You being real selfish right now, Hope," Brendon said.

"I don't wanna grow old in here. I didn't do this. You and the kids believe me, and Mona believes me; so do my closest friends. Promise me that you won't let the kids forget about me."

"Don't talk like that."

"It's time, Brendon. I'm tired."

Brendon lowered his head. He palmed his head and held his hand over his face for the longest. I wanted to remind him that we didn't have much time, but I wanted to give him his moment.

"Shit ain't right, Hope," he managed.

"I'm tired. I'm tired of living like this; this ain't living at all, babe, and I can't take it anymore."

"So what about me and the kids; what are we supposed to do?"

"Brendon, get real; I'm never coming home. This death machine is gonna do what it does. There's nothing we can do about that. Go on with your life, babe. I don't expect you to wait around for something that ain't never gonna happen."

"So that's it, you giving up and to hell with the rest of us?"

"I don't want you to look at it like that. I thought by talking this out with you, you'd try to see where I'm coming from; you'd try to see that I'm doing what's best for all of us."

The guard chose that moment to let us know, our visit was over.

SEVEN
ADENA

I t was approximately 2:15 p.m. by the time we arrived in Huntsville, Texas. There were four of us in my vehicle and another car following behind.

When we pulled up, the spectacle I saw nearly floored me. There were so many people gathered outside of the death house, the scene was simply amazing.

"Are those satellite trucks over there?" Michelle Jones, the office manager at True Justice, asked. She was like my right hand and second in command.

To the right, there were three satellite trucks. As far as the amount of people, I wasn't even about to try and guess how many were out here. I was so glad that, for once, the pros seemed to outnumber the damn abolitionists.

"What time is your interview?" Michelle asked.

"I have my first one at three-fifteen, then you know how it works; someone else will probably piggyback off of that. So I expect to be quite busy this afternoon."

"How many do you think are over at the Hospitality House?" Michelle asked.

"Not sure, but I wish like hell I could shake some sense into these clowns who are out here trying to support such a vile individual. If anybody deserves to die, it's Larry Wooten, the sick bastard; he killed an elderly couple for a measly five hundred dollars! What a waste of breath he is," I said.

"We're gonna drop you here, park, then come back. Do you want someone to accompany you for the interview?"

I had done this so many times, I thought I'd be fine, but Michelle seemed a little worried. I didn't want to make a huge thing out of this.

"Cindy." Michelle turned over her shoulder to speak to the secretary of True Justice. "You should go with Adena; this crowd seems a bit rowdy."

"I'm fine."

"No, it's okay, Adena, I'd be happy to," Cindy said.

We stepped out of the car and signs were everywhere.

No man has the right to kill!

Texas, you have blood on your hands!

An eye for an eye!

Huntsville, TX: Judgment Day

The moment Michelle pulled off, the reporter charged toward me.

"Mrs. Binnaz, good to meet you," he said.

"Pleasure." I smiled.

"Where would you like to do the interview?"

"Here is perfectly fine with me," I said.

He and his photographer looked a bit surprised. But I stood firm. The signs in the background would make a great backdrop.

Cindy and I stood by as the photographer set up his tripod and clamped the camera on top. The reporter took his position and handed me a lavalier microphone to clip to my shirt.

The red light on the camera went on, and the reporter asked, "Why are you here today?"

I smiled. "Well, I can't think of any place else I'd rather be. Today, October 21st, the dry spell comes to an end out here at the Walls unit behind me. It's been awfully quiet at the death house.

The last execution was on back on August 17th when Peter Cantu finally met true justice, so I wanted to be a part of this big day."

He seemed a bit taken aback by my answer, but I stood poised and ready for his next question.

"So, what are your thoughts about some of the signs you see out there; the fact that some feel no man has a right to take another's life?"

"Larry Wooten deserves to be put to death for killing eighty-year-old Grady Alexander and his eighty-six-year-old wife, Bessie, in Paris, Texas back in 1996. Do you realize Wooten stabbed the elderly couple repeatedly and cut their throats? Before killing the couple, he pistol-whipped the wife with such force that portions of the pistol broke off."

The reporter looked like he wasn't expecting me to be well versed on the case.

"After that," I continued, "Wooten robbed them of about five hundred in cash. Now, stop and think about the horror of that night. Try to imagine the terror eighty-six-year-old Bessie was feeling as she was being beaten to death with a pistol by this piece of trash. Now, imagine that Bessie was *your* elderly grandmother. Let's take it a step further—try to imagine what kind of monster it must take to be able to inflict that kind of torturous and brutal pain and injury on *anybody*, much less helpless old people.

"Now I ask you, how dark is a person's soul to be to be able to carry out that crime? You tell me how do you rehabilitate that kind of hate and darkness? The answer is, you can't. That's why death is the only suitable punishment for a rabid animal like Larry Wooten," I answered with a straight face.

After two more questions, the interview was finished. I did a couple more, then saw Michelle and the others walking toward us.

"You did great as usual," Cindy said.

I smiled. "Let's head over to the Hospitality House."

By the time 5:00 rolled around, we were taken by van, provided by the State of Texas, from the Hospitality House to the Walls Unit where the executions took place. We were escorted into a room. We were searched for any undesirable elements.

"There will be two sides. Witnesses of the victims on one, and the inmates' witnesses on the other," a guard said.

After more rules and regulations, we were told there would be no cameras or tape recorders permitted. By 6:20 p.m. we were moved into another building and then escorted to another room. We were told to wait there.

"What's going on?" I asked, hoping he hadn't received a last minute reprieve.

There was some type of a delay. An officer came back and spoke.

"The delay is normal and it could be as much as fifteen minutes to an hour or longer."

But it seemed as if the moment he finished speaking, we were escorted into the viewing chamber. At that point I saw Larry Wooten strapped down to a gurney, which strongly resembled a horizontal cross with intravenous tubes inserted into both arms.

Once everyone was situated, I heard a voice ask Larry if there was there anything he had to say. Larry issued his final statement. The only part I heard was, "I don't have nothing to say. You can go ahead and send me home to my Heavenly Father."

Then he turned his head to the chamber that I was in. By 6:35 p.m. the lethal injection began. Larry's body made that familiar sound.

It was the sound of his body actually exhaling all of the air from his lungs. The sound was very loud. After that his heart was stopped by a chemical used in the injection. I saw what looked like tears flow from Larry Wooten's eyes, which were wide open and looking straight up toward heaven.

He had the nerve to look like he was totally at peace. At 6:43 p.m. a physician entered the execution chamber and examined the body. He called the time of death at 6:45 p.m. At 6:46 p.m. we were escorted out of the prison and back into the van. We were taken back to the Hospitality House.

By 8:20 p.m. we were escorted back to the prison where those of us, three men and me, who had witnessed the execution, then spoke to the media and to the people there.

I felt good. My members and I were planning to drive back to Houston to have a celebratory dinner and drinks. But nothing could've prepared me for the most wonderful phone call I received during the drive.

EIGHT
BRENDON

I didn't know what to do or who to try and reach out to. Hope said she needed to keep this under wraps because anything that leaked about her had a way of going viral fast. And honestly, after the media circus we went through early on, I didn't want to put my kids through that again.

After spending hours on the Internet, I saw that what Hope had done had essentially set her up for execution a whole lot faster than if she'd waited out her appeals. Some inmates were on death row for twenty-plus years before they were executed. I was sick and pissed at the same time. How could she do this?

"Who's there?" I called out when I heard the door open.

"It's me," Chastity said.

"Oh, in the kitchen."

Chastity walked in and looked around. As usual, she looked really nice. Chastity was curvaceous with a real nice body. And the way she was always there for me and the kids, I didn't know what I would've done without her.

"Is everything okay?" she asked.

"No, it's not." I brought the beer bottle to my lips and took another long swig. Chastity stood off to the side and watched me. I didn't know if she was more worried or curious. It was almost like she wasn't sure if she should take another step. "Hope is giving up," I said, then took another swallow of the beer.

At first, Chastity didn't say anything. She stood there and looked on like I'd never said a word. But she didn't take her eyes off of me.

"Just like that, to hell with the rest of us and what *we* want; *she's* tired. So she gets to decide when it's over."

I slammed the bottle onto the table and Chastity jumped. I didn't mean to scare her, it wasn't her fault that I was pissed and wallowing in misery. Still, Chastity didn't say a word. She was leaning up against the doorway.

"She wrote a letter to the court of appeals asking that they withdraw her appeal and set her execution date immediately."

My eyes were burning and I wasn't sure how much longer I could sit there and not look like I was having a meltdown. I was waiting for Chastity to say something, or at least react, but she didn't. She never even moved.

"Oh, but you can't tell anyone; we don't want it to leak to the media. I don't know how I'm gonna tell the kids, so right now, nobody knows."

Chastity still didn't say anything. She stood and stared at me. I felt like I was going to be sick. I had talked to Hope's lawyer. He had said there was nothing he could do because the choice was hers, and she was well within her right to withdraw the appeals. I asked him who I should contact, and told him she was making a mistake, but he didn't seem to be much help.

"I knew Hope was going to eventually die; we all knew it, but I don't understand why she wouldn't fight up to the very end. She didn't do this shit! Even Q said Trey implicated her because he was coerced. I don't understand why she won't keep fighting."

"I was gonna start dinner," Chastity said.

I turned to look at her. Hadn't she heard a word I'd said? Didn't she understand that Hope was making a huge mistake?

"I can get out of your way," I said. Before she said anything else, I bolted from the kitchen and rushed to my room. I wanted to punch a hole in the wall or do something. I didn't understand how Hope could make a decision like that without even talking to me first. It was like she knew for sure how this thing was gonna end.

"I can't believe she'd make a decision like this all by herself!" I was pissed.

As I lay stretched out on the bed, I closed my eyes and started thinking about the arrest, the conviction, and the loans. But then I started thinking about the madness that greeted us outside the TV studio after we taped that segment for *Watching Execution*. After we stepped outside and realized that crowd was waiting, I was pissed.

It never surprised me how they were able to follow me around anytime I spoke, made an appearance, or attended a rally. They hated Hope something fierce. Thinking about it now and there I was, back in the midst of the outrage, back right outside the TV station for all the passers-by to see. *These people are sick!*

"Your wife deserves to die!"

"That bitch needs the needle!"

"True Justice now!"

The crowd was rowdy. I wasn't nervous about walking through the crowd, but I didn't like listening to all the crap they'd throw at us as we walked.

"Just keep moving." I grabbed Mona's arm and tried to steer her toward the waiting car. "Don't say a word to them," I whispered.

But Mona wasn't good at ignoring them. Suddenly she stopped. I sighed hard. *Here we go*, I thought.

"My daughter ain't done a damn thing! She didn't kill nobody! She didn't even know Q and Trey had held up that store!" Mona yelled.

"Then why were her prints found on the gun?" a reporter shouted back.

Mona looked in the direction of the question. I wasn't sure if she knew who had asked; I couldn't tell. There were so many of them.

When Mona lunged toward a couple of guys standing too close for my taste, I didn't know what she was gonna do. Her face was twisted into a menacing frown. "Her purse spilled on the floor and she touched that gun by accident when she was reaching for her stuff!" Mona said. "That DA only said her prints were on the gun; he didn't explain *where* on the gun they were!"

I could see the veins in her neck throbbing and her body shook uncontrollably as she spoke through gritted teeth. No matter how much I told her to ignore them, not to say a word, not to answer their questions, she couldn't stop. It was like she couldn't help herself.

I nudged her forward. "Let's go, Mona. Don't say anything else; not another word!"

Microphones were shoved in our faces, and we could barely move because of how closely they followed us. They were like an angry pack of wolves, hoping we'd drop some raw meat. The sad part is the media was mixed in with the protestors. As far as I was concerned, they were all one in the same, always trying to keep the shit brewing.

"Hope is innocent! She ain't killed no damn body!" Mona yelled as I gently pushed her into the car. When she resisted, I pushed a little harder. But I didn't shove too hard; Mona would swing in a heartbeat, so I knew better. At the car, I rushed her in, then stumbled around to the other side and slid into the backseat. Chastity took off before I could close the door completely.

When I turned to look out of the back window, a few of the

reporters were actually running as if they were trying to catch up with the damn car!

"They're like blood-sucking vultures," Mona said.

"I keep telling you to ignore them. I don't know why you won't listen."

Mona turned her body and looked at me. "And I don't know how you do it. She's innocent! How do you listen to all that foul shit they constantly yell at you and keep walking in silence?"

I looked Mona square in the eyes. "Because, Mona, I know in my heart of hearts that Hope's not capable of what they're saying. I block them out because they're just trying to get the perfect sound bite for the six-o-clock news. They don't give a damn about Hope and whether she did it; they need a good sound bite! And I ain't giving 'em shit!"

Mona didn't say anything else. She turned in her seat and we all rode the rest of the way home in our own little world. All I could think about was, now that Mona had talked to them, I knew for sure we'd make the first block of every station's evening newscast.

The screaming in the hallway pulled me away from the memory.

"Breanna, stop fighting with your brother!" I yelled from the bed.

I walked back into the kitchen to get something to drink.

NINE
CHASTITY

I stood there looking at Brendon for the longest. Had he said what I thought he'd said? Was Hope really about to give up? I wasn't sure how I felt about her decision. I would never utter these words aloud, but there was a tiny part of me that wanted this to be over, even if it meant what I knew it meant. I was tired of being tired. I wanted us all to move forward.

When he came back into the kitchen, and started talking again, I really felt bad for him.

If my cell hadn't interrupted while we were talking, I'm not sure what I would've said to Brendon.

"Where the hell are you and can't he get somebody else to wait on him and them damn kids?" Trevor's voice boomed in my ear the minute I said hello. I could tell he'd been drinking.

"Is everything okay?"

"Naw, ain't shit okay! Were you at Hope's again? Damn, tell him to get his own damn woman!" Trevor screamed.

Again, he slurred his words and I rolled my eyes. I wasn't really in the mood to fight with him. After what Brendon just told me, about Hope and the look on his face, I knew he needed to talk. And I wanted to be there for him.

"I'm coming over there, and when I leave, I ain't leaving without yo' ass!" Trevor threatened.

"I was um, about to get dinner started," I said. I turned my back to Brendon, hoping he wouldn't hear this conversation. I had a feeling he knew there was trouble with Trevor and me, but I didn't want him thinking it was about him, even though it was.

I jumped when Brendon touched my shoulder. I turned back to face him. That's when he mouthed something and pointed toward the door, telling me he was leaving. I didn't want him to. I would've preferred to talk to him instead of Trevor, but getting off the phone with Trevor would all but guarantee he'd show up within the hour.

"So I can't see my woman 'cause you over there playin' house is what you tellin' me, right?"

"Trevor, come on, I try to keep up with the kids over here during the week; it's easier. If I knew you were coming over, I would've stayed home," I lied.

Sometimes when Trevor was drunk, it was best to simply tell him what he wanted to hear, or at least try not to aggravate him. It didn't take much for him to flip out, so I had to tread lightly; especially when he was juiced up with vodka or gin.

When I heard cabinet doors slamming, I knew for sure he was definitely in a mood.

"So what the hell am I supposed to do here all by myself, while you over there serving that fool?"

"Trevor?"

"Ain't even shit in here to eat," he growled.

I needed to keep him calm. The last thing I wanted was for Trevor to get so mad that he decided to come over and kick up some drama.

"Hmmm, I was there earlier. There should be some leftover pasta casserole in the fridge, and uh, there's some of that cheese dip you like," I said, trying to sound as cheerful as possible.

"So I'm supposed to fix all that shit myself?" He sounded put out. "You know I don't know how to cook!"

"Trevor, all you have to do is put whatever you want into the microwave."

"I don't believe this shit," he whined. "I gotta be over here fixing my own fuckin' food and shit, while you serve that fool like he's a king!"

Again, I didn't say anything. And, when I exhaled, I tried to do it as quietly as possible. I didn't want to set him off.

I stood holding the phone and listened as Trevor fussed about looking around in the refrigerator. I'd always been a magnet for guys like Trevor. I can remember as far back as high school, when it started with Brian Ashton. Back then he was the ultimate catch. Everyone wanted him, or at least that's what I thought. Brian was spoiled by all the women in his family; he recognized no boundaries and needed someone to do everything for him.

"Oooh-weeee, girl, he's coming this way. Don't look now, but I think he's checking you out!" My classmate Pamela Craig and I made a habit watching Brian and his every move. He was perfect; the epitome of Mr. Popularity. He was the captain of the football team, he played basketball and he seemed poised for great things.

"How's my hair?" I asked. I popped a few Tic Tacs into my mouth.

"You good, you good; here he comes." Pamela giggled.

We watched as Brian seemed to float in our direction. Even in the early days he took very good care of his body. His muscles were more popular than him.

"Hey, Chastity, Pamela." He smiled.

I wanted to melt right where I stood. My young heart knew then that I wanted to be connected to him for the rest of my life.

As he floated by, Brian's eyes connected with mine. He smiled that killer grin that had melted many a heart and seemed genuine when he abruptly stopped by my locker.

"Oh, I was wondering if you wanted to go to homecoming with me," he said.

My tongue felt like it was playing a game of Twister and the words seemed to jumble as I tried to push them out.

"Hhh-omecoming?" I stuttered.

"If you're busy…"

"Oh, no! I'm not! I wanna go! I can go!" I screamed.

He smiled.

It didn't help that Pamela was jumping up and down behind him like a clown. I couldn't keep a straight face. I couldn't wait to go home and brag to Hope, Stacy, and Betty Jean. Everyone knew how fine Brian was and he wanted me.

Brian and I went to the homecoming dance after I cheered for him from the stands during the game. After that, we became joined at the hip. I was lucky to have a boyfriend that everyone wanted. It was no secret that a few of the cheerleaders had tried their hardest to turn his head, but he wanted me. I was on cloud nine, so nothing could've prepared me for what happened one afternoon after we'd been going steady for nearly three months.

I left school early and walked home alone, thinking I'd invite Brian over after practice. My cramps were unbearable so I figured the rest would do me some good.

When I unlocked the door, I heard sounds but figured it was Mona in her room. Maybe she had company, which was fine with me. I wanted to lie down for a bit.

After dropping my books on the couch, I walked down the hall and to the back room I shared with Hope. Imagine my disgust when I opened the door and saw Brian's naked behind humping up and down between Hope's legs.

I screamed.

They jumped up and tried to scramble for cover.

"Hope! How could you!"

Brian rushed out, leaving my sister and me to duke it out over him. We tumbled and rolled all over the floor, pulling hair, scratching, and screaming until Mona rushed in and pulled us apart.

"So, when you coming back?" Trevor asked.

His question pulled me back to the phone call. He couldn't be serious about me coming back tonight, but deep down I knew he was.

At that moment I felt like crap because I wanted nothing more than this mess to wrap up. I was sick and tired of feeling stuck between two men; especially when one was completely unstable.

TEN
HOPE

One of the major problems with being behind bars were the memories that haunted you. Scenes from my past played out in my head over and over again. It was like torture. I wanted it to be over. I needed the end to come quick. One of the scenes that seemed constant was my days in court.

There were lots and lots of cameras and when they flashed, so bright, so fast, they made my eyes hurt. The sound of shutters firing from all those cameras in such a rapid rhythm made my heart thump louder. I was more nervous now than I had been in the last six weeks. I already knew the verdict wouldn't be good. Thanks to the smear job the prosecutors did, people hated me. They said so on the news every night. But today, there was something different in the air. It made me feel like a million bugs were crawling all over my skin. I was shivering. Even though everybody shuffled around me as if someone yelled *fire* and they wanted to be first to the door, to me, everything seemed to move in slow motion. That's when you know for sure something bad is creeping up on you, and no matter what, I couldn't shake the feeling. Then, it happened.

I had an outer body experience. I felt myself leave my body; it was like I was a fly on the wall looking down at the scared petrified me. I saw myself literally trembling as I sat on the little wooden chair that was too hard. I was cold, I was hot, I was anxious and nervous, but mostly I was terrified. I was a wife, a mother, a daughter, a sister, and a best friend. My future was bright, and there was no way in hell this could be my life. But it was, and until now it never felt so real.

I turned to my right and stole a glance at my mother; she had aged right before my eyes. These past six weeks may as well have been sixteen years. That's how quickly and how much my mother, Mona, had aged.

Her olive-colored face looked sunken in, dark circles were around her hallowed eyes, and lines had suddenly sprouted around her dry lips. When our eyes met, she shook her head like she felt so sorry for me. My father, the once big and strong man, who was always around, now cried before anyone had uttered a word. He and my mother never married, but he was ever present in my and my sister's lives. But it was the lost look in my husband, Brendon's, eyes that scared me the most.

I wanted to walk right up to him and lead him out of the courtroom. I remembered how, in the beginning, I thought this would all go away once I explained that Q and Trey were a couple of knuckleheads from the neighborhood.

I figured if I told the District Attorney, Joel Conley, that I had only accepted that ride because the car Mona let me borrow, which wasn't even her car, broke down, and I was desperate, he'd understand, but nobody cared. Back then, I dreamed of the ways I'd say sorry to Brendon and tell him how this was all a nightmare. I'd explain to my young children that Mommy really made a bad choice but it was going to be all right. Because that's what happened; you made mistakes but you learned from them. I had certainly learned a lot from my mistake, but it didn't need to destroy me completely.

Suddenly, the judge's voice made me whip my head around and focus my attention on him.

"Will the defendant please rise?" Judge Roman asked, like I had a choice.

Judge Wayne Roman was a tall, older man who, according to what I read, was a conservative. He was hard on crime and much harder on criminals. His salt-and-pepper hair was slicked back in an oily style. He had that no-nonsense appearance that made me wish I were a close family friend, instead of one of those criminals he didn't like. But I wasn't.

I swallowed back tears, and when I tried to stand, my legs felt like they were about to give out on me. I stumbled but held my balance. The courtroom was packed; about every TV station had a camera present. During the trial that lasted six long grueling weeks, there were so many cameras I wondered if they were filming around the clock.

Every time my eyes shifted or any time I flinched, I noticed reporters jotting things down on their notepads. Were those the ones who had called me the femme fatale? For months, I was the biggest story on the local newscast. They'd even gone and dug up my kindergarten teacher; imagine that!

But I had some support; my entire family held vigil from day one. They were at every last one of the hearings and each night on the news, I could expect to see someone I knew being interviewed.

"Baby, they even had a Japanese reporter interview me," Brendon had said after the state rested.

But in addition to the negative things I heard, there was no doubt, I was a celebrity. Vigils were being held in Rome, Australia, and in other parts of the world I never knew existed. I heard the President of Mexico even sent a letter to the Governor of Texas on my behalf. But that obviously didn't work; the trial still continued.

"Hope Jenay Donovan, you have been sentenced to death..."

Those words, they played over and over in my mind. It had happened several years ago now. It took almost two years for me to go to trial, with delays, continuances, and us switching attorneys. Q's death also caused a delay. I was locked up while I waited for my day in court, because bail was denied. It's been years, but every night when I closed my eyes, I still remember those days like it was a few minutes ago.

"Aeey, Party Girl," Latrice called out to me.

Latrice Huff worked next to me in what we called the stitching room, so naturally we became close. Our job was to sew for three to four hours a day. Because we were work capable, we were able to socialize with each other. We worked in threes, so it was Latrice, Pauline and me. There were two other shifts of three and two inmates who chose not to work. Latrice was cool.

She and the other inmates called me "Party Girl," because everyone knows under Texas' Law of Parties, I was eligible for the death penalty for a crime I didn't commit simply by being in the wrong place at the wrong time.

"What's up?"

"Your ol' man coming through this weekend?" Latrice asked.

Each Friday before we got off, Latrice would ask that same question. That was part of what bothered me most about being in here. Every day was exactly like the first, second, third, and day number 1,092. But I imagined it would all be the same until the State made good on its promise to put me to death by lethal injection.

After what I had told him, I wasn't sure if Brendon would ever come back to see me again. I figured only time would tell, and hopefully I wouldn't have much of that left.

ELEVEN
ADENA

It amazed me to see the power I still had over the press. Years after my husband's tragic and untimely death, I was still able to command a crowd. I had called the press conference outside the small storefront that housed the headquarters for True Justice's offices and was nearly taken aback by the number of people that showed up.

Flanked by my oldest son, Raakin Junior, members of my board, and other victims' family members, I cleared my throat to indicate I was ready to start.

"I'm so glad you could make it here this morning," I began. There were so many microphones on the podium I was afraid the thing might tumble beneath all of the weight. In addition, there were several large boom microphones hanging overhead.

"As most of you know, I sleep, eat, and breathe images of my nemesis finally meeting True Justice. It's been five years since Hope Jenay Donovan was sentenced to death for her role in the brutal murder of my beloved husband. I have sat by over the years and watched as various groups rallied to support this murderess. I have waited patiently for her to receive True Justice. I want to thank Allah for the glorious news that I'm about to share with you today. As of yesterday, March 21st, Hope Jenay Donovan has dropped all appeals and has asked the Fifth U.S. Circuit Court of Criminal Appeals to expedite her execution."

I waited until the gasps subsided. Reporters wrote feverishly and suddenly the questions were fired at me like they were coming from a high-powered rifle.

"*What is your reaction?*" a dark-haired reporter asked.

"*Has she received a new execution date?*"

"*How do you feel about this decision?*" a tall reporter standing next to a cameraman asked.

"*Where were you when you received the news?*"

"*What about Hope's claims of innocence?*"

I held up a hand to try and quiet the crowd. I wasn't finished, and I wanted to answer every single one of their questions.

"As you know, I have long been an advocate of the death penalty and remain steadfast in my resolve to be front and center when Mrs. Donovan takes her last breath. I want her to look into my eyes and let my face be the last she sees before she's sent to her Maker."

Glancing up from my notes, I smiled and pointed at one of the local TV news reporters who was familiar to me.

"Ty?"

"Yes, Adena, Hope has maintained her innocence from day one, and even now, she insists she had nothing to do with your husband's murder. Have you ever given any consideration to her claims of innocence?"

"Ty, that's just what they are; *claims*. Hope Donovan is a murderess who doesn't deserve the humane treatment she's about to receive. You find me a guilty person on death row and I'll show you someone who hasn't learned to beat the system yet. They all claim innocence," I said and looked beyond her.

"John?"

I answered each question and beamed with pride at the thought of being able to witness Hope Donovan's date with True Justice.

TWELVE
BRENDON

I woke up at 4:39. That's what the digital clock flashed when I turned over and realized I was in bed and not arguing with Hope. In my dream we were arguing about some of the things she did. In the darkness I clutched my pillow and remembered the bottle I was sipping on before I must've passed out.

"Shit!" I nearly stumbled as I tried to get up. I needed to piss like a racehorse.

After the bathroom, I navigated my way back to bed, grabbed the fifth that sat on my nightstand, took a swig, and swished it around in my mouth before swallowing it.

The burning sensation warmed my insides and made me feel good for a minute.

"Why couldn't she listen? Why couldn't she listen?"

I flopped down onto the bed, my eyes plastered to the ceiling, and I was wide awake. Then I started thinking about all of the times I tried to talk to Hope about leaving some people behind.

See, Hope was the kind who still had friends from elementary school. She hung with the same group she knew back in the day. She thought there was something wrong with outgrowing some people, and we couldn't see eye to eye on that.

"You don't think you're better off cutting ties with *certain* people?" I had asked after one of our heated arguments about the touchy subject.

Hope's doe-shaped eyes focused in on me. She was pretty. I could see why even the guys from her past didn't want to let go, and she had a big 'ol heart, too, but I didn't want my wife rubbing elbows with the underbelly of the hood.

When she shook her head saying no, I knew she meant what she said. I didn't know back then that she'd get caught up in this kind of mess. I don't think anything could've prepared us for what happened with Q and Trey, but something was bound to happen because Hope never met a stranger, and to her, people who forgot where they came from are the real lowlifes.

"I can't walk down the street acting like I'm better than everybody else, just because we got good jobs and we're trying to live the good life," she said. "I mean you're a friggin' bus driver and I'm an admin assistant at Workforce; it ain't like we're rocket scientists!"

"I don't give a damn what we do, Hope, the point is we work hard, and if some of those people are still doing the same things they used to do when y'all were sixteen, that's not cool, Hope!"

We were in the kitchen. Hope was standing there opening mail, but we'd just come back from the store. What set the argument into motion was what happened as we left the grocery store.

I spotted dude as he walked toward us. His pimp stroll was outrageous and I couldn't tell whether he was coming to snatch her purse or about to pull a gun on us both. You shouldn't judge people like that, but you can never let your guard down.

"Hold up, Hope," I had said, immediately ready to protect my wife.

She looked around, confused. I thought her confusion was about what we should do next, but it wasn't.

"What's wrong?"

I'd tried to step in front of her when she started pushing me to the side.

"What?" Hope had sounded irritated.

I wondered if she didn't see this character strolling in our direction with a street swag that told me to cross the street and let him do his thing on this side alone.

"What's wrong? I wanted to say hi to K-Dogg," she'd said.

I stopped in my tracks. Now I was the one who was confused.

"What? Who the hell is K-Dogg?" I'd asked.

Hope motioned toward what I thought was a possible threat, then broke out grinning like she was happy to see this filthy-looking thug.

As he got closer, his expression changed, too, and they quickly embraced like two long-lost friends.

"Aeey, Tiny!" he screamed as he held my wife in a way that made me uncomfortable. Tiny was her nickname growing up, but I didn't like using it or when others used it around me.

"K-Dogg, what's up? What you know good?" Hope never really spoke the King's English, but I was more than stunned to hear her ease into the gritty street slang she shared with this dude.

"So, shorty, what's crack-a-lackin'?" He stepped back, grabbed his crotch, or where it was supposed to be since his starched jeans hung so low; his crotch was more like at his knees. I watched as this man talked, he kept bopping around, used his fingers to flick at his nose, and he kept sniffing.

"Oh, oh, K, this is my husband, Brendon," Hope finally said, after the two had held what was like a mini-reunion.

"That's what's up!" He reached in and gave me the brothaman hug, with a quick two slaps on the back. "I heard you'd done that shit, Tiny," he'd said.

I felt like I was witnessing an encounter between two strangers. Hope was a different person as she stood there confirming or denying gossip from the neighborhood with K-Dogg.

Each time I tried to give her the *wrap it up* look, it seemed like she thought of something else to ask this dude.

"Yo, K, it was cool meeting you, but we've gotta get going," I'd finally interrupted when the conversation turned to the escapades at an old house party.

Enough was enough!

Hope was from around the way, and I understood that when we decided to move back to the neighborhood she'd grown up in, but sometimes I was still surprised by certain aspects of her life.

Later, as we got ready for bed, I tried to think of a way to ease into a conversation about K-Dogg and others like him.

"Dude earlier today, he was a trip," I said as Hope sat on her side of the bed putting lotion on her thighs. The kids were asleep; she'd just showered and we were about to shut it down for the night.

"Really, what was such a trip about him?"

"What's he, about thirty now? He still dresses like he just came off a gangsta rap video set," I joked.

When she didn't laugh I should've left it alone, but I didn't.

"His pants were sagging so low, I never understood what those young cats get out of that, but to see a grown-ass man looking like that?" I blew out a breath as I shook my head at the absurdity.

Hope still hadn't said a word. But her expression had changed.

"I think it's cool that we live in your old neighborhood, but sometimes I worry about the way these dudes feel like they know you so well."

"Ah, that's because they do," she said.

Her tone told me she was really mad. She always got all defensive when I started talking about the questionable characters from her past. It was no secret that when I met Hope she thought I was one of *those* guys. By the time she learned the truth, that I was from the suburbs and not an inner-city thug, I guess she was already hooked.

"Everybody's not from the burbs with two parents and a perfect childhood like you, Brendon," she hissed.

That's when I knew for sure I had gone too far. Every married couple had their issues, but a main one for us, was Hope not being able to let go of the past.

"Hope, my childhood wasn't perfect. I don't know anyone whose was, but when are you gonna leave the past in the past?"

"I don't feel like listening to that straddling the fence bull again!" she yelled.

"You can't even try to see my side, huh?"

"Your side is for me to be fake and deny where I'm from and the people I've known all my life. It ain't gonna happen!" she snapped.

"That's not what I'm telling you to do. How you think it makes me feel, knowing all these thugs behave like my wife is some kinda hoodrat?"

What'd I say that for?

"Oh, so now I'm a hoodrat, huh? What does that make you? You married me!"

"Hope! That's not what I'm sayin' and you know it," I said.

By now I was in the dark, talking to the back of her head. She switched off the light, jumped under the covers, and turned away from me.

She had shut down the night in a way that I wasn't expecting.

I can remember all those years ago, lying there in the dark, trying to think of a way to get my wife to see there was nothing wrong with leaving *some* people behind.

THIRTEEN
CHASTITY

I should've known when I didn't go back to the house that Trevor would be ready to act the fool the next time I saw him. But I didn't stop to think when the next time would be. I wish now that I would have.

The kids had just left for school and I was cleaning up the kitchen. I wasn't trying to be all up in Brendon's business, but he seemed to be moving slowly that morning.

"You okay?" I asked.

He sipped his coffee before answering.

"Didn't really sleep good last night," he said.

"Were you sick or something?"

"Yeah, I guess you could call it that; sick from bad memories mixed with Patrón," he confessed.

I wanted to laugh, but I didn't want to seem like I was making fun of him. Brendon was such a lightweight. I didn't understand how he and Hope made it as long as they did. They were so different. She was street-wise and rough around the edges while he was different.

"Patrón will do it every time," I said. I didn't know much about alcohol, but I wanted to keep the conversation going.

His eyes twinkled, even though he was tired. And his smile was still as bright.

He looked at me. "Like you would know!" And then he started laughing.

I had to laugh at myself, too. I had never been much of a big drinker. As a matter of fact, I could count on one hand the number of times I had gotten really drunk. Usually heavy drinking was only an option for me when something went wrong and I couldn't figure things out. He went back to his room and I went back to mine. I laughed again about his comment.

The first time I was on the losing end of a battle with a bottle of Hennessy was after Hope had done what she was so good at doing, hurting me. First, there was Brian, and if that wasn't enough, there was Chris.

"Chastity! What are you doing home?" Betty Jean yelled the moment I walked into the living room. I should've known something was wrong. I wondered what was going on. She and some guy had been hugged up, but then suddenly I walked in and she started screaming.

I didn't think about where Hope was. I needed to get to our room, change, and head back out. Hope and her friends were always ditching school, so it was no surprise to find them there in mid-afternoon. I had a job after school and was able to leave campus before the last period.

I didn't even answer Betty Jean. I rolled my eyes at her and started making my way down the dark hallway.

When I opened the bedroom door and saw Hope lying across her twin bed and the love of my life at the time between her legs, I wanted to fight.

"What the hell, Hope!" I yelled.

They jumped up and started trying to cover their naked bodies.

"Wait, Chastity, it's not what you think!" she had the nerve to say.

The guy, Chris, looked at me and acted like he didn't see the problem.

"You bitch!"

"Why you getting vexed with me? He's been trying to get with me for more than a minute now," Hope said, like that was a legit defense.

First, she slept with Brian; now she'd slept with my boyfriend in our bedroom and was behaving like she wasn't to blame. Hope and I didn't care too much for each other, but it seemed like she wanted and took everything I had.

"We came back here to talk, and one thing led to another," she said.

I was so mad at her. Each betrayal pushed us farther apart and I didn't understand why she felt the need to go after every man I ever looked at twice, or at least that's how it felt.

"Chastity, you're blowing this thing way out of proportion. Be glad you found out now, instead of later. I keep telling you, these guys ain't nothing but dogs!"

As I looked at my sister, I wondered what it was about her, about me, or even us, that made her think doing this was okay. By now Chris was dressed and had the nerve to try and talk to me.

"I don't wanna hear it!" I said in his direction.

"So, it's like that now?"

I shot him the look of death and he knew the answer to his question. It wasn't that Hope and her friends were sluts, but it seemed like at least one of them always wanted to show me up and I was getting tired of it.

It didn't take long for me to move away from Hope and her friends. Although my friends and I weren't as tight as she was with hers, I didn't have to worry about them trying to sleep with every man I wanted.

Over the years, the relationship with Hope and I turned from sisterly to barely friends. There were times I had no idea what was going on in her life and that didn't bother me in the least. As a matter of fact, it made me feel like I was doing a good job of keeping my business under lock and away from her.

Mona was always off doing her own thing. If I needed advice or female help, I started turning to my friends' mothers. Mona was no help and Hope was on a path to self-destruction. I remember being home one evening and wondering where she was. It wasn't that I was concerned about her, but some friends were over and I didn't want her coming in and getting all up in our business. The phone rang and I started not to answer, but did anyway.

When the collect call came in, I first thought it was a mistake. I finally accepted the call and it was Hope.

"Where's Mona?" she asked.

"I dunno, why?" I was already bored with the phone call. "And why you calling here collect anyway? You know Mona's gonna blow a gasket when she sees the bill," I said.

"Chastity, I'm in jail!" Hope said.

That moment stood still for me. Jail? That was where our friends' and neighbors' older brothers went. Some girls from the neighborhood got caught up, but we didn't know any of them personally, so their arrests were more like urban legends.

"In jail?"

"Yeah, I need you to find Mona; she needs to come and get me out," Hope said.

"What are you in jail for?"

"I ain't got a lot of time. Find Mona and tell her to come get me before they start talking about transferring me to the county."

How did she even know about transfers to the county? What was she doing in jail? We weren't close, but had she gone that far to the left that she was a complete stranger to me?

"Chastity, I need you to find Mona!" she screamed.

"Why you in jail?" I screamed back at her. The nerve of her;

she wanted my help but was trying to boss me around from behind bars?

"They talking about me shoplifting, but it wasn't even me. Just go find Mona!" she demanded.

I knew where to find Mona. She was at a weekend card game over in the projects. It usually started Friday evening after work, and lasted until Sunday night. But suddenly thoughts of Brian and Chris flooded my mind. I was wrong but I felt like some time in the slammer may be what Hope needed.

The knock at the bedroom door made me leave the memory behind.

"Yeah?"

Brendon opened the door and stuck his head in.

"Hey, Trevor is here for you," he said.

My heart nearly stopped.

FOURTEEN
HOPE

"What the hell?"

Sounds of a scuffle jarred me from my sleep. I heard a few bumping sounds, then tumbling and finally, groaning.

"Get her legs, get her legs!"

I rubbed my eyes. It was dark, but I could see the shadows off to the side of my cell. Once I woke completely up, I knew exactly what was going on.

"Ooouch! You fuckin' hurting me!" a woman screamed.

The voices sounded like they were right outside my cell. When I heard what sounded like someone being slammed against a wall, I knew for sure the C.O.'s were once again treating someone else like shit. This was nothing new.

These women in crisis management were brought in there at all times of the day and night in various stages of hysteria, fear, or anger. A lot of them came in cut up from attempted suicides. An inmate died in there not long ago.

She was brought over from another unit right after force was used on her there. She came over on a Friday to the crisis management part of this building, very hurt and sick. Because it was a weekend, there was no doctor on the unit and none called in to see her. They had one officer working that Friday night on third shift at 3:00 a.m.

When the officer looked in on this woman, she was covered in feces black as tar, which meant it had blood in it, and no one would clean this lady up because there was only one officer. She sat in that cell all weekend with blood and fluids coming out of every hole in her body.

By the time Monday rolled around, the doctor, who was actually a physician's assistant, wouldn't see her and she died that following Wednesday. If she'd gotten medical attention sooner, she'd probably still be alive.

The tumbling noises continued outside my cell. There was nothing I could do. I couldn't say anything, and I damn sure couldn't go back to sleep. I was so sick of this place, the way they treated us and nobody cared. If we didn't work, we were forced to stay in these little cells all day long simply because we were on death row; with no TV and no room to move around.

We didn't even have a stool and table to eat or write on. We had to eat our meals on our bed, floor or toilet. They had come in there the other day and covered up one of the outlets in our cells, so now we only had one outlet to use for all our electrical appliances.

Sometimes I thought about writing letters to give people a glimpse of what it was like in there, but then I reminded myself that they probably couldn't have cared less. Many people think if you're on death row you don't deserve humane treatment, but they're wrong. I was on death row, but I was innocent, and even if I wasn't, I didn't deserve to be treated like that.

Eventually, I must've drifted off to sleep because when I woke this time, food was being shoved into my cell. The slop they served wasn't even good enough for hogs, much less humans. I picked through it enough to stop my stomach from growling and stretched out on top of my bed.

I wondered who they were fighting with last night. I wondered why they felt the need to treat women the way they did.

As time passed, my hour of rec came up. C.O. Martinez pulled the door open and yelled at me. "Donovan, let's move it!"

I took my time getting up and making my way to the door. What the hell was she going to do? I mean-mugged her just as much as she was staring me down. I didn't want any trouble, but it was like they came to work with a chip on their shoulders every day.

As I walked down the hall and passed the officers' bay, I started getting even more vexed.

"We had to spray that nut four times. She just sat there batting that pepper spray up," a C.O. said.

Then they had the nerve to sit around and laugh. There were four correctional officers laughing and carrying on about what they had done the night before.

"Man, she was so loony," another C.O. said, and again they broke out in laughter.

If I heard all the commotion going on last night, everybody else heard it, too. It was such a trip to me that so many women were subjected to gassings with pepper spray and all kinds of other foolishness for different reasons. Each time something like that went down, it instantly affected everyone around the area.

And how could it not? We were trapped in those cages with no windows open in the building. The things we'd seen were enough to drive anyone crazy. Then after something like whatever went down last night, to come out here and listen to the officers sit around laughing and making fun of those women, it was all enough to make somebody crack, for real.

The only thing that kept me going today was knowing I had a visit coming later. But the way they treated us during the visits was enough to keep my blood boiling.

Later as I being escorted over to the visiting room, I had mixed emotions. I was still pissed over the guards for laughing it up after beating someone's ass, but I was glad for the visit.

I stepped into the cage and held out my wrists for the C.O. to unlock the cuffs. I was surprised to see a lawyer and wondered who had wasted both their money and their time.

My mind was made up.

She was petite with big brown eyes and dark brown hair. Her hair was long with a part down the middle. She looked like she could be in her forties or fifties; I couldn't tell.

The officer stood off to the side as the lawyer pulled her black bag onto the desk and started digging into it.

"Hope, my name is Anna Rich. I wanted to talk to you about your recent request," she said.

She was all business. There was no time for handshakes or even too much eye-to-eye contact. Before I could sit, she was flipping through a thick file she'd pulled from her bag. When I saw my mug shot on one of the pages, I realized it was mine.

I looked around. The transport officer had left and we were locked in. I always wondered what we would do if a fire ever broke out, and we were stuck, locked in there like animals.

"Mrs. Donovan," Attorney Rich said. Her voice was so stern I snapped my head and looked at her.

"You're wasting your time and mine; nothing you're gonna say is gonna change my mind," I said.

She looked at me. "You must be mistaken. I'm not here to change your mind about anything. I'm here to give you information about your expedited execution."

Suddenly the cage felt like it was closing in on me.

FIFTEEN
ADENA

I had been working the phones for days trying to verify the information about Hope and trying to get someone to explain the next steps to me. I had been more emotional with my prayers to Allah.

The prize was finally in sight. So many times these killers sit on death row, eating away at taxpayer dollars, and I was sick and tired of it. True Justice lobbied the state legislature every chance we got. We wanted stricter laws to govern this process. Once they are convicted and their conviction was upheld by a higher court, we saw no reason to prolong the process. We wanted them put to death immediately.

We understood the magnitude of the appeals process, but there had to be a way to cut that down. If the criminals realized they could survive for years as appeals make their way through the justice system, I didn't think capital punishment was the deterrent we needed it to be.

As I sat on the phone holding for one of the legal scholars I talked to often, I thought about the day when we would see justice carried out as swiftly as the crimes these maggots committed.

Suddenly, a voice broke my train of thought.

"Ms. Binnaz? Are you still there?" she asked.

"That's Missus Binnaz," I corrected. "And yes, I am."

"Doctor Willis is available now. I'll transfer you."

"Thank you."

Doctor Vincent Willis was a leading authority on capital punishment in the country. When abolitionists, lawyers from the Innocence Project, and lawyers from the Defender Services tried to jump on the bandwagon over the legality of the three-drug cocktail used to carry out executions, Willis was on our side.

I can remember the deep sense of depression I felt when Texas followed suit with other states that halted executions while the justices determined whether the Kentucky case that challenged the cocktail use held any merit. It was such a waste of money and time. Texas held out for a while, but under mounting pressure from the liberal do-gooders, our state joined the makeshift moratorium.

The Harris County District Attorney's Office was in turmoil at the time. Former DA Chuck Rosenthal, a staunch supporter of capital punishment, and a friend of ours, was caught up in a sex scandal with his then secretary, and it looked like the liberals were trying to ease their way in.

Luckily, Pat Lykos was able to beat out the former Houston Police Chief C.O. Bradford and all hope was not lost after all.

The next voice I heard was that of Doctor Vincent Willis.

"Missus Binnaz, what can I do for you?"

He was gracious enough to take my calls and help me understand some of the laws regarding the death penalty and the rights death row inmates had.

"Did you hear Hope has dropped her appeals?" I asked. I was still as excited as the first time I heard the news.

"I did."

"Well, you know I was thrilled to get the news. I'm trying to figure out what this means; how soon can I expect her to get the needle?"

"I've been expecting your call," he said. "If you give me a moment, I can tell you what I know and what you can expect."

"For that wonderful news, I have as long as you need," I said.

I waited again as Doctor Willis did what he needed to do.

So many thoughts ran through my mind. I had dreams about confronting Hope and looking into her eyes as she lay strapped to the gurney in Huntsville. I could also remember the endless lonely nights when I laid awake wondering if I'd ever see sweet justice.

There had been so many vigils, so many rallies, and fundraisers. It was almost as if they'd turned her into a martyr and, each time, I wanted to tell these people not to worship a false prophet.

"Missus Binnaz, thanks for your patience."

"No problem, Doctor Willis."

"So no one knows for certain, but now that she's dropped all of her appeals, she can get a new execution date immediately and thereafter she can be executed within months."

"Months?" I said slowly.

I couldn't stop the tears that rolled down my cheeks. They were tears of pure joy.

"Yes. Your next call should be to the District Attorney's Office. Once they set a new date, according to the current schedule, we should see an end really soon."

I could've kissed him.

"Months," I repeated.

"Yes, months."

"Thank you," I said sincerely.

"I'll keep my eye on this. If you have any more questions, please feel free to call me again."

"You've always been so supportive," I said.

"It's not a problem."

When I hung up the phone, I wanted to break out in dance. I was so excited. The thought of Hope Donovan finally meeting true justice after all of these years was overwhelming. Tears of joy tumbled from my eyes and, for once, I did nothing to stop the flow.

"All praises to the almighty Allah!"

I called my son's cell phone again. He didn't answer, but nothing could dampen my spirits.

SIXTEEN
HOPE

"She's no stranger to the law. She's been arrested three times before. Once, maybe we could understand that, but to be arrested again and yet again, well, that's just a clear disregard for the law." The prosecutor, Conley, pointed at me before he turned and faced the jury. The courtroom was so quiet. I could hear the humming noise of the air conditioner.

"Ladies and gentlemen of the jury, Hope Donovan has continuously flirted with the underbelly of society. At eighteen, she was arrested for shoplifting. Most people would've learned, but no, not Hope; she likes walking on the wild side. So after spending six days in jail, instead of trying to walk a straight line, nine months later, she was back in the slammer; only this time it was for prostitution!"

Again he turned and looked at me, then back at the jury. "Yes, this mother of three who friends and family would have you believe is harmless, and deserves leniency, although she confessed to this heinous crime, claims it was a misunderstanding. But again, she gets off with a slap on the wrist and what happens? You guessed it; she was arrested yet again! Well, this time, she was arrested for assault. I don't have to tell you, ladies and gentlemen of the jury, each time Hope has had a run-in with the law, her offenses have gotten progressively worse."

He walked over to the table where I sat next to my attorney

and looked at me, then sighed. I wanted to spit in his face. He shook his head, then looked back at the jury.

"I think, and Hope's record clearly establishes, there is a high probability that given the opportunity, she will continue to commit criminal acts of violence. Ladies and gentlemen of the jury, *that* constitutes a continuing threat to society." He took a dramatic pause and started a slow stroll back toward the jury box. As he walked he counted down on his fingers; first the pinky, then the ring finger.

"Secondly, we know that there was no mitigating circumstance that could justify the heinous crime Hope participated in, and lastly, we know Hope realized who she was rolling with. She should've anticipated that a human life would be taken in the event their robbery took a turn for the worse. She knew that by *rolling* with Q and Trey there would be bloodshed and an attempt to leave no witnesses behind."

As he stopped right in front of the jury, he again turned to me. His beady gray eyes focused in on mine.

"Ladies and gentlemen of the jury, you need to send a message to Hope Donovan. You need to tell her that in the great state of Texas, we don't take kindly to her *kind!* As a matter of fact, here in the great state of Texas, we believe that ultimate punishment is reserved just for her *kind*, the kind of criminals who know no boundaries. And ladies and gentlemen, the way to send that crystal clear message to Hope Donovan is to make her pay for her crime with her life. I want you to go back there and let her know with your sentence that we won't stand for such heinous acts in this great state of Texas. Send a message to Hope and others who would consider walking in her shoes."

As I sat listening to closing arguments, I felt like there was no way in hell he could be talking about me.

"Yo, Donovan!"

Pauline's voice snapped me back from that memory. I was on my bed reading a magazine, and I started thinking about the things that were said about me in court.

"That crazy bitch from True Justice is talking about you again!" Pauline screamed.

"What the…" I scrambled up from my bed and rushed to the door to try and catch what Adena was yapping about now.

"She's holding a press conference?"

"I'm so glad you all could be here today. I wanted to be the first to share wonderful news. As you know, the woman who helped her friends kill my husband and two innocent people has been on death row for the past five years. Well, I received word that she has written a letter to the Fifth Circuit Court of Appeals. Now she's requesting that all appeals be dropped and her execution date be set as quickly as possible." She had the nerve to grin like she was excited.

Every head in the day room turned in my direction.

"Party Girl, no!"

"What the fuck?" Pauline said.

"Don't give up. If those mofos wanna take you, make 'em work for it, Party Girl; make 'em work!" she added.

As I watched Adena take questions from reporters, all I could do was think Brendon must've lost his mind. What part of "don't say a word" did he not understand?

SEVENTEEN
BRENDON

"So you expect us to believe, you sitting up there with that fine-ass thang, Stacy, right across the street from your house, and you just palming it every night?" my boy Desmond Ford asked.

Desmond was the suave playboy of our trio. His main concern daily was making sure his fade haircut was properly lined up. He was always sharp because he wasn't sure when *GQ* was calling for his cover shoot, but he wanted to be ready. He wanted to screw every woman he saw. Most women fell for his lame-ass lines and threw their panties at him every chance they got.

"Shiiit, you a better man than me!" Jemar Charles chimed in.

Jemar loved the ladies, too, but nothing like Desmond. Jemar was more discreet with his womanizing. Regardless of how different their approach, the results were still the same; women fell all over themselves for their attention. Jemar was a playboy with a heart, which meant he was often caught up in drama because he kept falling in love.

I had met lots of people over the years. But I didn't have many close friends, except for Desmond and Jemar. With Hope's situation, I'd seen people come and go, but these two were there before, during, and they would be there long after. Those were the three categories that now defined my life.

Before Hope got into trouble, during, and of course, the future; and what will happen after the state kills her.

"Can I get you fellas anything else?" the young waitress asked. We were at Buffalo Wild Wings, drinking and shooting the shit.

"Another round," Jemar told her.

She gathered several empty bottles before bouncing away from our table. The restaurant was like a man cave, bustling with other sports fans and even some families. Massive flat-screens were all over the walls displaying games from mostly every sport.

It felt good to be out with the fellas. These days they were the only ones I went out with and we didn't do that often. I hated to leave Chastity alone with the kids; she was already going far above and beyond for us.

"So seriously, Bre-Man," Desmond continued, using the nickname he'd created when we were sophomores in high school. "You not hitting that?"

"That's one of my wife's best friends!" I said.

"Yeah? And, I ain't tryin' to be all outta order and shit, but Hope's been gone for more than a minute now." Desmond pulled the beer bottle to his lips and took a long swig. He sucked his teeth like he was trying to get his words just right. "She gotta know life goes on for you, dawg," he said.

"Nah, I'm good, man, seriously. It's all good over here," I said.

"Man, you can lie to yourself all you want, but you can't lie to us 'cause we know you better than you know yourself," Desmond said.

"I'm cool, man. Stacy is cool, but ain't nothing going down in that department," I said.

"Yeah, lying to yourself, man; lying to yourself," he repeated.

"Maybe there's nothing going on," Jemar said.

Desmond looked at Jemar skeptically. Then he chuckled.

"Don't tell me you buy that shit, man," he said.

"There's nothing to buy," I insisted.

"You seen Stacy lately? It's like her stock shot way up since that divorce. Her shit's like *bam*!" He clapped his hands together. "I mean, that body, that ass. On a good day a man wouldn't be able to resist. Talk about a man whose woman is on lockdown, and you got a recipe for disaster," Desmond explained.

"I'm telling you, ain't nothing popping off with me and Stacy, or any of those other broads on the block," I said.

"You probably wise to stay away from that one, dude," Desmond finally said.

I frowned. "Stacy?"

"Yeah, I heard she had something to do with the fire at Tamera's shop," Desmond said.

Those rumors were flying around the neighborhood, but I never paid that mess any mind.

"You think she had something to do with it?" I asked.

"You don't find it strange that any woman who came close to you suddenly bounced? I don't think it's a coincidence," Desmond said.

I shook my head and took a sip.

"Think about it, Jackie Smith, Tamera, Betty Jean?" Desmond said.

"What happened to Jackie?" Jemar asked.

"Wasn't she arrested for transporting drugs or something like that?" I asked.

"Nah, dude," Desmond corrected. "Drugs were planted in her car, then she was arrested. *Bam*! Tamera, once the shop burned down and she didn't have any insurance, she moved back West. Then we still don't know what happened to Betty Jean. All we know is Stacy and Chastity are the last two standing."

"C'mon with that," I said, trying to laugh off his conspiracy theory.

"Whassup with Chastity?" Jemar's eyes lit up.

"You can forget about that," I said. "Besides, she seeing ol' boy from around the way."

"Since when?" Jemar asked.

"I'm not all up in her business like that; she helps out with the kids and that's about it. What she does in her private life is her business."

"Yeah, okay," Desmond said.

"You barking up the wrong tree over there," I said.

"I think she wants to give it to you, man," Desmond said. "And if y'all know what's good, y'all would keep it away from Stacy; mark my words!"

I started cracking up. He had to be smoking something.

Jemar looked at Desmond like he was crazy, but then he turned to me. "It ain't like Hope ever has to know; besides, dude, the way she looks at you!"

"I'm with Jemar, Bre-Man; you needs to get on that! Seriously, dawg, you need to take it all the way! You making us all look bad," Desmond said. "But just watch out for your stalker across the street!"

"Getting involved with Chastity would be nothing but more problems and more headaches. I don't need that shit right now. I wanna keep my head on straight, focus on what's going on with Hope, and keep things copasetic between Chastity and me, the way it should be," I said.

"But you should get a pass on Chastity. Everybody knows how much she and Hope hate each other," Desmond said.

It was my turn to swallow some beer.

The bitterness between Hope and Chastity was legendary in our neighborhood, but everything changed when Hope went away, or at least that's what I told myself.

I hated when we got on this subject. I hated when my buddies felt like they had to help a brotha out by hooking me up with some easy hoochie, having the sex talk, or even paying for a stripper for me like I was some kid who needed assistance losing his virginity. I kept telling myself, but the truth was completely different.

They meant well, but the truth was, Hope was gone for good, A lot of shit went wrong with us. I kept telling Hope she needed to leave her past in the past but she wouldn't listen. Despite that, never did I ever think we'd wind up where we were today. The worst I thought would happen was she'd leave me for some loser from her past. Let the prosecutor, Joel Conley, tell it, I should've predicted something like this. I chuckled at the memory. That man hated Hope something fierce.

Most of that crap they said about her wasn't true, but there was no way I could convince my boys it wasn't. Yeah, let the D.A. tell it, my Hope was a modern-day Bonnie running with two Clydes who didn't move until they had her permission. By the time the District Attorney was done painting that picture of Hope, she made Bonnie look like Cinderella.

EIGHTEEN
CHASTITY

I didn't say a single word when he stepped into the room and closed the door softly. He was close to me and that's all that mattered. I inhaled and held his scent in my chest for as long as I could. We didn't need to speak; there was an unspoken understanding between us. Neither of us asked for this. We were victims of circumstance and we were trying to make the best of it.

He reached for me and I welcomed his touch. I wanted whatever he had to offer, no matter how meaningless and shallow it was.

His lips covered mine, and even though the room was dark, I kept my eyes open, trying my best to look deep into his soul. He tasted good; I could sense the hunger he must've felt because I felt the same way.

"Oh God!"

When his hand stroked me just the right way, I wanted to melt where I stood.

"You smell so good," he broke our kiss to say.

The kiss was rough, yet gentle, and mostly it was good because I wanted it. We stumbled toward the bed, but we wouldn't end up there. Anywhere but the bed was okay.

"I miss you," he said.

And I wanted to believe him, I wanted to think those words were meant for me, but I knew better. That's when I closed my eyes. This was the part I couldn't stand to see.

We kissed some more and this time we moved together toward the wing chair. It was either there, on the dresser, the nightstand in the bathroom, or even on the floor, anywhere but in the bed. I decided that made it feel less like betrayal and more like two people trying to help each other out.

When he tugged at my clothes, there was nothing gentle about his touch. He grabbed at my blouse like it irritated him to have to go through this each time.

"I got it," I said.

He always kept his pants on, only his fly was undone, and I wondered how that worked for him, but I didn't dare ask.

I sensed his impatience, I was eager, too. Once I got out of the top and wriggled out of my jeans, he grabbed me by the shoulder, and shoved me over the edge of the chair. He entered me with force, but I understood.

"Oh God!" I bit my lip to stay quiet.

He fit me perfectly, and I moved to his rhythm, rocking my body back when he pushed forward. It felt so good.

"You hittin' my spot," I managed.

His hands gripped my hips, and he held me tightly, like he thought I might try to get away. I wanted to move toward the magical mixture of pain and bliss.

"Shhiiit," he moaned.

"Yes, right there, it's yours!" I cried.

"Shhiit!"

He never expressed himself in a way that told me it was good for him; I had to assume.

When he grabbed my shoulder and held me in place, I realized it was time. Our passion was explosive but it was what we both needed. It always lasted just long enough. It was always so intense.

When we were done, he eased into the bathroom and that was

my cue to tip out of the room. I didn't leave any of my things and was careful to move quickly, but quietly.

As usual, the guilt was almost immediate. As I undressed for the shower, I wondered whether the seconds of bliss were worth the hours of torture I'd endured. It felt so right, but was wrong; we were wrong, but that never stopped me from going back for more.

In the shower, I scrubbed and scrubbed but still felt dirty. My tears always mixed with the scorching water but nothing ever changed. I still felt awful for a long time. This was a sick cycle, but neither of us knew how to make it stop.

I turned off the water, grabbed a towel and walked back into my bedroom. All I had to do was keep telling myself that things would get better soon. And I had to believe it, but it was so hard at times.

I jumped at the sound of the knock at the door.

I looked at myself in the mirror and couldn't stand the reflection looking back at me.

"You're going to scorch in hell for this," I said to my reflection.

But as usual, the bitch ignored me.

When my eyes snapped open, I realized I had been dreaming. Everything felt so real. Being awake and realizing that this had simply played out in my mind, made me feel even more pathetic.

Then I remembered the sheer awkwardness before I finally convinced Trevor to leave and go home, without me.

"So you just gon' leave me hanging like this? You up in here playing house and what am I supposed to do?"

Reluctantly he did, and I was relieved.

NINETEEN
HOPE

We were still reeling from the death of the mentally ill inmate on the row. In my opinion, the Texas Department of Criminal Justice was more of a murderer than those of us who are wrongly accused and convicted. Of course TDCJ found a scapegoat for everything that happened, so it was no surprise to us when we found out they had fired two nurses and one doctor. But that was it.

I had seen many inmates suffer because of a lack of proper medical care. Those of us who were work capable put in seven and a half hours a day sewing aprons. And, for our seven-and-a-half hours of work, we were able to get extra hours of recreation and are able to socialize more than the two who stayed in their cells just about all day. We had no TVs down our unit, unless you count the little one in the day room.

We had been separated from general population because we were death row inmates. We were cuffed, put in a day room and left alone when they were searching our cells.

If something were to happen while they were searching our cells, we had no way of helping ourselves. There had never been any violence on the female death row in all the years I'd been here, but yet, they treated us like it was the most dangerous part of the prison. When they started making it harder for us to use our radios, fans, typewriters, hot pots, curling irons, and blow-dryers, I was fed up. I wanted out, either through the bars or in a body bag. I was tired.

Back in the day, we did have some newspapers and magazines to read—a nearby school brought them over for us—but suddenly the warden said death row inmates couldn't read them anymore. We found out, a short time after he pulled that punk move, that general population inmates still read the papers and magazines.

At work I stood next to Latrice and we were both in our own worlds. Thoughts were running wild in my mind. I wanted to say bye to everyone in person, but that wouldn't be possible.

Then, as if she could sense what I was thinking, she leaned over and said, "Party Girl, don't do it! Fight until the very end; make their asses work for it!"

I couldn't figure out why people couldn't understand all my fight was gone! I was tired. My kids didn't know me, my husband was probably building a life with a new person, my mother was as disconnected as she'd always been and my sister didn't even talk to me. What was there for me to live for?

"These people don't care about innocence."

"Look at Anthony Graves; he was on the row for eighteen years before they realized he was innocent," she stressed.

"Eighteen damn years?"

"One eight," she confirmed.

"What kind of shit is that? More than half that man's life was spent in a damn cage, and he was innocent! I don't want to live like that. I've given this system more than five years of my life; it's time to end this shit! I'm tired."

Latrice didn't say anything else. I thought about the number of people on death row who really couldn't say they were innocent. They didn't want to die, they were remorseful, they were full of regret and given a second chance, they probably would be able to contribute to society, but they knew they were guilty as hell. Me, on the other hand, had gone through so much emotionally. I'd never killed, but at times I wished I had. At least if I had committed the crime, a small part of me would've felt like okay, you deserve to be in here, but I didn't do it. And the fact that no one with any real power cared made it that much worse for me.

Yes, I made the right decision. When the lady lawyer came to see me the other day I thought Brendon had gone and gotten someone else to try and change my mind. She was there to make sure I understood the ramifications of my decision.

I wanted to ask if she realized how long I had been caged up like an animal and if she did, did she know how sick this life was. I wanted to know what the hell did she not understand about me wanting to take control of the situation.

Brendon was mad. I figured Mona probably had something to say about my decision, too, but what everybody didn't realize or care about was that this was my life and I was tired of living it like some helpless animal. I didn't see Brendon's last appearance on TV, but everyone told me about it. They told me how he represented and how I was so lucky to have a man like him pulling for me on the outside.

While they were telling me all of this, all I could think about was how I could get him and everyone else to see the logic behind my decision. Brendon was a good man, but I wondered when he was alone with his thoughts and the only one that could hear him was God, what he said then.

"I hope you change your mind," Latrice said at the end of our shift.

It was funny; I didn't feel like going back to the cell, even though I had no choice. I wanted to stay around people. I wanted to hear voices other than the ones inside my head, and even though I didn't want to talk about my decision, I wanted to not feel so lonely. I wanted to not feel anything anymore. This was no way to live.

TWENTY
ADENA

I had been waiting for nearly an hour, but still I was patient. Everyone at the city knew me and they knew how determined I was when it involved something I wanted. But I was a little concerned now that Houston's crime victims' assistance office had moved over to the police department. Many of our groups were concerned about what that move would mean for our rights and the man who had done so much for victims.

Andy Kahan has long advocated for victims and our families. I could remember back in the early '90s when Harris County was a parole haven. Parolees would be released from prisons, given a one-way ticket to Harris County and allowed to roam free with no real destination. But it was Andy who informed elected officials that inmates were being dumped in Harris County at an unprecedented rate. Not only did Andy expose the problem; he ultimately helped find a resolution. In the national arena, Andy was perhaps best known for his fight against murderabilia, a phrase he coined.

By definition, murderabilia was the artwork, evidence, or personal effects of a murderer made available for sale. I couldn't imagine this was legal; victims' survivors and most decent people found this deplorable. But it was Andy who embarked on a ten-year mission to stop it. He pursued it with such vigor that the international awareness caused eBay to ban the sale of murderabilia. He spent his days accompanying victims' families to trials and parole hearings, even executions; forging an alliance with local and national media with the objective of publicizing victims' rights issues; convening with government leaders to discuss those same issues; and driving to Austin during legislative sessions to present them to lawmakers, along with suggestions for solutions.

I know personally that when we called him, he got right on it. I remember during Hope's trial, when there was news of a possible plea deal, I was trying to get an appointment with the district attorney. They would not return my calls. When I got Andy involved in it, within fifteen minutes after he called, they suddenly got my messages and we did finally meet with the DA. He had done so much in his nearly two decades as crime victims' director for the Houston Mayor's Office. He'd brought twenty pieces of legislation to fruition, including creating a capital offense for those who murdered a child six years old or younger; abolishment of mandatory release of convicted felons; and extension of statute of limitations on hit-and-run fatalities from three years to unlimited, as in other cases of homicide. I knew he'd be able to guide me in the right direction about adding pressure for Hope's swift execution.

I was familiar with some of the older detectives, but not so much with patrol officers. I had been talking with Andy Kahan for years. He was a friend of True Justice and he understood my need for justice.

"Would you like something to drink while you wait? Mr. Kahan's meeting is just about to wrap up," the assistant said with a smile.

"I'm fine, thank you. I expected a wait since I didn't have an appointment."

"Okay, it'll be just a few minutes more," she said, then disappeared behind the large monitor that sat on her desk.

As I waited, I used my cell phone to check emails and text messages from the office. Michelle texted me to say they were rerunning a program on which Hope's husband had appeared. I wondered if he was talking about her decision to end the appeals or whether it was an old show.

When Michelle texted back that she wasn't sure, I made a mental note to look it up later. I hated to miss out on anyone who spoke up on Hope's behalf. Frequently, they were trying to raise money for her defense or some kind of testing. Those rallies and vigils used to depress me. I wondered why the killers garnered such sympathy and support, when their victims were always forgotten.

We can't readily recall by name who Karla Faye Tucker killed, who Cleve Foster, Peter Cantu, or Frances Newton murdered. But their names have gone down in infamy in the state of Texas. There were people still today who would try and defend them.

Finally, Andy stepped out and greeted me with a smile.

"Adena, sorry about the wait," he said.

I followed him into his office and sat.

"I want to make sure there's nothing to stop this fast track for Hope's execution," I said.

"I knew you'd be here soon to talk about this, and I was actually going to call you," he said.

"Should I be worried?" I asked.

I didn't need anything or anyone coming up at the last minute and changing the course we were on.

"Well, I have a feeling about this one. Hope isn't like most of the death row inmates we're accustomed to dealing with."

I frowned. I hoped Andy wasn't getting soft on me. What did he mean she wasn't like most death row inmates?

"I happen to know about a massive effort that's underway to introduce new evidence in this case. The international community is crying foul even louder now as Foster's case was commuted."

Panic flushed my veins as I sat listening.

"Are you telling me that there's a chance she won't meet True Justice?" I asked, deathly afraid of the answer.

TWENTY-ONE
BRENDON

I opened the front door on an unusually quiet Saturday afternoon to find Stacy standing there staring at me with sad eyes.

"Whew! It's about time they left," she said. "I thought I was gonna have to come tell Chastity they'd miss the movie if she didn't leave soon."

My eyebrows went up a bit. I wasn't in the mood for company, but with Stacy, my mood didn't matter. She looked at me as if I was missing the obvious.

"Aren't you going to ask me to come in?" She huffed. A hand flew to her hip.

"Well, since Chastity took the kids out, I wanted to catch up on some sleep. I ain't been sleeping too good lately."

Stacy looked around. "It's such a nice day outside, we should be out enjoying it." She smiled.

We? I yawned, and leaned against the doorframe. "Nah, I need sleep. What's up?"

"I wanted to talk, you know, about us," she purred. I could sense her softening up a bit, but that always spelled trouble for me.

She reached out and stroked my chest. That caught me off-guard a bit. Her wicked smile was inviting. There was no *us*. I explained to Stacy I couldn't get emotionally involved with anyone while I was going through everything with Hope. I thought she understood, and not to mention, Stacy was a good friend of Hope's, or she used to be.

"I heard about what Hope did, and I knew you would take the news especially hard. I wanted to come and talk to you about it and what it really means," she said. "I don't blame her; I would've done the same thing a long time ago."

Was she serious?

Although I was looking into Stacy's eyes, my mind wasn't really focused on her. I didn't want to talk about Hope, and what she'd done. I didn't want to talk about her former best friend and me either.

Despite what my mouth was saying, Stacy heard what she wanted to hear. Soon, she was sashaying into the living room where she planted herself on the sofa and crossed her shapely legs. Her tight dress showed off every curve in her figure. She looked good, delicious even.

"I think it's time you let go." She began the talk I didn't want to have.

I was still standing near the door. I wasn't in the mood to fight or dodge what she was really there to give up. I was weak.

"Think of the kids and their future. Chastity's doing the best she can, but how much longer can you expect her to ignore her own needs?" Stacy looked around the room. "Besides, this place could use a real woman's touch. And I don't mean your sister-in-law's taste either." She smirked. Stacy glanced around the living room. I really didn't care what she thought about the place. I tried to tell myself it was best if she left. She knew how to get to me.

"Besides," she said, "It won't be long before you won't know what to do without me."

Stacy was always talking in crazy riddles and this time was no exception. I used my palm to go over my face and stifled another yawn, but she didn't seem to notice or care. Stacy was persistent.

She crossed, then uncrossed her legs, and I noticed everything about the way they moved. I even began to imagine how they would feel. It was like the devil was on one shoulder telling me to go with the flow. But common sense tried to seep in to warn me about what could happen if I fell for her antics, again.

"...who would blame you? You've been an outstanding husband to Hope. She didn't value what you all had. You've gone above and beyond; most men would've walked the minute she was arrested with those hoodlum friends of hers. I don't think anyone can blame you for wanting to enter the next phase of your life," Stacy said.

She was working me.

By now I was looking at her breasts. The battle in my head had started and this was what I wanted to avoid.

Stacy licked her lips.

I looked away and told myself I didn't have to kiss her. Stacy was looking for a husband but I was already taken. I glanced up when she licked her lips seductively again.

"We should think about a future together; it makes sense. Our kids are already best friends, and your sister-in-law really needs to focus on her own life. Trevor isn't gonna allow this thing to go on much longer. Besides, I'm here for you," she said. "And none of those other women would've been willing to wait on you the way I have."

I frowned. What other women? What was she talking about? Desmond's warning flashed through my mind.

"Hey, you ever hear from Betty Jean?" I asked.

Stacy stopped cold and looked at me with wide, curious eyes.

"What a blast from the past," she said. "Last I heard, she got knocked up by some married dude she was seeing." Stacy shrugged. "What you asking about her for?"

"Just curious," I said.

Stacy started caressing herself and she looked good. Thoughts of the other women quickly faded. In my mind I rolled around the pros and cons of sleeping with her again. Stacy said she didn't expect anything, but since her husband left, she'd been on me like I was the last man left on earth. I think her plan was to move him out and me in, even after I told her that wasn't going to happen; it seemed to me like she was trying to up her game.

Before I realized what was happening, I was up against the front door, my shorts around my ankles, and Stacy on her knees in front of me. My throbbing muscle was exploring her mouth and she felt so incredible. But this was wrong. Every little misstep on my part told her if she kept at it, she'd eventually be able to break me down.

I couldn't deny that she felt damn good. But still, I wanted it to end there. I didn't need her in my bed. But no matter how much I told her nothing would come of us and those stolen moments, she kept coming back for more. I wanted to be strong enough to turn her away before it came to this, but I couldn't.

Still on her knees, she grabbed my bare ass, pulled me in deeper, and moaned. She was driving me crazy. I shut my eyes and pretended Stacy was Hope. In my mind I told myself I had to do what I had to do. I justified what we were doing by reaffirming that Hope was never coming home. I hated myself for the pleasure I was experiencing and enjoying, while she was suffering.

"Ssstop!"

Stacy was relentless. When I moved, she moved.

"You gotta stop!" I screamed. I didn't really want her to stop, but I needed her to end this here. Instinct caused me to grab her head. I was going down fast and hard.

Was this really going to be over in a matter of months? Would Hope really be gone for good? What would happen with the kids and me, and what would happen with Stacy and Chastity?

Stacy was still on her knees, working. In the past she said she only wanted to please me because I deserved it and then some. But eventually she knew this would translate into some pleasure for herself, too.

I grabbed fists full of her hair and tried to pull her head off.

"What's wrong?" She looked up at me.

"I can't keep doing this; I need to get some sleep," I said. I realized my breathing was still rugged. I shouldn't have let that happen.

"C'mon, let's go to the back," she offered. "We'll be more comfortable there."

I shook my head. I didn't have the strength to keep fighting her.

"I'll be real quiet. I won't do anything you don't want me to do. Let me give you a massage. You seem so tense; let me help relieve some of the stress." She had started rubbing my thighs.

Her touch felt good. I started telling myself it wouldn't hurt to be with her. But I was also tired of having to look over my shoulder when I stepped outside. I hated to have to quickly dart from the door to the car, hoping she wasn't looking out of her window.

"I wanna help make it better," she said.

I watched as she fell back onto her butt and started caressing her breasts. She was relentless. And she knew sexy always won out.

Before I could lock the bedroom door, Stacy had undressed. She walked over and began to undress me. I didn't try to stop her; what was the use? Naked now, I stood there as she touched, stroked, and licked me like I was her favorite flavor.

I watched her as she pull a chair in front of the full-length mirror. I looked at it, then looked at her.

"Trust me, sit," she said seductively.

I sighed hard, but did what she said. I was crazy hard and ready for action.

Stacy mounted me.

"Ooooh," she cried.

I grabbed her hips to steady her.

She felt so good, so warm and so inviting.

"You could have this all the time, anytime you want it. You deserve this," she purred as she wiggled her hips.

I was under her spell. I closed my eyes. I didn't want to see her or what we were doing in front of the mirror.

I tried to bite down on my lip so I wouldn't make a sound. I didn't want to encourage her. But she didn't need me to cheer her on; she was performing like her life depended on pleasuring me.

"Open your eyes," she huffed as she worked.

She wiggled some more. "Open!" she commanded.

I finally did.

"Every time you look in the mirror," she huffed.

Sounds of our skin connecting filled the room.

"I want you to see me, see us, see what you could be having," she said.

Stacy was working overtime; she ground her hips and rode me mercilessly.

TWENTY-TWO
CHASTITY

I didn't need to turn around to know he had walked into the kitchen. I was at the sink washing dishes. The kids were already off to school, and I should've started work, too, but I wanted to wait for him, like I did most every morning. When he walked in, it was as if my spidy-senses had kicked in. I smelled him, sensed his presence, but more importantly, I felt him.

Brendon's scent was so enticing, so intoxicating, it was like torture to me; his voice sent my juices flowing into overdrive. Everything about him was sexy. He looked good, smelled good, and it had been five years, and each and every single day I'd tell myself that this was not right. He was off limits, but the heart wants what the heart wants. And I couldn't help that other side of me that kept thinking, how during the day we move around each other like two people who have never been intimate. Then at night all of this passion is oozing out of our pores.

I'd never fucked on so many different pieces of furniture. Sometimes I was grinning so hard, like when I was dusting during the day. It wasn't that I liked cleaning house, but an image of us would flash through my mind and it was like a done deal.

"What do you feel like eating tonight," I asked, trying to erase the taboo thoughts from my mind.

"It don't matter. Don't tell me you ain't got no hot date tonight?" he said more than asked. He already knew there was no other man for me.

I turned to face him, hands on my hips.

Brendon Donovan had gotten a raw deal. You know that cliché, when you think you got it bad, you should look at someone else because they have it worse? Well, Brendon was the worst they were talking about.

"Besides, you know Mona was talking about fixin' somethin'," Brendon said, talking about his flighty mother-in-law and my mother. He said that because I knew he felt what I was feeling. He figured if he talked about Mona, that would remind me of my role. The mention of Mona's name would make me remember that I was supposed to be there caring for my sister's kids, and I was. I was taking care of her house, her kids, but it was her husband I really wanted. And I wanted to do all sort of things to and with him.

I shook those thoughts from my head.

Who knew it was gonna go like this? We thought Hope was getting out, we thought she'd get probation; after all, what had she done? Sure, she had done some shit in the past, but who hadn't? We knew for certain the best lawyer money could buy would mean her freedom. But here we were, almost six years later, her kids were looking at me like I was their mother, her husband was looking at me with lust in his eyes, and Hope was closer to death. God help us all!

"What'd you make for breakfast?" Brendon asked, pulling my thoughts away from our sad reality.

"Made pancakes for the kids, but trying to think of something for dinner tonight." I had to turn away; looking into his eyes too long wasn't good for me. I'd become weaker by the day.

"God forgive me," I whispered under my breath.

"What you talkin' 'bout over there?" he asked.

Brendon was muscular, and tall, about six-two; he had a clean-cut thing going on. His eyebrows, thin mustache, and long side-burns were black, and made for a dramatic contrast against his caramel-colored skin. So many nights, I had dreamed of what it might feel like to have his multicolored lips pressed against mine. It was wrong, but it was how I felt. It was what I dreamt about.

"I asked what do you feel like eating for dinner," I said.

I whipped around to look at him. It was becoming more and more difficult for me. His eyes threatened to see right through me and I was more than a little ashamed of what they might see.

I had stopped accepting letters from Hope the moment I realized what was budding between us. It was the right thing to do. There she was sitting on death row, and me, her sister, the woman who vowed to step up in her absence, was trying to take her place. I was there daydreaming about fucking her husband.

I promised to take care of her family, become the mother her children needed, the wife her husband was missing out on, but never in a million years did I think I'd be sitting up falling in love with Brendon. Trevor had been right all along, but I didn't want to admit it to myself.

"I have a taste for some chili but only if you making that corn-bread with it." Was that a twinkle in his eye? Did his lips pucker too long on the word *with*?

He knew anytime I made chili, I made cornbread. He flirted with me in his own little ways, and I didn't know how much longer I could resist. God, forgive me.

"You are a mess." I smiled.

"What?" He smiled, and melted my heart in the process.

"Whatever, Brendon!"

"Whoa!"

We heard her before we saw her. I rolled my eyes.

"Whoa! Whooooooa!" Mona screamed.

If I didn't know any better, I'd think she'd hit the numbers or something, but Mona was loud and always overreacting. She called herself moving in about a few months or so ago. But the truth was, she couldn't pay her mortgage anymore and was about to be foreclosed on, so she popped up there, talking about she wanted to bond with her grandkids. She kept saying she wasn't gonna stay long.

But the minute she realized I was there cooking, washing, cleaning, and taking care of her grandkids, she fell in line and started acting more like an extra kid sitting back for me to wait on her hand and foot, too.

"Girl, I'm feelin' lucky today!" she screamed as she came running up the hall.

Mona was so full of it, so fake. But who was I to judge, when I was a phony myself?

"You make pancakes this morning?" she asked, stopping dead in her tracks.

"I did for the kids; you want some?"

TWENTY-THREE
HOPE

"How could they have found my fingerprints on a gun that I didn't touch?"

I was frustrated. It was so convenient to me, how the prosecutor needed to put the gun in my hands, so suddenly my prints were on it. Then, when he needed to place me at the scene of the crime, a witness said I was there. Then a jailhouse snitch conveniently claimed I confessed to her. But the thing that bothered me the most was Trey's confession. He confessed, saying it was my idea to rob the place and get rid of all witnesses. It made no sense; it wasn't true, but no one seemed to care.

"I didn't touch that gun!" I was adamant. I wasn't about to admit to doing something I didn't do. I knew the lawyer, Mona, and Brendon were frustrated, but so was I. So many times I dreamed of someone proving the DA was dirty. Trey was lying, but that lie turned into a life sentence for him. Since no one could talk to Q, I was stuck. Last I heard, he and Trey had fallen out before Q was killed anyway. I'd never know why, but so many people from the neighborhood placed me with those guys and that didn't help.

Of course I'd been with Q and Trey. When you had wheels in the hood, you were popular. I had accepted countless rides from them. Our families knew each other, but none of that mattered. When it really counted, all of that was twisted to help the DA's case against me.

Everything after the arrest moved like the speed of light. I remember back when I was first delivered to that ol' wicked and infamous Harris County Jail. It was beyond wicked. On average there were about twenty-two deaths here a year! Actually recently, in April, a prisoner who was brought in for a hot check died because of some sort of choke hold administered by one of the guards. Stories like that ran rapid throughout the system. I know from experience before being transferred out to the Mountain View unit. Even now, years after my time there, the memories still haunted me.

From what I heard the Feds were coming in to investigate the string of deaths and wondering what else was being violated. A quick glance around and I didn't have to wonder what they'd find in Harris County Jail. I was wondering what they were willing to do about what they found. Jail wasn't supposed to be pretty or else people wouldn't mind coming, but processing itself was like a thirty-six hour nightmare.

The only way you could enjoy sleep was if you liked sleeping on a cement floor where a stream of women had come and gone for days. Plus, it was crowded, and it was cold.

I sat and watched as a woman got up, grabbed a roll of toilet paper, and wrapped her legs. Another woman pulled the plastic garbage liner out of the trashcan, ripped a hole for her head, and pulled it over her body.

Remembered by the time I made it there, me and my business were plastered all over the news, and every newspaper, so I was certain I got double time in the cold holding cell because a guard took a real disliking to me and put my processing papers back for the next shift.

They told us over and over again, "We can turn out the lights and nobody will know you're even there." It wasn't a veiled threat. It was a real threat. Around six-o-clock the next evening I was ordered to go into a medical unit with fifty other women. Every seat on the only metal bench was taken. At least twenty women were sprawled on the floor. I was one of them; it was either that or stand. When I lifted my head, I felt dizzy. I hadn't had any water in two days, but liquids were one thing those guards were not big on.

My breath was beginning to stink, but it didn't even matter; everybody in this cell was stinking. For once it wasn't cold. This time it's hot, and fifty female bodies made it worse. This was the medical unit. I tried to recall the last time I was in there, but way back then, dying on the floor wouldn't have gotten you into the medical unit. You could've bled to death and it seemed as if no one would have been a little worried. So I wondered why all of us were in there.

I listened as one of the girls explained to the crowded room, "The feds are coming in next week," she said. I wasn't sure who she was talking to, but I listened because I had nothing better to do. She was rail thin, her wiry hair was all over her head, and she was missing several teeth. She used her bony arms to emphasize her words as she preached.

"Yup, they checking who is and who ain't getting medical attention if they want it. They also gonna see who died, and what were the circumstances around their deaths. That's why everybody coming in now goes straight to medical after thirty hours of a processing."

I wondered what was up, but I didn't dare ask a soul. In one corner of the room, another girl, who looked Hispanic, was going off on a hysterical frenzy.

"I'm a model, and I got me a college degree. I got five boyfriends and they all love me. The only reason I'm even in here is because someone stole my oven!"

Near her on the floor was a young black girl, who looked more like she was twelve instead of twenty-one. Her belly was huge; she was eight months' pregnant. "I know two women who lost their babies right here in this same jail!" she said.

That's when I noticed she was sitting in water. It looked like her water was leaking and she was bleeding.

"I'ma be okay! I'ma be okay," she repeated every few minutes.

Another inmate said, "Don't you dare talk to those investigators coming here. You'll end up dead!" she warned. "My own daddy died right in this same jail. Then they had the nerve to rule it a suicide. Now you tell me how he could've killed himself. There wasn't no way he could've, where he was found!"

Another inmate was trying to convince her to talk about it. "I saw a woman die right there," she said and pointed to a low cement bench in the unit we was in.

"Lucinda was her name and right before she died, she said to me, 'Lookey here at all these sores, lookey here.' Lucinda had two huge cankerous sores, one on her chest and another on her arm, and guess what, she died right there. Turns out she had diabetes and a staph infection."

She sat back, nodding. "You know there was a bad outbreak in here last year. It's a shame!"

I shook my head as I looked around and listened in on all of the conversations going on around me. I had a thought that we'd be in this unit for a very long time.

A few seconds later, a guard came in and said, "Y'all gonna be here a very long time. Might even have to pull y'all out in the morning for court, then throw y'all back in."

I sighed at that news. Just when I thought things were about to settle down a bit, the model with the oven goes crazy and some of the other inmates start howling to be let out of the room. A different girl looked at the melee and said, "I don't know why they making such a fuss. Don't matter; it's crowded upstairs, too. Wherever you go in here, it's crowded."

Hours later, when I thought it couldn't get any worse, it was time for the strip down. And I mean total strip down, worse than having a baby. I was getting a little sick with the whole thing and tried to imagine myself in a room all by myself. But, by the time my turn came around, I was one of twenty women in the middle of a strip down; worse than having two babies at once.

Finally, I was issued my orange jail outfit and ten minutes later, I calmed a bit, thinking in a few days, this would all be a bad dream to stash away with all the other bad experiences in my past. Little did I know that for years to come, I'd be stuck in a cell with the lights out. Soon, I'd feel as if nobody realized I was even there.

Now, as I thought back about that time, the early days in the county jail, what I wouldn't have given to be in a crowded cell. I wondered what the model with the oven was doing? I even wondered whether the girl delivered her baby. Even that crowded room waiting in the medical unit would've been better than being locked up in this tiny cell alone for most of the day.

TWENTY-FOUR
ADENA

Depression settled in fast. Over the next few days, thoughts of Hope Donovan walking out of prison a free woman haunted me. I couldn't allow that to happen. It felt like I was being victimized all over again. I had to be strong; so many people depended on me and my strength. They looked to me when they were weak and vulnerable. But very few knew of my dark moments. I didn't want to look up one day and see pictures of Hope hugging her husband or her children. I didn't want a reunion outside the courthouse after she was freed.

Everyone I talked to said the same thing. The decision was hers. She could literally be on the gurney in thirty to sixty days or she could change her mind and the appeals process could once again take more years.

My ringing phone forced me to try and pull myself together. I needed to be strong. I had to see this thing through. The truth was I'd be crippled by grief for as long as that woman was breathing.

"This is Adena," I answered as cheerfully as I could. "Yes, this is Adena," I repeated.

"Missus Binnaz, I'm returning your call," the attorney said.

"Yes, I have specific questions about Hope Donovan." I waited for the normal pause that was nothing new when I tried to get information about Hope.

When he didn't speak up right away, I started in.

"I understand that lawyers on her behalf are pushing for a new trial. I want to know why she claims she has ineffective counsel," I said.

"Ma'am, I'm not sure I can have this discussion with you."

"Why not? My husband was the victim in her crime. I have questions. If this woman is freed, I fear for my safety, so I don't understand why she deserves protection and I can't get simple information."

"Ma'am!" he shouted.

"Yes?"

"I'll help with what I can, but understand, I was Hope's court-appointed attorney. I did the best I could before her family scraped up money and hired private representation."

"Yes, I know all of that. But the kind of information I'm looking for now has to do with how after all of these years, she could claim ineffective counsel."

"I'm not sure I'm the best person to help you."

I wanted to be the judge of that.

"So, she claims she never touched the gun. Why then were her prints found on the weapon? Can you tell me that?"

"Ma'am, that was nearly seven years ago. Like I said, I was on the case but I was replaced. Much of what I had consisted of statements from family and friends. I didn't get a chance to dig too deep into the evidence before her family hired private counsel."

"So if I asked you what, if anything, you could think of that may get her a new trial, or if there was anything that stuck out about her case, what would you say?"

"Well, I'd have to think back. Again, that was so many years ago. I've handled so many other cases," he said.

"Yes, but how many death row cases involving women have you handled? You can't tell me that nothing about that case sticks out in your mind!"

He was making me angrier by the second. I happened to know for a fact that very few women were charged with capital punishment. There was no way he couldn't remember details from the case. When I researched, she was the only female defendant he'd ever had.

"What about the witnesses?"

"Again, nothing really sticks out in my mind. It's been so long."

As I was on the phone with him, a news tease caught my attention.

"Lawyers for a Houston mother who is on death row say they need more time. We'll have details about what's next for Hope Donovan, the local mother of three who sits on Texas' death row after being convicted and condemned under the state's controversial Law of Parties."

"Sir, thanks for your time!" I hung up abruptly. "So she's got a date!" I closed my eyes and this time, nothing but tears of joy seeped from my lids.

TWENTY-FIVE
CHASTITY

Brendon didn't want to talk, but I needed to hear it from his own mouth. Was he really seeing Stacy? She caught me on my way in from the mailbox and was bubbling with excitement.

She looked around as we stood on the sidewalk near the house.

"Girl, come on over here," she said, all but dragging me to her house.

"I was um..."

"I wanna give you something Breanna left over here yesterday. Wait right here," she said as she dashed down the hall.

I didn't want to be inside Stacy's house and I damn sure didn't want to be chit-chatting with her about Brendon. A few minutes that felt like hours passed and she still hadn't come back.

"Stacy?" I called out as I ventured down the hall. Her bedroom door was ajar. I stuck my head in and called her name.

Something flickering in the corner near her window caught my eye. I couldn't understand how she had a candle burning so close to her sheer curtains.

"I'll be right out!" her voice yelled and I nearly jumped out of my skin.

"Oh, okay," I said.

But instead of turning around and going back to the living room, I stepped into her room to get a closer look at the candle.

What I saw made me jump and run from her bedroom. I rushed

through the front door and was headed back across the street until she stopped me.

"Chastity, here; it's Breanna's shirt. I had to dig for it, but I didn't think I was that long." She giggled.

I was spooked. I grabbed the shirt from her and turned to leave when she touched my arm.

"Oh, yeah, I just want to say a huge thank you, to you." She giggled.

I frowned. I had no clue what she was talking about. What was she thanking me for? I hadn't done a thing for her and didn't plan to.

She leaned in like someone might be listening to our conversation.

"Brendon, he's getting closer and closer to realizing that hanging on to what he had with Hope is a waste of time. When we were together a few days ago, he finally broke down and told me he's just waiting for word on a new execution date."

How did she know these things if she and Brendon were not together? And after what I had just witnessed with my own two eyes, I couldn't find any words. I turned abruptly and walked back to the house.

"Chastity!" she screamed after me.

But I didn't listen, and I didn't stop. I kept walking. I entered the house and walked straight to the back and closed the bedroom door behind me. About an hour passed when there was knocking at the door.

"Who is it?"

"Chastity, can I come in?" Breanna eased the door open and poked her head in. "Where were you?"

"Oh, in the shower," I said.

"No, I mean earlier. I was looking for you, 'cause I wanted to ask you something."

Breanna was ten years old and she liked to talk. Usually, she wanted to talk about *Hannah Montana*, *I-Carly* or another one of those Disney shows she was addicted to.

"What is it?"

"You remember Selena Gomez, right?"

I sighed, but Breanna didn't notice or didn't care.

"Yes," I said.

"Well, I heard she's gonna have a concert at the Toyota Center," Breanna said. "Everybody's talking about it."

"And?"

"And, I wanted to know if you'd take me and McKenzie," Breanna asked.

McKenzie, Stacy's daughter, was her best friend.

"I might," I said.

Her eyes lit up and the big Kool-Aid smile grew even wider.

"If your dad says it's okay," I added.

"I was looking for him. I couldn't find him either. You think he went to the store or something?"

I turned away from her and started fidgeting with my clothes.

"You can ask him later; now let me get dressed," I said.

"Okay, but you're the greatest, Tee-Tee!" she cheered. After she left, I started thinking about Stacy and the foolishness in her house. I needed to tell Brendon, but with the kids around, that would be hard to do.

Soon, the door slammed and I could hear Mona yelling as Breanna went down the hall.

"B.J., don't start fighting with your sister," Brendon said.

We were all seated around the small dining room table for dinner. I understood the importance of having family dinners together, so I tried my best to make sure we did it at least four to five times a week.

Tonight, I had made mashed potatoes, green peas, and smothered chicken with dinner rolls. But I kept thinking about Stacy and what the hell she was trying to do over there.

"She started it," Brendon Junior said. He was eight, and the middle child. He frowned, crossed his arms at his chest and poked out his lips at his older sister, Breanna.

"Anybody want more dinner rolls?" I asked, trying to lighten the mood as I passed the breadbasket to Breanna.

I didn't like when the kids started wilding out. Brendon worked hard, he had enough on his plate and the last thing he needed was to come home to a bunch of unruly children. When they misbehaved, it made me feel like I wasn't living up to my end of this deal.

I didn't want Brendon thinking I couldn't handle his kids. I was there to help him out, keep order in the house and handle the family.

Breanna took the basket of dinner rolls and placed it down on the table so hard I thought she'd crack the glass.

"Bre, chill," her father warned.

"I want more juice," Blake, the youngest, yelled. He was six.

These kids weren't bad, but they could be more than a bit active at times. I tried my best to keep things in check and keep them under control. I was hoping they wouldn't pick tonight as the time to act out. I hadn't said a word to Brendon about what I saw over at Stacy's or even what she'd said, but I wanted to. I wanted him to clear up what had to be a huge mistake on her part.

Brendon looked at me. "Dinner is really good tonight, Chas. We're so lucky to have you."

I smiled. But what I really wanted to do was send the kids to their rooms, use my arm to clear a spot on the table, and jump Brendon's bones right there in the middle of the dining room table. But instead I blushed. "I'm glad you like it."

The words hadn't really left my lips when a big wad of potatoes went flying across the table and landed on the wall behind Breanna's head. She ducked.

I don't know who started laughing first, but it was on.

Before I could say anything else, a massive crowd of peas flew toward B.J. I'm not sure where the rolls came from, but they were being fired like missile rockets searching for their target.

"Cut it out!" Brendon screamed.

But it was too late. Before long, we were caught in the middle of a full-fledged food fight, and I didn't know what to do. S*hould I laugh or try to act like the adult in the room?*

"Stop it! Stop it!" I yelled.

But the clump of food that smacked me across the forehead made me stop for a second, forget where I was and soon, I started flinging food, too.

"This is crazy!" I said.

"Cut it out!" I heard Brendon say before I saw him grab a fist full of dinner rolls.

Soon, the room was filled with laughter and screams. Food was flying so fast I could hardly keep up with which direction I should duck.

"Stop it, this is crazy!" Brendon yelled, but I could've sworn he hurled a wad of chicken in my direction.

The melee finally stopped when the house phone rang. We all froze and looked in its direction. My eyes quickly glanced toward the clock. It was probably Hope's nightly call. Sadness fell over the room. Everyone's demeanor instantly changed.

The children went from laughter to somber faces. Brendon

looked as if he wasn't sure what to do. When the phone rang for the third time, my eyes darted to Brendon; I wondered why he hadn't jumped for it.

My heart started racing and I suddenly got excited. It was sick, but was his devotion fading? I quickly told myself there was no point in reading anything into that.

"Phone, Dad," Breanna said as she wiped mashed potatoes from her cheek. "It's probably Mom."

That's when Brendon moved and I started trying to clean up. I didn't want to hear him talking to his wife. I didn't need to hear the sweet exchange. Each night I replayed those words in my dreams and that was enough for me.

Brendon caught the phone and started picking up the food that had fallen to the floor. I didn't want the kids to see the sadness on my face.

They, too, were victims in this mess. I didn't need Blake questioning me like he'd suddenly started doing.

"Tee-Tee, whas wrong?" he'd ask when he found me crying.

"Tee-Tee, who hurt your feelings?" he'd ask.

The truth was I loved these kids and I had no idea how this mess would end, but I didn't like the idea of them being caught up in the middle of it.

"Hey, Chas, the phone's actually for you," Brendon said.

He caught me completely off-guard. I didn't want to talk to Hope. I wasn't in the mood. I'd been successfully avoiding her calls and I wanted to keep it that way.

"Um, I'm a little busy," I said with a hint of an attitude. *Why would he even try to put me on the phone with her?*

"Yeah, but it's Trevor," he said.

"Oh." I dropped the napkin I was using to wipe up green stains, and rushed into the kitchen.

"Thanks," I said to him.

"Don't worry about the mess; the kids and I will get it," he said as he walked back into the dining room. My eyes were glued to his ass like there was no place else to look.

"Hello?"

"Chastity, what are you doing?"

Could Trevor read my mind? Did he sense how I was looking at Brendon? I shook the paranoia from my mind.

"Oh, we're just finishing up dinner. Why, what's going on?"

"I wanna come by and see my woman! Is that gonna be a problem for dude?"

Trevor wasn't one to mince his words. He was still pissed about the other day when he came to fight and I shut it down before he could start. So it came as no surprise to me that I'd get an earful when he called claiming he wanted to *see* me.

"Uh, yeah, you can."

"You see that woman on TV?" he asked.

"What woman?"

"That woman, you know the one whose husband your sister killed—you know, your boyfriend's wife," he said.

"Brendon isn't my boyfriend," I said, lowering my voice as I spoke.

"Well, if you ain't screwing him yet, it's only a matter of time."

"Trevor, what's really going on? Is this why you called?"

"What? Shit, I can't joke with you anymore. I don't understand how you could put your life on hold like this. You over there playing house with your sister's husband, and meanwhile, shit is falling apart between us," he said.

I had heard this so many times; it hardly fazed me anymore. When I told Trevor I was going to help out with Hope's kids, he looked at me like I said I was about to reproduce with an alien.

He forgot he was lying up with me when people were already talking about him and his wife getting back together.

"I don't like this shit one bit," he had said.

Then when I told him I was moving in with Brendon and the kids, he was fit to be tied.

"What the hell is he over there telling you? You expect me to sit by while you play house with some other man?" He had yelled so loud, I was sure everyone in the Breakfast Club knew all my business.

Trevor had the nerve to lean forward like he was about to lower his voice; instead he yelled right in my face.

"I left my wife to be with you and now you wanna go and play concubine to your sister's husband! Damn, you a cold piece; your sister's in the slammer! You got your own life to live, but yet you gon' be over there laying up with her husband?" he yelled.

I was so embarrassed, but when it was all said and done, I had already made up my mind about what I was going to do.

"I didn't see the interview," I told Trevor. "Is that all you wanted?" I wasn't worried about him coming to see me. He liked to use that line when he was pissed at his wife.

"Why you rushing me? Massa say it's time to get off the phone?" he asked with a chuckle.

I rolled my eyes at his comment; it wasn't funny.

"Look, I need to get the kids to bed. I'll call you back," I lied.

"Ain't even got time to talk to your own damn man," he said. I wondered where I was when he became my man again.

I chuckled and said, "I'll call you back," even though I had no intention of doing that.

After hanging up the phone, I stood there for a moment, wondering how much longer I'd have to suffer.

TWENTY-SIX
BRENDON

I t had been a long time since I was accosted outside my house by anyone other than Stacy. I nearly jumped when the woman approached me and thought Stacy was gonna come running out of her house as she stood watching the woman talk to me.

"I'm Jennifer Crowe and I'm working on a story that could help your wife's case. I understand she wants to die now, and since she's got the new execution date, I may be able to help. First, I wanted to ask you a few questions."

She was a thick white girl with long stringy hair. Looking at her, I wouldn't think she was a reporter for anybody's newspaper, but she had the plastic badge around her neck and a digital recorder with a microphone plugged into it if I needed evidence.

"What's your name again?"

Stacy was still at the window watching us, but I ignored her.

"Jennifer Crowe," she said.

"Jennifer, why didn't you call me? We could've set something up. I'm running late for work."

"I was hoping we could start the interview now, but obviously we'd finish sometime later. I was turned on to your wife's case because of a lawsuit being filed against the DA that prosecuted her. If all goes well, some of the information I've already uncovered may help Hope."

I stopped walking. I wasn't in a real talkative mood. I had lots on my mind, between Hope, Stacy, and Chastity, I didn't know if I was coming or going. These days work was more like an escape for me.

"What do you do for a living?" Jennifer asked.

"I work for Metro. I'm a bus driver," I said.

"Oh, how long have you been with the company?"

"Nearly ten years; why do you ask?"

Jennifer's green eyes looked a little red. I wondered if she smoked weed, but I didn't ask.

"Have your bosses been supportive?"

"Yeah, pretty much." I stopped walking and looked at her. "Listen, Hope didn't do this. Most people who have followed her case realize that she made a bad decision. What happened to Hope really could've happened to any of us. It's that simple."

Jennifer looked at me. "You know what, I believe you. It doesn't make sense. She had so much to lose; I think it's a shame that she's giving up. Another man, Jerome Singletary, was released last year after some of the former District Attorney's tactics were revealed. But mainly, I don't want Hope's case to turn into a situation like Todd Willingham; you know, after he was executed, we found out he really didn't do it."

Until Jennifer mentioned that, the thought hadn't crossed my mind. I wish Hope understood what she was doing. The thought that even after she's executed, we could find the evidence to prove she didn't do it? I'd be sick. Suddenly, I wondered if Hope had considered that. I wondered if she realized that then it would be too late.

"Listen, Jennifer, I need to run. Call me and we can set something up for later. Is that okay?"

"Yeah, that'll work; sorry about showing up unannounced, but I wasn't sure if you handled your own media so…" She shrugged.

I didn't have time to think about what she meant by that. I was grateful she told me about Todd Willingham. I knew all along my route that my mind would be stuck on that Willingham case. He was the guy who was executed because fire marshals ruled a fire at his house was arson. They said he set the fire, he was convicted and given the death penalty. After he was executed, we learned the fire marshal's office doesn't even have legitimate standards to properly identify arson.

As I pulled out of the driveway, I noticed Stacy on her front porch. I wasn't sure if she was about to go and say something to Jennifer. It wouldn't surprise me if she did, but I couldn't worry about that.

Later, I was anxious to talk to anybody about the Willingham case. I even called several attorneys. I was trying to find out everything I could about his case and get enough information to try and change Hope's mind. I wondered if it was too late. I needed to know she wouldn't have the final say.

When I walked into the house, Mona came rushing around the corner.

"I'm so sick of this bitch right here!" Mona snapped.

"Who, what's going on?"

"Oooh, that damn Adena, she was on the news earlier today talking some more shit about Hope. Lord knows I'm so sick of that woman!"

"What's she up to now?"

Mona was on fire. Her hands flew to her hips and her neck started twisting. "The bitch don' went and started a petition! Can you imagine? She wants people to sign a damn petition to put my baby to death!"

That news nearly broke me down. Here I was all day long excited about the idea of using the mess with Todd Willingham's case to convince Hope to change her mind only to hear this. It was like we took a step forward only to fall three steps back!

"What do you mean she's starting a petition?"

"The bitch says she wants to make sure Hope doesn't get cold feet, so she's going around gathering signatures! How could people be so damn insensitive? I know she doesn't believe Hope is innocent, but why go to this extreme? The girl has already said she's ready to die. She don't need no damn help!"

"Calm down, Mona, calm down. You know Adena is nothing but a media ho. The minute she sees an interview or article about Hope, she feels like she needs to speak out. I'm sure all this news about Hope dropping her appeals is making her feel restless."

"I wish I could go slap some sense into that girl! Why she wanna go and make it easy for them murders is beyond me! I'd be kicking and screaming all the way to the death house. Some people live on death row for years; why she so ready to give up?"

"She won't listen to me. I told her this was a huge mistake. She's giving up too soon. I really believe someone is gonna look at one of those appeals and give her a new trial."

"Well, it ain't enough if she don't believe it," Mona said. "That damn Adena; she better be glad murder for hire is frowned upon!"

"Mona!"

"I'm serious, Brendon; that bitch gonna make me wait for her in a real dark parking lot late at night!"

Mona was a real character, but she was good for keeping it real. I'd hate for something to happen to Adena, because as many threats as Mona had dropped against that woman, homicide wouldn't have any problems solving that crime.

★★★

The week dragged by so slowly I thought I was gonna lose my mind. I couldn't wait to visit Hope. She had to hear me out. She had to listen to what I had to say about the Willingham case.

I wanted to say something to Chastity, who seemed to be upset about something. But each time I tried to talk to her, one of the kids came barging in or Mona was cursing up a storm about Adena. All of the news stations ran her story several times in all of their later newscasts.

Two nights in a row, Chastity fixed food, got the kids settled, and then she left. The funny thing was, I thought she was turning in early, but when I eased back to her room, I was shocked to find out it was empty. I wondered where she was, not that it was really any of my business. Unfortunately, I didn't get the chance to talk to her about what was going on; if it wasn't the kids, it was Mona. To me, not much got past Mona; she seemed to notice everything and this was no exception.

Even before I could put a finger on whatever was happening with Chastity, I started noticing the glances Mona threw our way. She'd purse her lips and her beady eyes would go between the two of us like she was confirming what she already knew.

"Mona, you wanna come see Hope with me?"

"Can't, baby, but you tell her I'm thinking about her. And you tell her I said don't worry about that damn Adena."

The visit with Hope wasn't one of our better ones. The whole time I spoke, she looked at me like I just didn't get it.

"I should have a new date in a week or two," she said.

"Hope, haven't you heard a word I said? Don't you care about Todd Willingham?"

"Brendon, he's a white man," she said unenthusiastically.

I shrugged.

"The rules are different, even when it comes to death row. You see that man is dead, but still his supporters are struggling to keep his memory alive. They want the state to admit they've killed an innocent man; well, with me it's different. If no one cares about this stupid law that could really get anyone caught up, all the fussing and evidence in the world won't be enough to save me from that death chamber."

"What happened to you, Hope?"

She looked confused.

"Seriously, what happened to you in here?"

She didn't answer.

"It's like you're already dead," I said.

Hope didn't deny it. She stared at me but I could tell she was only looking through me. It was like she was going through the motions, waiting for the guard to give us the signal so she could slip out of this conversation.

"It doesn't have to be like this," I said.

I couldn't imagine anxiously waiting all week to talk to her about this, then having her stare blankly at me like I'm wasting her time.

"Nothing's gonna change, Brendon. I need you to accept the facts. I'm going to die for a crime I didn't commit. And if I had it my way, I'd die tomorrow! I'm tired of this shit and I want it to be over as soon as possible! So, I'm glad that the state of Texas is now looking into whether they executed an innocent man. I'm sure he hasn't been the first, isn't the only one, and he damn sure won't be the last."

We got our cue; this visit was dead. But it was the dead look in Hope's eyes that really scared me shitless.

TWENTY-SEVEN
HOPE

Days after our last visit, I was still thinking about Brendon and his excitement over the Todd Willingham case. What did he think that was gonna do for me? When it was all said and done, he walked out and went back home to our family. I was returned to my small cell where I was reminded of how pathetic life on earth was for me now.

I had written letters to radio stations, newspaper reporters, blog writers, and still no one believed me. I didn't try scare tactics, but I did tell people that what happened to me could literally happen to anyone. Still, nothing!

How did anyone expect me to get excited after all I'd experienced and I was still there?

During my time in the rec room, I caught a glimpse of Adena on TV. She hated me so much I almost ached for her. How could you hang on to so much hatred for a person you've never personally met?

Latrice was watching TV with me.

"She's on one, for real, huh, Party Girl," she said, talking through the bars.

"It's crazy. I wonder if this woman has a life. She seems to spend all of her time making sure I'm going to die."

"You ever reach out to her? To tell her your side, how you didn't do it?"

My eyes were glued to the screen. They were showing pictures of Adena and her husband. I could see how much she had aged; I wasn't responsible for her misery. But she didn't want to hear it; she needed to have me to blame. Her man was gone and I was still around; she wouldn't rest until I was dead, too.

"She doesn't want to hear my side; she needs me to be the bad person. Think about it, for her to be confronted with the idea that I'm innocent, she wouldn't know what to do."

"Yeah, you probably right. But, Party Girl, I wish you'd change your mind. Why make it easy on 'em? Make those bastards come drag you up outta' this bitch if they wanna give you that needle."

I laughed at the thought. I could see myself refusing to leave the cell. It would take three or four C.O.'s to come in and drag me out.

"Wouldn't that make news around the world!"

"Shiiit! You know we'd be cheering you on from our own death traps."

Another inmate walked into the rec room.

"What y'all over there hacking about? Y'all sound like old hens," she said.

Latrice turned to answer.

"I was just telling Party Girl she need to withdraw that move she did, dropping her appeals!"

"Oh, fo' sho'!" Pauline said. She sat down at the table next to us. Her shoulders were so wide, and her haircut really made her look more and more masculine.

"I was wondering why you went and did that shit anyway!"

"Just tired," I said. "I'm sick of being in here, sick of this shit, and I want it to be over!"

"Yeah, but anything could happen. Who's to say your sentence won't be commuted?" Pauline asked.

I looked at her like she was crazy. Commuted sentence? I want out! I don't want to spend the rest of my natural life caged like an animal.

"Pauline, that's what I'm saying; I don't wanna be here! The state has already robbed me of damn near eight years of my life. First, the nearly two years I spent waiting for trial, then I've been on the row for five years. It's too much; you think I wanna grow old up in this place?"

Pauline eased back in the chair that looked like it might crumble under her weight.

"Shiiit! I plan to go senile up in this bitch! I plan to appeal every single aspect of my trial and when that runs out, I may try to appeal some of yours, too!"

She rushed over to the cell and slapped high-fives with Latrice.

"I say let them Mofos provide me with three hots and a cot until I'm in my golden years. Then after that, I'ma' call on the governor, the state attorney, and even the U.S. Supreme Court if I have to."

In theory Pauline's point sounded good, but emotionally I realized I couldn't hang in there that long. I shouldn't have let what people said get to me, but I couldn't help it. My skin wasn't that thick. Even if I ever got out, which I wouldn't, I couldn't imagine walking down the street and having people whisper.

"You think she did it?"

"What if she did?"

"Did she get away with murder?"

No, all of that would be too damn much for me. I wasn't strong like Pauline, Latrice, or even Evelyn. Her petite housewife image was just that, an image. One thing I learned by being on the row is that those women weren't taking shit from anybody!

I was glad when Adena's story went off. I was sick of her and

her victim role. She made me so sick. Every time she was interviewed, she talked about me and only me. What about Q or Trey?
Had the bitch forgotten I wasn't alone in that car? Oh, just like
the DA, she probably used only the information that sounded
good in her sound bites.

"Your ol' man, how's he handling this?" Latrice was always
concerned about Brendon.

"He's not. He's pissed. Wants me to change my mind, says I'm
being selfish. I absolutely hate it in here!" I looked around to
make sure none of the C.O.'s were listening as we talked. They
didn't need much to start holding a grudge and I didn't need any
trouble.

"You think any of us like being in here?" Pauline asked. "I'd
give anything to spend some time in general population. Ain't
nobody stupid enough to let my big ass out of prison, but if I was
in population, I could *live* like that."

She looked back at Latrice and started laughing again.

As I watched the two of them, I could see how they'd do well
in population. They were both really friendly and outgoing. People
gravitated to them. But it was different for me. I was a little outgoing, but mostly with the people I knew. It usually took some
time for me to warm up to people I didn't know. That's probably
why it was so hard for me to do what Brendon wanted and that
led to so many of our fights.

I never understood how he expected me to act like people from
my past didn't exist. It was easier for him; he only had a few close
friends anyway. But it was different for me. People from my old
neighborhood felt a special connection to each other. I keep
thinking maybe Trey implicated me because of the way we made
fun of him throughout the years.

It wasn't like we picked on him, but he couldn't get any play whatsoever. And he tried. I think he tried everyone from me, to Stacy, to Betty Jean, Jackie and even Chastity. He didn't realize it wasn't really about him. But I suppose he did finally get the last laugh. I know for a fact Conley had nothing on me without his confession. I didn't do it. I knew it, Conley knew it, and so did Trey.

I simply wished those jurors had known it, too.

TWENTY-EIGHT
BRENDON

I was meeting Desmond and Kemar at Fox Sports Bar and Grill to watch the game. I got there before either of them so I grabbed us a table and quickly ordered a drink.

As I sat there I kept thinking about the mess my life had become. Shit was all jacked up and I had no idea how to fix it. I was trapped between two women and at least one of them was unstable. I kept thinking this shit couldn't get any worse, but the truth was, it could. What if Hope ever found out? She had to know I was doing what I needed to do to survive, but I was sure she would never guess this situation I was in right then.

The really jacked-up part was, I didn't know what to do because picking one over the other would do nothing but cause more drama than I needed.

"Say, Bre-Man, you look like you lost your puppy." Desmond slapped me on the back from behind before he walked around to take a chair at the table.

"Nah, dude, what you talking about? I was tired of waiting on y'all slow asses; that's all!"

"Save it, man! You looked like you were seconds away from tears. Shit, I felt like I had to rush over here and talk you off the edge. What's up?"

"I'm good, I'm good. I don't know what you thought you saw, but I'm straight!"

Desmond flagged down a waitress who came over right away.

"Miller Lite on the tap, and another round for him," he said before she could say hello. "It's been one of those days," he added.

The waitress looked at me and smiled. "What are you drinking?"

"Oh, I was drinking Budweiser, but since he's buying, make mine a Heineken!"

She looked at Desmond and he nodded. "It's all good." He chuckled. "The poor bastard is having a horrible day," he joked.

He waited until she walked away before he started in on me again.

"Seriously, I heard about Hope giving up and shit. I can imagine how that's got you all messed up in the head."

I didn't really want to talk about Hope; I wanted to drink. I felt like drinking would help me forget about all the shit that was wrong, even if it was only for a little while.

"Yeah, Hope's gonna do what Hope wants to do. Damn everybody else!" I shrugged like it was really nothing. But Desmond knew better.

Our drinks arrived.

We sipped without saying anything else at first. We were watching the game and I looked at my watch.

"Where the hell is Kemar?"

"Probably caught up at work; you know how it is," he said.

"If that fool spent more time working and less time trying to chase skirts, he'd be okay," I said.

Desmond started laughing. He knew I was telling the truth.

"He'll be here. We were talking about you last weekend. He said it's been a while, and shit, it has. What's been keeping you so busy?"

"Man, this stuff with Hope is killing me. Then a bunch of other shit, too; after a while, it feels like it's too much!"

Desmond sipped his beer. He nodded slowly. Without commenting on what I'd said, he looked up at the game and frowned.

"I can't think of a single person who would blame you for walking away, man. Think about all the time and money you spent. It's not like you didn't warn her about them shady characters in the first place."

There was a time when a comment like that would've really pissed me off and ruined my night. But now, I'd accepted the truth for what it was. All she had to do was listen to me. I'm not saying our life would've been perfect together, but damn, we wouldn't have been dealing with shit like this. Whose wife is convicted of capital murder and sent to death row? Sometimes I look around wondering if the cameramen are gonna jump out of the bushes.

"Hope always worried about what other people would think," I said.

"Yeah, but everybody knows that you can't expect everyone from high school to take the ride with you. There's a reason you need to leave some of 'em behind."

I held up my hand. "Preaching to the choir, dawg, and I'm not in the mood for a sermon today!" I pointed at my beer. "This is all I want right now."

"I feel you, I feel you," he said, then sipped his drink again.

An out-of-breath Kemar slid into a chair next to Desmond. "Sorry I'm late. I had some business to handle in the parking lot of my building."

Desmond and I eyed each other and started laughing.

"Some things never change," I said.

"Hey, what's up with Hope?" Kemar asked.

Desmond tried to warn Kemar by clearing his throat, but it didn't work. Kemar looked at me. "Why in the world would she basically request a speedy execution? She giving up just like that?"

"It ain't been *just like that*," I said. "It's been more than seven years, I'm broke, we're damn near out of options, her kids don't know her anymore, her mother and sister have all but left me to deal with her, and she's frustrated. Can't say I blame her. I'm not happy about it, but it's her life, not mine."

They both looked at me like they never expected all of that from me. I said I didn't wanna talk about that shit anymore. It wasn't like I was passionately in love with Hope anymore. The love started seeping away when she couldn't let go of the past. I got tired of fighting over those thugs and hoodlums she couldn't stop mingling with. Guilt was what kept me loyal for as long as that lasted. I felt guilty about some of the shit I was doing myself while trying to judge her. Then, of course, I needed the kids to see that I had control over this mess.

By the time I lost control, it was too late. I looked up and I was stuck between these women and the one in prison. Who knew how the shit would turn out?

The waitress came back to check on us. "You guys okay over here? Oh, a new one. I turn my back and you multiply."

She spoke to us all, but her eyes seemed to lock on Kemar. Desmond shook his head and I already knew what he was thinking before he said it. "Another round."

"Yeah, and add a Miller Lite from the tap for me," Kemar said.

We watched as she smiled seductively at him, then she asked, "Is there anything else I can get for you? Um, I mean, you guys?"

"Nah, that's good for now." Kemar's eyes rolled up and down the length of her body.

"Why don't y'all take it to the room?" Desmond asked the minute she turned and walked away.

I started laughing.

"Nah, I barely had enough energy to get over here. The new receptionist at the office; she's a beast!"

I shook my head. I couldn't believe it. As I was about to take another sip, something on the news stopped me cold.

"A Houston woman now has a date with death. We'll have details about the new execution date for Hope Donovan, the Houston mother of three who sits on death row, convicted and condemned under Texas' controversial Law of Parties!"

Desmond and Kemar looked at me; we were all speechless.

TWENTY-NINE
CHASTITY

I had no idea how Brendon even made it home. I saw head-lights turn into the driveway and I heard keys dangling at the front door, so I jumped up to see what was going on. When I opened the front door, he stumbled in and nearly landed flat on his face. He reeked of alcohol and I knew he had drunk some bar completely dry.

"Chastity." He fell into my arms. "Where you been? I thought you were mad."

"Did you drive home?" I asked. I grabbed the keys from his hand.

"Nah, the waitress drove me," he said. "Kemar's waitress."

"Oh, okay." I had no idea how his friend had a waitress, but what-ever. I was glad he'd made it home in one piece.

"I'm good though, I'm good."

He didn't look good and he smelled like he had been soaked in alcohol.

"Damn, how much did you have to drink? And what were you drinking like that for anyway?" I was so scared for him; I didn't want him to die from alcohol poisoning. He was so drunk.

With his arm draped over my shoulder, I did my best to help him back to his bedroom. I was hoping the kids wouldn't wake up before we made it back there. "Did you have to drink every-thing in the place?"

"So Hope's got a date, huh?"

It was now obvious why he was staggering drunk. I'd heard the story on the news, too, but I'd turned it off before they'd said the date, so I didn't know if Hope was dying tomorrow, next week, or two months from now. I really didn't care.

Thank God his door was open. We stumbled to his bed and when I let him go, he fell onto it. But then he pulled me down and I landed on top of him. He was so drunk, I swear alcohol was coming out of his pores.

"I was stupid to think anything would change," he said.

Our lips were so close. Even though I told myself he was pissy drunk, and he didn't mean any of this, my heart still fluttered at being so close to him.

"You beautiful, Chastity," he slurred.

I tried to wiggle out of his embrace, but he wouldn't give. He held on to me tightly. I didn't struggle or anything like that, but I at least wanted to make it look like I was making an effort to avoid what seemed like the inevitable.

His breath was hot and I felt myself falling. I closed my eyes when our lips touched. It felt like an electric bolt of something rushed through my veins. He tasted nothing like he smelled, his lips were sweet and so soft, and his tongue flickered back and forth so easily that it nearly drove me insane. I wanted more; I wanted him all to myself.

In my head, a voice screamed loudly that I should not be doing this. I needed to wait; it wouldn't be long. But my body was tired of waiting; I wanted him now.

He sucked my neck and the sensation had never felt better. His hands traveled along my body, caressing me intensely, like he loved me. I knew he didn't, but I told myself that didn't matter. He was drunk, I was sober, but I didn't want to do the right thing.

I wanted us to go with the flow. This time, when I couldn't bear to look at myself in the mirror, I wanted to feel like it was at least worth it.

I tugged at his shirt. I kissed his neck, the side of his face, and his earlobe. He felt so good. It felt even better to be in his arms, in his bed. I wanted him so much more than I thought, and he seemed to want me, too.

"We..." He kissed me again. This time he sucked my tongue so hard it was like he was trying to taste traces of dinner.

"We can't..." I managed. But I didn't even believe me.

I felt him shake his head. He was saying no. He agreed. That was good; he agreed we shouldn't be doing this. I knew that was because we were on the bed. When our eyes met, even in semi-darkness, I could see the sadness in his. I wasn't sure why he was doing this, but I suddenly couldn't go through with it. I felt like I was taking advantage of him while he was down, emotionally.

"I should go; you're safely in bed now. And, you're drunk. I don't want you to do anything you don't want to do."

As I was getting up, Brendon eased up onto his elbows. The next words he uttered shook me to my core. "Hope is never coming home, if that's what are you're worried about. I'm ready to move on now."

He didn't sound all that drunk after all. Did he?

THIRTY
HOPE

I learned about my new execution date by watching TV. It was so pathetic to me, how less of a human being I was because I was on death row. How could it not matter that I be told first? How could they give this information to the press before they gave it to me? I was the one on death row!

I told myself that it really didn't matter. I wanted out of that cage, and out of the life that had amounted up to nothing.

According to the news reports, I had two months left to live. Two months. Most people have no idea when they're gonna die. They don't know if it'll happen on the way home after work, after a bout with cancer, or during a home invasion. In a way, I was fortunate because I knew my exit day right down to the very minute.

"Looks like the state of Texas will make good on that promise after all. On Tuesday, November Sixth at six-thirty p.m., I will die by lethal injection in Huntsville, Texas," I mumbled aloud.

I wasn't sure if I felt better knowing, but I was happy about not having to be there for the next twenty-five to thirty years. I didn't agree with Pauline. She could have that shit for the next quarter of a century. I was tired of imagining how my life would have been if I hadn't accepted that ride. In my head, I'd gone through every single scenario possible.

A while back I got a letter from a newspaper reporter asking me to add her to my visitation list. I wasn't sure why she wanted to visit me, but I said, what the hell. In Texas, Tuesday was the day for media visits. I was sure she was probably working on a story and wanted to get my side—again.

"Donovan, visit!" the C.O. yelled.

I got up and prepared myself for the cuffs.

Later, as I sat across from her, my mind was all over the place.

"Almost immediately after your arrest, Trey cut a deal with the prosecutor. In exchange for a lesser, second-degree murder charge, he agreed to testify that it was you and Quenton who'd committed the murders. There was also the jailhouse snitch?" she asked.

Our introduction was quick and she jumped right in. Jennifer told me she was working on an investigative piece she hoped to turn over to the Innocence Project. I had heard that one before, but it wasn't like I had something better to do.

"Yeah, pretty much, and did you know Trey failed a lie detector test, and that while he was the only one of the three of us who tested positive for firing a gun, the detectives still ran with his lie about what happened?"

She was writing faster than anyone I'd ever seen. I saw her recorder sitting there, so I kept talking.

"The prosecutor illegally kept Trey's polygraph report from my lawyers. It totally contradicted his trial testimony; in fact, the prosecutor was on the news talking about how he gave Trey a deal because he had passed his polygraph. Meanwhile, Q and me? Well, the media kept running these crazy stories labeling us the modern day *Bonnie and Clyde*. Even though he claimed he wasn't gonna try the case in the media, he was on almost every night. He called us thrill-seekers, talking about we killed for the fun of it. I was first to go to court. What a waste; no surprise there. I was quickly found guilty and sentenced to death. The most persuasive evidence the DA had was Trey's testimony! And of course, the only other person who knew what happened was Q, who was dead by the time I went to trial."

She looked up at me, her green eyes wide in disbelief.

"I don't get how the DA made a defendant with no previous felony convictions eligible for the death penalty," she said.

"Hmm, well, that's when they pulled out their star witness. Some chick that was being held on drug charges around the time I was at the county. Linda Brown said under oath that we were cellmates for a hot minute. Now you tell me how it sounds that on the first night we met, I suddenly confessed to the murders, told her how much I enjoyed it, and how if pushed, I'd do it again!"

Remembering how that bitch had lied made me want to kill her right then and there in court!

"What did you do while all of this was going on? What'd your lawyer do?"

"Well, I sat there looking around the courtroom like, am I the only person here who has a problem with what this crackhead is saying? Imagine sitting there listening to these folks lying on you and there's not a damn thing you can do about it, 'cause your attorney acts like he's so riveted by what they're saying, he doesn't even object!"

"Why didn't you tell your lawyer to say something?" she asked.

"I did. I was like, I can't believe you're just gonna sit there and let that trick bitch lie like that!"

"Is that what you said?" she asked.

"I know it wasn't the best way to put it, but I was mad, and I was stunned!" I tried to calm down a bit. If this reporter was really going to help, I didn't need her thinking I was some crazy freak who *deserved* to be locked in a cage. I took a deep breath, then continued.

"When the judge spoke up, I was even more amazed that he threatened to put *me* out! He had the nerve to talk about me disturbing the proceedings. Who spills their life story to some stranger who looked like she was high on the stand? Oh, and I'd confide all of this to someone I'd just met? I tried to point out that when I was in the County, it was so crowded, there was no way this conversation could've ever taken place, but guess what?"

She stopped writing and looked up at me.

"No one gave a damn! They didn't then, they don't today, and they won't tomorrow!"

"So what did you guys do?" she asked.

Thinking and talking about it now made me mad all over again.

"Well, at that point we got rid of our court-appointed lawyer. We mortgaged our house and hired one of Houston's best firms. They quickly brought in some high-powered lawyer from Atlanta. Mitchell Monroe had me convinced I actually had a chance with him in my corner."

I blew out a breath and shook my head.

"He had us sold, telling us his job was to create reasonable doubt in the minds of the jury. He recalled the officer who had searched the car after we were stopped. That officer testified that in addition to the murder weapon, he found some of the stuff that fell out of my purse. Then he recalled the lead detective. I remember what he said, word for word." I swallowed hard as I replayed that day in the courtroom. "My attorney asked that detective, his name was Anthony, whether it was possible for my fingerprints to have gotten on the murder weapon when I was trying to pick up the stuff that fell out my purse."

"What did he say?"

"He said it was possible," I explained. "Then, he cut the detective off and excused the witness. Then, Mitchell went after Linda, the jailhouse snitch, and attacked her credibility. He questioned her about her drug use. She'd lost her kids because she used crack, and she'd been arrested on a bunch of theft and hot check charges. He called that bitch out, letting the jury know the only reason she was testifying against was because DA Conley promised her a lesser sentence in exchange for her testimony.

"But the icing on the cake was when he recalled Trey to the stand," I continued. "He had told Brendon to make sure all of my girls were in court, dressed to the nines and sitting in the row right behind me on that day. Trey couldn't help but see them from the witness stand."

I fell silent as my mind raced back to that fateful day.

"You've known the defendant for a long time, haven't you, Mr. Montgomery?"

"Call me Trey," he said.

The judge's eyebrow inched up a bit.

Mitchell turned to the jury. "Okay, Trey, you've known the defendant for a long time, correct?"

"Yeah, you could say that; we came up in the same neighborhood."

"What do you think of her; do you like her?"

His big ol' eyes wandered over to me and I felt dirty.

"She a'ight."

"Isn't it true that you never liked the defendant because of the way she and her friends made fun of you throughout the years? Isn't that why you're really testifying against her?"

"Objection!" Conley screamed.

"Withdrawn." Mitchell walked over and stood behind our table.

"It wasn't that they picked on you, but you couldn't get any play whatsoever from any of these women." He pointed at Stacy, Betty Jean, and Chastity. "And you tried."

"Your Honor, please. Is there a question in this?" Conley asked.

"Ask a question or move on, Mr. Monroe," the judge said.

"Mr. Montgomery, that's quite a scar you have there. Would you mind telling us how you got that?"

"I got it in a fight." Trey used a bony finger to trace from his ear to the edge of his mouth, like he was showing it off.

"Really? Well, back in my *neighborhood* in New York we called a scar that goes from your ear to the edge of your mouth the mark of the snitch."

"Objection, Your Honor!" Conley jumped to his feet. "Objection!"

"Withdrawn," Mr. Monroe said as he walked away. "I guess you've been snitching on your friends for a long time."

After that I remember feeling good about my chances. It was actually starting to look like the jury might return a verdict of not guilty. I guess Conley saw it, too. Later, we learned that he went to the judge and had the judge issue a special instruction. That the jury could still return a guilty verdict under Chapter 7.02 of the Texas Penal Code called the "Law of Parties," which says a person can be criminally responsible for another's actions if that person acts with "the intent to promote or assist the commission of the offense" and "solicits, encourages, directs, aids, or attempts to aid the other person to commit the offense, whether the defendant actually caused the death of the deceased or did not actually cause the death of the deceased but intended to kill the deceased or another or anticipated that a human life would be taken. Furthermore, If, in the attempt to carry out a conspiracy to commit one felony, another felony is committed by one of the conspirators, all conspirators are guilty of the felony actually committed.

I caught myself and snapped out of my trip down memory lane. Hell, it was no sense in replaying that anyway. And judging from the stunned look on the reporter's face, I wasn't sure she believed me anyway.

THIRTY-ONE
ADENA

"We're doing really well. We need to wait for the call back from the DA's office first, but we can handle this one on our own," I said.

"We can't allow this man to walk the streets again; what he did was wrong," Cindy Rucker said. She handled social media for True Justice.

She had to know a killer walking the streets was not about to happen if I had anything to say about it.

"What are our friends saying on Facebook and Twitter?" I asked.

When I wasn't keeping up with Hope Donovan's case and pending execution, I worked on behalf of other victims, survivors, and their families. I was proud of what we had accomplished with True Justice since its inception.

We especially liked getting in on a case at the very beginning. The sooner we introduced ourselves to the families, and let them know our interests in the outcomes were similar, the better we got along. In most cases we recruited without even trying. Our members were all brought together by tragedy; we were fueled by a thirst for justice and worked well because we'd traveled in each other's shoes.

"They're ready to sign a petition, show up at his arraignment in droves or whatever we need," she reported.

They usually were, but still, I liked to ask so that I could remind everyone of the work we were doing and reinforce that we were not alone.

"Good." I turned to Sabrina Collier. "What is his criminal history looking like?" She handled research.

"This is his second DWI. The only problem I see is he's well-connected. If you have money, you can buy freedom. Oh, and I got that from a source, but they're not identifying him yet."

"Why are they keeping his identity under wraps?"

"We're not sure, except, it must be that he's really connected."

"Hmmm, looks like this is a case where we need to get the media machine working right away. We don't have time for the police to be protecting a murderer. We need the mother in front of the cameras; we need her crying at the drop of a hat." I looked up from my notes and smiled. "All in all, I think we've had a good week. We got a date for Hope, and we're working on making sure this creep is put under the jail cell."

"You think we can push for the death penalty?" Michelle asked. That familiar twinkle was in her eyes. And I was not about to disappoint.

"I'm sure with the right amount of pressure the DA will do the right thing."

She smiled.

"If not, I'm sure we can organize an effort to make sure she knows how her constituents feel about her being soft on crime," Michelle warned.

I was so proud; I had trained them well.

We were wrapping up a meeting at the True Justice offices. We were talking about a campaign to get the DA to file capital charges against a man who was driving drunk and killed a father and his child. He fled the scene, but was recently taken into custody.

So far, authorities were keeping his identity hidden. I suspected it was until they figured out exactly which charges to file, but still I didn't like it. In my heart of hearts, I knew they were probably not going to be keen on the ultimate justice.

In Texas, anyone who kills a child under the age of six is eligible for the death penalty, but in this case, the child was seven, and it was vehicular manslaughter at best. But, if he had a record, he'd fled the scene and posed a future threat, anything was possible.

The child's widowed mother, Bethany Hicks, was understandably distraught. She wanted justice, an eye for an eye, but the community couldn't be trusted in a case like this. One sad story about his horrible upbringing, an unfit parent, or substandard education, and they were ready to offer sympathy.

As we wrapped up the meeting, I dialed my son's number again. No answer. I hated his need for independence. Since he moved out, I'd had to hunt him down like I was a bill collector.

"Raakin, this is your mother calling again; it's been four days now."

I hung up when we looked up and saw Houston Police preparing for a press conference.

THIRTY-TWO
BRENDON

Here lately, I tried to work as much overtime as possible on the job. I didn't want to face Stacy, and I didn't want to have to look at Chastity. Things were spinning out of control and I wasn't sure how much longer I could hang on. My wife was about to be executed so I was allowed a few tantrums.

Two months! November 6th!

Two fucking months!

The reporter had called three times after the last time we met. But what good would another story do? After all these years, after all of the rallies, vigils, and fundraisers, what did anyone think yet another damn story would change? Hope was still on death row.

She had sped things up anyway.

No, another story couldn't help us at all. Besides, we all knew the facts! Hope didn't do it. She accepted a ride from Q and Trey, Trey was first to make a deal, but by the time it was all said and done, Q and Hope were screwed. Even if Q would've survived, he wouldn't have been screwed like Hope.

The Law of Parties.

Fuck the law of parties!

Fuck the state of Texas!

And fuck Hope for deciding that she gets to run the show!

She simply couldn't listen to me. I remember one time when these two dudes ran through our back yard. Turns out, they were running from the police after a high-speed chase crash had ended on our street. I walked up right as cruisers screeched to a stop in front of our driveway. I didn't know what the hell was going on. At first I was scared, thinking something had happened to Hope or one of the kids. Boy, was I wrong.

I was relieved when Hope met me out on the porch. But that relief quickly turned to confusion, then grew into rage.

"What's going on? Why's the law swarming all around our damn back yard?"

Two officers swooshed by.

"Greedy and 'em running from the cops again," she said easily.

I looked at Hope and looked at the other officers rushing toward the back yard. I pulled her off to the side.

"Wait, you mean to tell me you know these clowns?" I asked.

"Everybody knows Greedy and his road dog, Jerome," she said.

My heart was racing. I was pissed. Why did these thugs feel so comfortable around her? Why was she not fazed by the fact that all of our neighbors were looking at our house as if we were the criminals!

"Hope, I don't understand; why didn't you say something?"

She jumped back as if I'd just disrespected her and Mona. Her face twisted into a frown and she looked at me like I was suddenly the enemy.

"What was I supposed to say? And what do you mean, *say* something? I ain't snitching to no cops. What you think, I'm a rat?"

Who was this woman?

Snitch?

Rat?

I couldn't wrap my mind around the fact that if a line was drawn in the sand, my wife, the mother of my children, was not siding with the law. Wasn't that the right thing to do? Where was all this hood in her while we were dating?

"Hey, aren't you Hope Donovan's husband?"

As the woman stepped onto my bus, her question caught me off-guard but it quickly brought me back to the present.

"Yeah, yeah, I am," I said.

"Ooooh weeee, chile, will you give her my best? I think it's downright horrible what's happening to her. Those cops should be out there looking for the real crooks; instead, they bullying the helpless."

I shrugged.

"Isn't that how it goes though?"

Her intentions were good. Her heart was probably in the right place, but I wasn't in the mood. I didn't want to hear about Hope or the case. I didn't want to think about the fact that she had gone and done something without even discussing it with me first.

The woman smiled, looked at me with pity, then walked to the back of the bus. I waited until the other passengers got on, then I closed the door and turned the wheel away from the curb.

We were told a private lawyer would cost up to six figures. We didn't have that kind of money. Who does? We mortgaged our house, but by then, it was nearly too late. The court-appointed attorney had already made a mess of everything. It was hard for the new pricey attorney to get a handle on things.

It was wild, watching the prosecutor roll his eyes to the jury in disbelief, every time a character witness came to speak on Hope's behalf. I wanted to kill him.

Then, once the DA got his conviction, he paraded these questionable people on to the witness stand during the sentencing phase of the trial and each one, including this one woman who claimed that Hope had made all kinds of confessions to her personally. It looked to me like the DA went to the jail, found the slimiest characters he could find, offered them something, and got them to say exactly what he needed.

It became obvious that we were losing, but we hung on to the idea that Hope hadn't done anything. There's no real evidence against her, so it would be a technicality. But once the trial went on, and the jury got the truth, they'd realize she hadn't done a thing and they'd send her home.

We had faith in the system. We thought justice really was blind, and the biggest crock of all, we thought you were innocent until proven guilty.

We were naïve.

THIRTY-THREE
CHASTITY

When the phone rang late, I braced myself for another battle with Trevor. He wanted to keep his wife, and be able to harass me about my relationship with Brendon. I wanted him out of my life because I was tired of waiting around for him to deem me worthy of his last name. That ship had sailed long ago, and I was glad it had.

I grabbed it without looking at the caller ID; I didn't want the noise to wake up the kids.

"Hello?"

"Chastity? It's late; you're still at the house? Brendon told me you spend more time over there and I'm glad you do, but it's really late," she said.

My heart dropped. I couldn't find my voice. How was she able to call? And it wasn't a collect call.

"Chastity," she called out to me again. I hadn't heard my sister's voice in years. Truthfully, I didn't think I'd ever hear it again. "You there?"

"Um, yeah, I'm here." Suddenly my throat felt dry, like it was getting tighter and closing in on me.

"Soooo, it's been a while, huh?"

"Yeah, it has."

"It's okay that you stopped taking my letters. Honestly, I didn't think I'd ever speak to you again. I guess you already know my time is running out, right?"

"Brendon told me. Says you dropped your appeals," I said.

"Yeah, he's pissed, but he can't understand what I'm going through. I'd rather be dead than live like this."

I wanted to ask how she was calling me. I wanted to ask if she had this planned. I wanted to get off the phone with her. I didn't want her asking me any questions about Brendon and me. Was there even a Brendon and me?

"There was so much I did wrong when it came to you and our relationship," she began.

I wasn't ready for this conversation. I wasn't ready for her to try and make things right between us; I wanted things to stay the way they were: me hating her, and she having time to think about all the times she'd done me wrong.

"I didn't know how to be a big sister. I should've been setting a better example for you; instead, I was too busy being jealous of you."

My heart slammed against my rib cage and I got scared, wondering if she could hear how loud it was beating.

"You, jealous of me?" I stammered.

"Yes, Chastity, you had everything. You were smart, you were pretty, and you had this perfect body. Everyone wanted to be around you. It didn't come that easy for me."

I felt tears burning in the corners of my eyes, but I refused to let them fall. Of course she'd say these things right now. She was facing her mortality. "Hope, you weren't jealous of me."

I didn't want to accept what she was saying. Accepting any part of this *end of the line* apology would mean things were good with us and they were far from good.

"I was horrible to you and there was no reason for it. You probably don't want to hear any of this right now, but I'm so glad I got the chance to get this off my chest."

"It has always been about *you*, Hope." For a moment, she didn't say anything. My comment threw her off, but I wasn't about to be sucked into whatever she was trying to do. If this was part of the long goodbye, she could keep it for someone else.

"You're right, and for that, I'm sorry. If I wasn't so jealous of you, we could've enjoyed a real sisterly relationship."

"You didn't need me; you had Stacy and Betty Jean," I said. I didn't like this conversation and I hated myself for answering the phone.

"Yeah, Stacy and Betty Jean, we were thick as thieves!" She chuckled. "I heard the minute I was convicted, they both started throwing themselves at Brendon. Man, you really find out who your friends are, huh?" She chuckled again.

I rolled my eyes. Suddenly I started to feel bad. If only she knew. I wasn't sure what to say about that comment. The last thing I wanted was for the question to turn to Brendon and me.

"Hey, I heard Stacy is divorced now," she said. Her voice ticked up a bit.

"Yeah, she's been divorced for a while now," I said.

My strategy was simple. I wasn't offering up any new information. I'd confirm what was probably already common knowledge, but I wasn't about to offer up anything new.

This wasn't about to be a moment to catch up. I didn't want to be on the phone with her, I didn't want to hear what she had to say, and I didn't want her to feel like I'd forgiven all the horrible things she'd done to me.

"So much has changed since I've been in here. The kids are probably almost grown now, and Mona, I'll bet she's still as crazy as ever."

"Yeah, all of that sounds about right," I said.

"I want you to know, Chastity, I don't blame you and Mona for not coming anymore. This place is depressing. That's why I told Brendon to stop bringing the kids; it made no sense. Every time they'd leave, I'd spiral into a deep depression. It was like torturing myself and them."

"Yeah, I could imagine."

"No, no, you can't imagine what it's like being in here. I wouldn't want my worst enemy to be locked in a cage like this."

What if I said I needed to go? How could she be on the phone this long? Didn't their phone calls have limits?

"You want me to tell Brendon you called?" I asked abruptly.

"Oh, you're gonna be there when he gets home?" She sounded surprised. I assumed Brendon had told her that I'd been living there, but it was obvious he hadn't.

"Yeah, Hope," I said.

Silence.

"Oh okay, then, yeah, tell him I called. Um, he did tell me you stay 'til he gets home."

But I could tell she was lying. She was probably having all kinds of thoughts about me being in her house with her husband, the same husband she hadn't been able to touch in more than seven years. I knew that it wouldn't be a far leap for her to think about what else might be happening between her husband and me.

I wasn't the least bit sorry. I felt absolutely no remorse.

And when the next few words fell from her lips, I knew she hadn't been sincere either.

"Well, Chastity, um, I hope you'll find it in your heart to one day forgive me for everything I've done to you, including Trevor."

That was the Hope I was used to. She wasn't sure whether anything was going on with Brendon and me, so she couldn't let me sleep tonight without confirming the long-running rumor that she'd always vehemently denied.

Bitch!

"Umph, well, Hope, I'll tell Brendon you called. He should be home soon," I said, and quickly hung up the phone.

THIRTY-FOUR
HOPE

When Pauline slipped me the cell phone because her cell was gonna be tossed, I had no intentions of using it. I had known about the illegal cell phone for a while, but I didn't need any infractions.

After hanging up with Chastity, I wished I had followed my first mind. That conversation went so far to the left, I didn't know how to bring it back. Maybe I shouldn't have gone in with the apologizing right off the bat. But I was nervous. I didn't expect Chastity to answer the phone and I didn't know what to say to her.

"So Brendon and Chastity?" Saying it aloud didn't make it any more real.

I had been through so much while in there, I'd seen so much and had been hurt in so many ways, but to know that Chastity was spending so much time with Brendon was to know real pain. I hadn't been fooling myself into thinking that my man had been celibate for more than seven years. I'd tried to avoid those thoughts at all costs.

"Brendon should be home soon..."

Looks like my little sister did learn from me. That was a Hope move if ever there was one. And it was designed to go straight for the jugular; no mercy whatsoever.

"I'll tell Brendon you called; he should be home soon..."

Sleep wouldn't visit me tonight, this I knew for certain.

I'd had nightmares about Betty Jean and Stacy fighting over

who would be with Brendon. But in my worst nightmare, never did I think Chastity would be the one. I was glad when she was stepping up and taking care of the kids, but it had never crossed my mind that she'd be taking care of him, too.

"I'll tell Brendon you called..."

I started wondering how long this had been going on, but then I told myself Chastity didn't have it in her. There's no way Brendon would come to the jail, look me dead in the face and pledge his love for me if he was fucking my sister all along.

I looked around the small dark cell and in all the years I'd been there, I couldn't think of a time I'd felt so lonely. I wanted to try and call him back later. She said he'd be home soon, but a part of me didn't want to give her the satisfaction.

Then I started wondering if that was the real reason Mona had started pulling away. Did she also suspect something might be going on between them? If she did, how did she keep that secret? Mona couldn't hold water.

Each time I closed my eyes, I pictured Brendon undressing Chastity. The pain I felt was indescribable. Why did it have to be her? When my girls Stacy and Betty Jean had abandoned me, that was difficult, but I'd said okay, whatever. That had hurt, too, but not like this.

This was the kind of shit I was tired of. I couldn't do a damn thing if there was a Brendon and Chastity. They still had their entire lives ahead of them. What did I have? I had nothing but damn memories that haunted me with a vengeance.

Where was Trevor? I couldn't fathom him standing by while Brendon and Chastity played house. And what about the kids; were they confused? No matter what I thought about, or how I tried not to think about, it stayed on my mind. I tried to tell myself I could be reading something into nothing at all.

Suddenly, I started thinking about something else. Why wait six weeks? What difference did it make if I went now? Who would give a damn? Brendon had already moved on, with my sister!

"I'll tell Brendon you called..."

Of course she'd tell him! But I couldn't help wondering why he hadn't told me, "Oh, Hope, since you're stuck in here, Chastity is gonna slide into your spot!"

I sighed. It was two-thirty in the morning and I wasn't sleepy.

I'd be tired at work but I couldn't help these feelings. What would I say when everyone else found out? How would I tell Latrice, Pauline, and everyone else that Brendon wasn't the stand-up guy they thought he was? What would I look like explaining he was now with my sister?

Shaking the thoughts from my head, I told myself I was piecing something together without knowing if anything was even really going on. But that pissed me off, too. Should I call back and ask flat out? If I called back now, I'd get Brendon himself. I could ask point blank and see what he said.

"Fuck it, fuck him, and fuck them!"

The more I thought it, the more I decided I had suffered enough. They probably weren't doing anything, but being in there and not knowing made me sick enough to wanna puke! I was tired. I didn't need yet another depressing thought to worry about. So, I decided to stop. I'd stop worrying, stop thinking about it, and stop everything altogether.

It was dark, but I knew my space well. I knew how to get around in the dark and if I did it now, the pain would soon be over.

I had paid for every wrong I had done. I had paid in ways that were inhumane and I was sick and tired of the suffering. This is what I thought about as I removed the pillowcase from my pillow. It no longer mattered who forgave me and who wouldn't. I was sick of being a burden to my family members. I was tired of Brendon having to live a double life because of me.

I removed the small mirror from the wall and used the pillow-case to wrap it tightly. It wasn't made of real glass, but I could make it do what I needed. Once I wrapped it several times until the pillowcase was more like a cushion, I banged it against the toilet.

"Damn!" Nothing happened.

I did it again, and again, and again. Finally, I felt the mirror break. I needed it to be sharp enough. For good measure, I banged it again and felt it crumble.

Because it was dark, I sat still listening, to make sure the C.O.'s didn't hear me. After a few minutes, there was no movement so I quietly unwrapped the mirror.

The pieces weren't as sharp as I needed, so I started scraping the biggest piece against some concrete. It took about twenty minutes, but it was finally sharp.

Without hesitation, I took the sharp edge and dug it along the thickest vein running up my arm. Warm blood oozed from it and quickly wet my clothes. By the time I got it right on my left arm, I'd started feeling lightheaded.

"Why should I give the state of Texas the pleasure?" Soon, everything went darker. Finally, I felt free, then the blackest black.

THIRTY-FIVE
ADENA

I was in a panic. This could not be! Michelle had been at my side for days since the news had broken. I was confused, distraught, and bewildered all at the same time. The phone rang and I dreaded who would be on the other end.

Michelle pounced on it before I could shed another tear. I had been sedated for two days, and every time I started to emerge from my drug-induced fog, I wanted to run and hide.

"No, she will not be making any statements," I heard her say into the phone. Michelle turned away from me, but her demeanor told me she didn't want to be in this position no more than me.

"We're trying to get a handle on this. Yes, I am aware of what the police said. It's obvious we weren't aware at the time."

I looked up in her direction. The phone had been ringing non-stop. The last time it had rung like that was right after my husband's senseless murder. May Allah have mercy on his soul! The press already had my number and they knew how to use it; they called around the clock.

The moment Michelle hung up the phone, it rang again. I didn't know what to do. She sighed and allowed it to ring a few times before picking it up again.

"Hello?"

I had never heard her sound so unenthused. She stood, shifted her weight to one side, sighed as she listened, then flipped her hair over her shoulder. Her eyes were puffy, too.

"We're not making any statements at this time," she said.

For years, I had been the media darling. I never had imagined a time when I'd try to avoid their calls or questions. Now I found it bothersome that they couldn't respect my privacy in my time of need.

Michelle hung up the phone and returned to my side on the sofa.

"Would you like a cold towel? I think you could use more rest," she said.

I didn't want to rest. I wanted to leave this life; this couldn't be mine. I wanted a do-over. What had I done to deserve this kind of cruel punishment? Was it not enough that my husband was gone? Now, my son, too? How could one single family experience so much devastation? I'd had my share. I needed misery and despair to find another place to call home. I was exhausted, both physically and emotionally.

"What am I going to do?"

Michelle looked at me with a combination of sorrow and pity in her eyes. I didn't want this to be my life anymore. I started wondering if this was some kind of wicked joke. Did I go too far with Hope? Had my relentless pursuit of justice in her case resulted in neglect of my own family?

"Have you heard anything more?" Michelle asked.

I snatched tissue from the box that had been at my side since we'd seen the news conference. I don't understand why someone didn't give me a heads-up. I had a few sources in the police department; someone could've called. I was completely blindsided by this.

"No, I'm waiting to see if Rusty Hardin will take the case. I don't understand why it's taking so long to hear something."

Rusty Hardin was one of the best defense attorneys in the

country. The thought of having to employ his services was nothing less that stomach churning.

"Rusty will take care of this," Michelle said. I wanted to believe her. I wanted to feel like Rusty would make this all go away.

"What are things like at the office?" I asked.

Michelle shook her head. She didn't need to say anything more. I already understood. I had been a staunch supporter of capital punishment. I was leading the charge when we'd found out that a father and his seven-year-old were killed by a drunk driver who'd fled the scene. I had made calls to the DA's office on behalf of the widowed mother, Bethany Hicks. Our team found out that this was his second offense.

Thinking about it and how hard I had tried to assemble a vigorous push for the death penalty in this case, made my head spin. I had been in talks with MADD. I was prepared to do a full aggressive media blitz that would've attacked PD if they didn't express utter rage over this inconceivable crime.

When Michelle's hand rubbed my back, I thought about this sick place I once again found myself in. First, I'd lost my husband, and now I faced losing my son?

How could I push so passionately for the death penalty now that my son was being accused of killing two people and fleeing the scene while driving drunk?

We were cursed.

THIRTY-SIX
BRENDON

Work! That's what would keep me focused. If I didn't think about what Carrie Jones had told me, my hopes wouldn't go too high. I had been working with the Defender Services and several other organizations. So my meeting with Carrie had been nothing out of the ordinary.

"Brendon, we think we've come up with a way to get Hope to reconsider her decision. We've got attorneys already working on it and we think we can make this appear as if she arrived at the decision herself."

Carrie was a hardnosed investigator who worked with the Defender Services. She was really down to earth, and she was hip. Most of the lawyers and other legal professionals seemed so out of touch. It was almost like they couldn't really relate to the people they were working to free.

But Carrie was different. She wore her hair in a slick ponytail and often wore t-shirts and designer jeans. She was really cool and laid-back.

"Okay, I'm all ears." I really was interested in what she had to say. The moment we realized Hope only had a couple of months left, it seemed as if time was suddenly on a fast track.

"Who does she look up to religiously?" Carrie asked.

The frown on my face probably told her we weren't the most religious people. Sure, we went to church here and there, and took the kids, but it wasn't part of our weekly routine.

I shook my head. This wasn't the time to draw a blank, but I couldn't name any one religious leader off the top of my head.

"Locally?"

"No, we were thinking someone on a national platform. And the reason we thought a religious leader is because they would more likely be sympathetic to our plight." Carrie leaned in. "Basically, we have a little bit of time to get some high-profile religious leader on our side. What's in it for them? The publicity they'll garner by convincing Hope to retract her decision."

"This might just work," I said, trying to keep my excitement in check. I had been trying for weeks to think of something.

"She likes the Reverend Al Sharpton!" I almost yelled.

Carrie started writing. Without looking up at me, she said, "Perfect. He's always looking for a worthy cause to champion."

I wanted her to be right. I didn't even bother asking what our chances looked like. She had an idea; it was better than anything I had come up with.

Several days later, I hadn't heard back from Carrie, but she'd assured me that she'd handle everything. Normally, I wouldn't keep the phone close while I was working, but I wanted to make sure I wouldn't miss Carrie's call.

But so far, everyone under the sun had called, except Carrie. As I looked at the caller ID, I wondered why life was funny like that.

I didn't feel like talking to this reporter or any others. She had gone to visit Hope. Why wasn't that enough for whatever story she was working on?

Jennifer had left several messages on my voicemail, but I wasn't inspired to return any of them. I looked at my phone and wondered what the hell was going on. I had four missed calls from Mona, a few from some other reporters, including Pascal, and several from Chastity.

Did I miss something?

My heart started racing. This was part of the problem with Hope being in prison. Every time I got a flurry of missed calls, voicemail messages, or something unusual, that typically meant bad news wasn't far behind.

Usually, I didn't like pulling out my cell phone while I was on the job, but since I was at the bus barn trying to decide whether I should work a few more hours, I figured it was okay. My phone showed a new voicemail the second I pulled it out. I hit the number to listen to the message Mona had left:

"Brendon, where the hell are you and why you not answering your phone? This is an emergency! Okay, I'm gonna call you back."

She hung up and apparently called me back to leave yet another message:

"I know you at work, but I just found out that Adena Binnaz's son has been arrested for vehicular manslaughter. I know you remember that crazy DWI accident where that man and his son was killed by a driver who took off? Well, apparently that driver was Adena's son! And if that's not enough, she and her group True Justice were demanding the death penalty for whoever had done it. I'm already doing a few interviews 'cause I wanna know what the bitch has to say now!"

Wow! Adena's son killed two people?

I needed a seat. I needed to let this information sink in. I wondered if her son was gonna get the death penalty. He killed two people? Oh, they would probably call it an accident and slap him on the wrist.

By the time I got Mona on the phone, she had already recorded two TV interviews and was waiting to do one for a local radio station. I wasn't sure who had set them up for her, but I could only imagine what she had been saying.

"Well, it's about damn time," Mona said.

"I was at work," I tried to tell her. But Mona was full of adrenaline so she was on autopilot.

"I want that bitch to come and look me in the eye and talk that shit now!" Mona screamed into the phone.

I moved the phone a few inches from my ear. She was loud and boisterous.

"So now that her own flesh and blood's got blood on his hands, she ain't out here yapping about no damn true justice anymore!"

If it was up to Mona, every news station in the city would have known that she felt Adena was now in hiding because of her son's crime.

"You still there, Brendon?" Mona asked.

"Yeah, I'm still here."

I didn't know what to think. I didn't want to rain on Mona's parade, but I wondered what good any of this would do Hope? I wasn't happy to know that Adena's son was now about to go through what we'd been going through, even though I suspected his journey would be far different than ours. His mother was well-connected, she knew the right people, and she had money.

"You hear what I said? Adena, her son killed two people and left the scene of an accident."

"I heard you, Mona, but what's that got to do with us? How's that gonna help Hope? That's all I'm concerned about."

"I ain't figured that out yet, but I tell you what. I wanna see Adena out here hitting the pavement, knocking on every law-maker's door and pushing for the death penalty now!"

"Mona, we've got four weeks. That's a month. If we don't get Hope to change her mind, she will die in thirty days!"

"You know how stubborn she can be. She don' made up her mind; I can't imagine what's gonna make her change it," Mona said.

I knew she was telling the truth, but I also knew that if Hope changed her mind, that would buy us more time. I was waiting for Mona to say something about how Adena's misfortune would work to our benefit, but she didn't.

"Ooh, I gotta go. I'll see you at the house. Make sure you tell Chastity to TiVo the news tonight."

It was like she was having fun. When I hung up, I told myself to let Mona do whatever seemed to be bringing her joy. I wouldn't start smiling until I knew for sure that Hope's appeals were back in front of the courts.

★★★

A week later, Adena was nowhere to be found. Now, I was convinced she had gone in to hiding. We hadn't heard a word from True Justice and that was unusual.

Carrie's phone number popped up on caller ID. I prayed she was calling with some good news.

"Hey, Carrie, what's up?" I held my breath. An entire week and a half had gone by since we'd talked about her brilliant plan.

"I've got some news," she said. I couldn't tell anything from her tone.

THIRTY-SEVEN
CHASTITY

"So what's up, you fuckin' him or what?" Trevor had me scared. I knew it wasn't a good idea to come over, but I was scared he'd pop up at Brendon's again and I didn't need the drama. Besides, I found myself running from some drama of my own.

"No, get real, you know I'm not," I said as calmly as I could. I hoped he wasn't able to read my mind and all of the salacious thoughts running through my head.

If only he knew.

Trevor looked at me like I was a kid caught in a lie and he was trying his best to be patient with me before going upside my head.

"That's what you runnin' with?" He looked at me like this was my last chance to reconsider my answer.

I shrugged my shoulders as if it was really no big deal. If Trevor sensed there was anything wrong with my response, or if I blinked too much or too little, he'd read something into it.

Suddenly, I wondered if being in the kitchen was the safest place to have this discussion with Trevor. He was already unstable, pissed because he realized he was losing me, and probably capable of anything. Thoughts of a crime of passion flashed throughout my mind.

I got up from the table and Trevor eased up in front of me.

"What?" I motioned to playfully shove him out of my way. He

was way too strong, of course. "Can I use the doggone bathroom?" I joked. I made sure to smile and ask the question lightly.

At first Trevor didn't move. He stood there staring at me like he wasn't quite sure how to take me, or what to do *to* me.

"What? You want me to pee on myself?" I chuckled.

He still didn't budge.

"C'mon, I need to go," I whined. I even started twitching my leg for good measure.

With his cold eyes focused on me, he slowly stepped aside. I didn't have to turn around to know he watched my every move until I rounded the corner and shut the bathroom door behind me.

I leaned against the door, closed my eyes, and took a deep breath.

What the hell was I doing? Why did I let him have this kind of control over me? I looked at myself in the mirror and tried to channel strength. Trevor didn't know what he wanted. He only wanted me to think he wanted me because he thought I wanted Brendon. I was so transparent when it came to him.

I also knew if I had to be honest with myself, I'd admit, it was really that last conversation with Brendon that had me here.

"She's a hustler, Chastity." Brendon looked at me with a smirk.

He and I were talking about Mona. Or at least that's how the conversation had begun. But suddenly, he started telling me I should be dating. He had crushed my heart into a million tiny little pieces.

"If you had plans like a date, Mona would step up more. She's only taking advantage because you're doing everything, and you don't really give her a chance to do anything."

I was so confused and hurt. Where was this coming from? Now he wanted me *dating*? And what's all this bull about Mona?

How could I tell him that I didn't mind doing for him and the kids because I was in love? How could I tell him that I felt like shit for praying the Governor would do what he'd been known for doing for years and ignore all of the pleas? Oh God, what kind of woman was I that I wanted my sister to die so I could take over her family and her husband?

"What the fuck is taking so long?"

Trevor's voice startled me. I literally jumped.

"I'm coming, dang! Hold your horses!" I screamed back. But I made sure my words were carefully laced with light humor. Keeping it light and easy was the way to go with Trevor.

My goal in going to the bathroom wasn't to use it, but to come back and move the conversation to the living room instead of the kitchen where sharp objects were all over and within reach.

I walked out of the bathroom, waving my hands like I was trying to air dry them. Instead of going back into the kitchen, I plopped down on the couch and sighed loudly.

"Okay, Trevor, what do you want me to do?" I didn't even turn back toward the kitchen. I wanted to make it clear that if he wanted to talk to me, he needed to bring his conversation out to the living room.

Before he could respond, there was a knock at his door.

I looked up but I didn't have to wait too long. Whoever had knocked was now using a key to enter. When she opened the front door and struggled to walk in with two kids in tow, it was obvious she didn't expect to see me.

THIRTY-EIGHT
HOPE

After more than a week on suicide watch, I finally got the clearance from the head doctor and was able to return to my cell. Besides the bandages around my wrists, life had returned to normal for me on the row. I got a few pitiful stares, but no one tried to talk to me about it and I was glad for that.

Imagine the state of Texas being so steeped in tradition? Even on death row, specific detailed procedures were in place. I sat reading the paperwork that was given to me. I was at work, talking to Latrice, when the subject came up.

"Who was that dude?"

"Oh, that was the Death Row Supervisor," I said.

"The what?"

"I know, right? Yeah, he presented me with the official notification of execution date. It's basically a form that lists everything that's expected of me to help the state facilitate my death."

"The nerve," Latrice said. "So what kind of shit they want you to do?"

"Well, I need to specify my religious beliefs, I have to submit a copy of my witness list, and decide whether I want to donate my body to research."

Latrice had stopped working. She was looking at me. "Party Girl, you say this shit like we talking about what to get from the store."

I looked at her. They didn't get it. I was ready. "Oh, don't trip, I'm just tired; that's all. But seriously, though, if you think my list is something, they have work to do, too."

"Who?" Latrice asked.

"The death row unit. I'm not sure who that is, but I guess it's the warden and his staff."

"So what they gotta do?"

"They have to get some papers over to the chaplain and the public information office. This is like fourteen days before the deed is done. They also have to get the execution summary, my trust fund withdrawal form, and my visitation list." I shrugged it off. "Oh, and an execution watch log."

"What the fuck is an execution watch log?"

"It's a trip. Seven days before, starting at six o' clock in the evening, they start watching me. Every thirty minutes, they start logging everything I do. For the last thirty-six hours, the log moves to every fifteen minutes."

"What the hell?"

"I know, right?"

We talked more about what I needed to do and what the prison staff was required to do.

"You didn't feel funny talking to them about all this stuff?"

"No, I swear, I'm ready. I'm sick and tired of being in here and I just want this over!"

Later that evening, we were in the rec room when the news came on, and I saw my mama's face plastered all over every single station.

"Party Girl," Latrice leaned over to look at me, "that bitch's son is now eligible for the death penalty. The same punishment she's been working overtime to push onto you."

"Karma is a mofo," Pauline said.

I couldn't believe it. But it took Mona to tell it like it really was. On Channel 13, she was acting the plum fool. "What I'm saying is, she lobbied for my child to die. She wanted to be front and center on execution day. I wanna know where she's at now? Oh, in the beginning, she was pushing for the ultimate punishment for this offender, but that was before she knew her son was the culprit." The reporter barely had to ask Mona a question and she was going off. "Where's her push for True Justice now?"

"You go, girl!" Pauline yelled. "Damn, yo' mama ain't no joke; she going hard!"

I watched Mona in disbelief. One thing about her, she knew how to cut up for sure.

"When I tried to tell her mother to mother, my child did not do this, she didn't wanna listen. I wonder what she's feeling now? She's looking at losing her own child; how's that death penalty working for you, Adena?" Mona was so furious, you couldn't help but wish you never got on her bad side.

Pauline and Latrice were cracking up.

"Yo' mama is off da chain!" Pauline declared.

"Yeah, she's something," I said.

I wasn't sure how I felt about Adena's new misfortune. I understood Mona knew her pain, but the big difference between her son and me, I was innocent! I hadn't done a thing. No one had called police and said I was drunk after I'd made it to the apartment.

Then how did they let him go, talking about he was at home and they gave him a ticket? How did they not know he had just killed two people?

The more I listened to the story, the more disgusted I became.

If that had been my poor black behind, I would've been under the jail cell while they worked things out. But he gets to take a ticket for driving drunk? Then they had to figure out he was the one who caused the accident that killed that man and his son?

"How perfect is this?" Latrice asked. "Here she is pushing for someone else to get the needle, but little did she know the life she was speaking on was her own son's!"

We all shook our heads as we watched the story.

"That's what the hell she gets!" Latrice added.

I didn't say a word. I didn't like Adena because she didn't like me. I didn't know the woman personally and I always thought if she'd only hear my side, she'd see I didn't kill her husband.

But back then, she didn't care what I had to say. She didn't care that Trey was lying.

"Where's the bitch now?" Latrice was getting all worked up and hyped. Me, I wasn't tripping at all. I had already said all I needed to say. In less than three weeks, all of this misery would be a distant memory for me.

I couldn't believe how Mona was cutting up. And those news people were so wrong for allowing her to get on TV and say all of those crazy things. The one thing she'd said during all of her interviews was that she loved me and she wanted to do everything in her power to convince me to keep up the fight.

"I ain't mad at her," Pauline said. "Shiiit, she just trying to save her child!"

"You can't be mad at her for that!" Latrice added.

★★★

Later that night, as I lay in the dark in my cell alone with my thoughts, I started thinking back to that night when I felt so tired

I was ready to end it all. Lucky for me, less than sixty seconds after I passed out, guards were in my cell. Shaking those memories from my mind, I started thinking about the irony of Adena's son and his predicament. I wondered what Adena would say to me. She'd pushed for the death penalty. She'd wanted to see that driver pay, but I really wondered how she felt now that she knew the culprit was her son.

I tossed and turned a bit, but I couldn't sleep. No matter how hard I tried, when I closed my eyes, colorful dots danced in front of me.

"I did the right thing," I mumbled.

Who wanted to spend the next twenty years living like this? My sister was fucking my husband, my kids no longer knew me, and my mama had gone and lost her mind. I laughed at Mona and her antics on the news.

Several days later, things had returned to normal. I was working when one of the C.O.'s came running in nearly out of breath. "Donovan! You got a visit!"

My eyebrow went up. A visit? What the hell was she talking about?

"I've been looking for you. You have a visit. C'mon!"

I looked around. What the hell was going on?

"The warden is in the visiting room taking some pictures. Do you need to go and change?" C.O. Ramirez asked.

I looked at her like she was crazy. Since when do they care about what I look like during a visit? I sensed something was up, but I wasn't in the mood.

"What's really going on?" I asked.

She didn't even cuff me as she escorted me back to my cell.

Suddenly, she stopped, turned and looked at me.

"Oh Jesus! Girl, nobody told you?"

Told me what? Did they move up my execution? Did something happen to Mona? I was dumbfounded.

"No one told me anything until you came looking for me. What's going on?" I asked.

"Girl, the Reverend Al Sharpton is here to see you!"

Now I knew for sure, she'd gone and bumped her head.

THIRTY-NINE
ADENA

"Son, don't say a word! Rusty is on his way." I felt odd telling my child not to talk to police. We bailed him out and agreed to this meeting because I wanted to see what the DA was thinking of doing.

I admit, it didn't look good. My son, who had been previously arrested for DWI, admitted that he was drunk when he struck those people. This was a huge mess. I couldn't remember a time when I was more afraid.

"I'm sorry," he muttered.

I snapped my head in his direction. I cupped his chin and turned him to me.

"Raakin, do not say another word! You have one of the best defense attorneys money can buy. I need you to sit here and be quiet. Do not say another word!"

I realized we were early, but I didn't expect to have to wait this long. Rusty's assistant assured me he'd be here so I wasn't worried. But Raakin was a complete mess. I wished I had gotten to him first. I didn't understand why he didn't come to me. Instead, he'd allowed his roommates to talk him into trying to hide. That really only made matters worse; authorities had to use valuable resources to try and track him down.

The calls, the letters, the emails; it was overwhelming. I had quite a few supporters telling me to do whatever it took to protect my son. But then there were those who were quick to call me a hypocrite. Hope's mother had been taunting me, all but challenging me, to come and speak out about what my son had done. She'd even asked me point blank if I still wanted the culprit to receive True Justice.

I was torn. I truly believed in an eye for an eye. But never before had I been confronted with such a gut-wrenching choice. Do I stand up for my beliefs even though it could mean the life of my firstborn?

Rusty came in like a true knight-in-shining-armor. He obviously had a relationship with both the officers and the DA.

By the time it was all said and done, we walked out of there and I began to feel like there was light at the end of the tunnel. I didn't feel quite as distraught as I had been.

"I'll set up a meeting with Lykos. We'll give it some time so people can forget, and then we'll start putting feelers out there for a plea agreement," he said.

"But what about the death penalty?" I asked.

Raakin looked at me like I was betraying him. Rusty looked at me like it wasn't a problem.

The crowd of reporters who waited outside the courthouse reminded me that I'd been avoiding the press for weeks now, and I couldn't get away with hiding forever. But the real surprise came when I saw the picket signs.

We don't want your son to die!

Now can you forgive?

An Eye for an Eye does no good!

Have a change of heart!

They didn't yell, they didn't chant. They stood with their signs. I had read their messages loud and clear.

"Adena, what a precarious position you're in. You were pushing for the death penalty; has your position changed?" a reporter asked.

"I don't want to speak about details of this case. My heart goes out to the mother who lost both her husband and her child."

Then I looked at another reporter and pointed.

"Hope Donovan's mother calls this karma; what's your response to that?"

"This is a misfortunate accident. Hope's mother is lashing out and I understand her concerns," I said, then tried to move on to the next question.

"A misfortunate accident? What was misfortunate, that your son was drunk? That he tried to hide what he had done? That he left the scene of an accident? Or that you had no idea it was your child's life you were pushing for the DA to take?"

It was like the crowd parted and Mona stood there waiting for the answer to her question.

My vision started to blur, and my throat started going dry. I wasn't ready for this. I wanted to talk to the press only because I knew they were getting frustrated. But I didn't expect Mona to show up. Although, this was the same tactics we used to confront her and Brendon anytime they spoke.

"True Justice is just that, true justice. Again, this was a misfortunate accident. My son is innocent until a jury of his peers finds otherwise. Our prayers and support are with Bethany Hicks during this difficult time. But we will not get into a sparring match over which crime was worse," I said.

"I'm glad you can at least admit there was a crime, because calling what your son did a 'misfortunate accident' is a bunch of bull!" Mona said. By now her neck was twisting and several cameras were going back and forth during our exchange.

Rusty stepped up. "We are looking forward to our day in court."

"Hmmm, sure wish I had Rusty Hardin money to help my baby when she was on trial for a crime she didn't commit!" Mona said.

I wanted the press conference to be over. Each time I looked up, I saw one of those signs or I had to look into Mona's eyes. She was getting immense pleasure from this. But Rusty and I agreed, I needed to say something to the press simply because being absent for so long could be seen as me admitting my son was guilty.

I pointed to another reporter, and when she asked the question, I wish I hadn't.

"Do you still feel passionately that your son should face the death penalty for this crime? You were pushing for it when we didn't know the driver's identity."

Thanks to Allah, I didn't have to answer that question. Rusty stepped in, declared the news conference over, and ushered us to a waiting car.

That didn't stop reporters from screaming questions in our direction; some even followed us to the car.

"What about those who say you're a hypocrite?"

"Do you still believe in the death penalty?"

"Are you still demanding a capital sentence in this case?"

I wanted to scream. As we slid into the backseat, I hugged Raakin. He collapsed into my arms and cried like the baby I couldn't help seeing him as.

As his mother, was it not my duty to do what was best for him? How did I agree to allow the state to take his life over an accident? He'd panicked. There was no way he'd maliciously hurt a fly.

He'd made a mistake.

FORTY
BRENDON

I was speechless, at a complete loss for words. My brain wouldn't work, but I was happy. As I held the phone and listened to Carrie, I wanted to jump for joy—literally. "So what happens now?"

"Well, we go back through the appeals process. It means her about-face has bought us more time."

"This is great news. I'm glad it worked out. Carrie, thank you so much for thinking of this. I didn't know what the hell to do and the clock was ticking so fast." I sighed.

"Our job isn't hardly done. While we do have more time, we need to use that time wisely. I wanted to run another idea by you. I wanna see how you feel about this. It's gonna be tricky, but I figured since we got this extra time, we need to make the most of it."

"I'm all ears, Carrie. What's up?"

"Have you ever thought about visiting Trey?"

That, I wasn't ready for. I had thought about seeing Trey face to face for years. I'd had dreams about him. I wanted to look him in the eye and ask him why he'd lied. The truth was if I did ever get the chance to see him, I couldn't promise we'd both walk away alive.

"Trey?"

"I want you to give it some thought. You don't have to answer right now. But I'm thinking if we could get Trey, or even Linda, to recant, that may speed up the process to a new trial."

"So I'd have to talk to him?" It was a dumb question. "You really think he'd admit to me that he lied? I don't even think he'd accept my visit."

"I'm trying to think of anything I can. I'm not saying it has to be you, maybe Mona—you know she's got quite a way with words. Or perhaps, Hope's sister, Chastity," Carrie suggested.

At the mention of her name, a crazy thought ran throughout my mind. It didn't last long, but it did flash. How would Chastity feel if she knew we were brainstorming ideas to free Hope?

"Her sister?"

"Yes, I was thinking she could befriend him and see where the friendship goes."

"I see where you're going with that, Carrie, but the problem is Trey knows Chastity and all of Hope's friends. Remember, they're all from the neighborhood."

"Again, that's why we're talking this out. I wanted to throw it out there, so you could start thinking along those lines."

"Okay, I'll talk to Mona about it and start thinking of ways we can get to Trey and Linda."

"I'll be in touch," Carrie said. "Oh, also, I talked with Jennifer Crowe. She's sending over some information she thinks may be helpful, so I'll keep you posted."

Blake came running into the room. He didn't knock on the door like I'd been trying to teach him to do.

"Daddy, get up," he said. He looked at me with Hope's eyes and I couldn't help thinking about how much he had grown since her arrest. Blake was one-and-a-half when Hope had gone to prison. Her breasts were still leaking.

"Where's Breanna?" I asked.

"She's with McKenzie."

I should've known. I tried to take the kids to counseling to deal with the fact that Hope was gone, but the more we talked about it with the counselor, the more it seemed to agitate them. Soon, we stopped going and if they talked to her, it was okay; when they didn't, that was okay, too. Breanna seemed to only want to talk to McKenzie or Chastity. A knock at the front door took my mind away from the kids.

The moment I walked to the door and opened it, I wish I hadn't. Stacy was not giving up.

I pulled the door open and smiled. "Hey, Stacy, what's up?"

She smiled. "Brendon, I'm good, was wondering if you had a few minutes."

Wondering if there was a way to close the door and pretend like I wasn't home, I leaned against the doorframe.

"Is everything okay?" I didn't really care, but I needed her to make it fast.

"I was thinking we could step out here on the porch and talk for a bit," she said.

Talking to Stacy on my front porch was the last thing I wanted to do. I wanted to go back inside and go over a plan in my mind to get Desmond or Jemar to talk to Linda.

"It'll only take a few moments," she said.

She was asking, but I knew I didn't really have a choice. Something told me to come up with an excuse so I could avoid a conversation I didn't want to have, but my excuse would mean nothing to her. She had to know I didn't want to talk to her.

Suddenly, McKenzie and Breanna come bouncing up the walkway. They were giggling and talking about something on a cell phone.

"Hey, Mom," McKenzie said.

"Hey, Dad," Breanna said.

They giggled into the house and once again, I was alone with Stacy.

Using a crooked index finger, she smiled as she motioned for me to come all the way outside. I eased out of the door and closed it behind me.

I sighed.

"What's going on?"

"I heard about Hope," she began. Her voice dropped to a low whisper.

Everyone had heard about Hope. That's been the story of my life over the past few years. I eased away from the front door. If she wanted me to say something else, she was about to be mad because I had stuff on my mind and none involved talking to her.

"Wwweell?"

My eyebrows went up. I wasn't sure what she was talking about or what she wanted me to say.

"Well, what?" I asked.

"You weren't gonna tell me that Hope's execution day is like hours away?"

Before I could correct her, she told me how she really felt.

Stacy sighed and smiled.

"To tell the truth, I'm glad it's over. I'm glad that we'll be able to move on soon. Don't think I didn't know you've been holding back." She stroked my arm. "Don't worry; I completely understand. That's why I made sure the others knew when the dust cleared, it would be you and me. I've worked hard all these years to make sure they understood."

"What are you saying? You wanted to make sure who understood?" I asked.

But Stacy kept talking like she didn't hear my damn question.

"You've been in a really tough situation. Why do you think I've been so patient?"

Instinctively, I stepped back when she got closer. I could see the hurt on her face, but the last thing I wanted was for our kids to walk out and see something I'd have to explain later.

"Brendon, is everything okay?" she asked.

"Yeah, but this is not a good time for me. I was in the middle of something when you popped up," I said without even thinking.

"Popped up?" Her neck snapped back. The pleasant expression on her face quickly turned sour.

"You know what I mean," I said.

I didn't need an argument with Stacy. What I needed was for her to sashay back across the street so I could try and figure out which one of my boys to sic on Linda.

"I was trying to ease into this, but I see that's probably not the best course of action. So I'm gonna spit it out so you can get back to whatever had you so *busy*," she said snippily.

I decided to ignore the sarcasm in her voice. The quicker she got to the point, the quicker I could get back to what really needed my attention.

"I need to know what the hell is going on between you and Chastity! I thought since the others were out the picture, *we* were working on something here. But I ran into Trevor yesterday and now I'm confused, and not to mention, highly pissed!"

Stacy folded her arms over her chest, and stood like she dared me to give her the wrong answer.

"Who are the others?" I asked, confused.

Her head tilted to the side, and then she frowned. "Uh, Jackie, Betty Jean, Tamera," she hissed. "I had no idea Chastity needed to be added to the list!"

What list? That's when it dawned on me. I never thought about how all of Hope's friends seemed to *coincidently* have issues that sent them away.

She had me there. Not to mention, Chastity's warning blared in my head.

"That bitch Stacy is crazy! You need to stay away from her!"

FORTY-ONE
CHASTITY

What, was I back in high school now? I'd had enough drama in my life, waiting to see what was gonna happen with Brendon. I didn't need the kind of foolishness Trevor was offering. My phone had rung like crazy after I'd left, but I was not interested in talking to him.

How dare he dog me out over Brendon, trip like he had a right to do so, when he knew he and Felicia were still messing around? I felt like such a fool. I wanted to tell her exactly what he had been doing before she let herself into the apartment.

As I drove back to Brendon's, my brain started thinking of all the witty things I could've said when she'd stepped to me instead of her so-called man. Who does that now? Everyone knows you take it to the man and not the woman!

"Who the hell are you?" When she finally made it into the apartment, her eyes zeroed in on me. If the atmosphere weren't so tense, I would've laughed at her question.

"Why you all up in my husband's apartment like you pay bills around here?"

Felicia knew good and well who I was. We'd had enough run-ins with each other for her to be sitting there, trying to act all brand-new now.

"Drop the act, Felicia; you know who I am," I said.

She turned her attention to Trevor. "What is she doing here?"

"Man, don't come with all that bullshit!" Trevor dismissed her question with a menacing frown.

Felicia ushered her kids into one of the bedrooms and quickly closed the door. "Mommy and Daddy need to have grown-up talk. Stay in here."

I started to get up, but she rushed to the sofa and instead of attacking him, she turned her rage toward me.

"You need to take a hint. How long are you gonna keep chasing someone who doesn't want you?" I couldn't believe she was serious. But she was. "Trevor don' already told me how you over there humping your sister's husband; ain't you got no shame?" She looked at me like I was less than dried shit on the bottom of her shoe.

I whipped my head in Trevor's direction. He didn't crack under pressure. I turned back to Felicia. "I don't know what Trevor has told you, or why the two of you are even talking about me, but you should be asking him why I'm over here."

Her narrowed eyes looked back and forth between Trevor and me, like she wasn't sure which one of us to take out first. When I glanced back at Trevor, I noticed he didn't look the least bit fazed by what was going on.

I got up. "I don't have time for this."

But before I could balance myself, Felicia shoved me back down into the chair. I was stunned.

"I'm sick and tired of you!" Her crooked finger was in my face. "How many years has it been? We are *married!* We have two kids. When are you gonna understand he doesn't want you!"

"Don't put your hands on me again," I warned. The last time I'd had a fight, I was in high school. Trevor's wife was pushing me around like she had the right to.

And, he stood off to the side looking on like he'd be happy regardless of who won.

Felicia walked up on me again. She was standing over me because I was still in the wing chair. As she towered over me, I wondered why I was going through this mess with Trevor and his wife, estranged wife, or whatever she was to him now.

Something must've snapped in me because I raised my right leg, kicked her in the stomach, jumped up, and rushed her before she knew what hit her.

"You wanna know what I'm sick and tired of, Felicia?" I rustled her back down. "I'm sick and tired of married men playing with my damn emotions!" When she was flat on her back, I jumped on her stomach, used my knees to pin her arms down, and grabbed fists full of her weave. "I'm sick of dumb-ass women who blame me when their husbands don't wanna act right!"

Slap!

Slap!

"I'm tired of make-up sex with your husband out of fear that he'll come and act the fool with my brother-in-law if he doesn't get what he wants!"

I slapped her again.

Felicia squirmed beneath my weight, but I had her pinned down real good. It wasn't until I heard a faint voice that I stopped.

"Mommy! Get off my mommy!"

That's when I realized I needed to get away from Trevor and all of his senseless drama. I jumped up, grabbed my purse, and bolted out of there. The sad thing was Trevor never lifted a finger to prevent the fight. Felicia didn't realize I had been frustrated long before she had tried to punk me. Thoughts of Hope and Brendon, Stacy and Brendon, and everyone else sent my blood boiling.

I was tired of being punked.

The moment I walked up and realized the scene that was unfolding right before my eyes, I thought I was about to fight yet again. That's when I realized I'd never told Brendon about what was in her house.

When Stacy touched Brendon's arm, I stopped, and watched the two of them for a moment.

It wasn't that he'd made any promises to me, but there were so many times that he'd denied being involved with her. I was disgusted. First, Trevor; now, Brendon; there must've been something in the water.

When I saw Stacy fold her arms across her chest, I walked up and let my presence be known.

"Am I interrupting something?" I asked.

Brendon was first to look in my direction. It was as if I'd caught them doing something they had no business doing. Both he and Stacy looked like they'd seen a ghost.

FORTY-TWO
HOPE

Tuesday November 6th, the day that would've been my execution day, passed without incident. It was simply another day on Texas' death row—same shit, different toilet.

At work, Latrice and Pauline commented, saying they were glad I was still among the living. But I was still thinking about the possibility of being on death row and living in a cage for ten to twenty more years. I had a new outlook, but some things remained the same.

When the Reverend Al Sharpton came to the Mountain View unit, it was a pretty big fucking deal! The C.O.'s were falling all over themselves and for once, I was treated like royalty instead of scum.

He was bigger than his persona. I didn't realize he really was a man of faith. After reading scripture and talking about no man having a right to take a life, he really had me convinced that I needed to fight for my freedom.

"So what was he like?" Latrice asked.

"He was real gentle. I don't know how to explain it really, but I could tell he'd studied my case. He knew all about Trey and Q, he knew about the confession, and the witnesses who claimed I confessed to them."

"So what did he say?"

"He mainly explained to me why I needed to fight and not give up. He made me see that my dying early, if that's what was gonna happen, wouldn't have the impact I expected."

"You think he really cared?"

"Yeah, he didn't have to come here. He wasn't paid to meet with me, and I don't know how true it is, but he says he's got some connection with the Innocence Project," I said.

Latrice's eyes grew wider than saucers.

"What?"

"Yeah," I said.

"Party Girl! You know what that means?"

I stopped what I was doing and gave her a *get real* look. I had been through too much. I had hung my faith on the wrong things one too many times.

"I can't believe you don't believe what he said."

"It's not that I don't believe him. But Latrice, get real! He's only a man. Regardless of his connections, he's only a man. If he is able to help me, I'd be grateful, but if he doesn't or can't, I won't be too heartbroken."

Latrice and I went back to stitching.

"I wish somebody would come and visit me on death row, and act like they care about me trying to give up," she said.

"I didn't look at it that way."

"Girl, you don't have to. But let me tell you something. I have felt for you since day one. I know in my heart of hearts that you didn't commit that crime. So when you were talking about giving up, I prayed every night that God would intervene. Never once did I think He'd send a famous man of the cloth, but whatever works!" She laughed.

Knowing that Latrice had prayed for me made me feel better. It wasn't that I was eager to die; I was tired of feeling like a wounded, trapped animal. But when I said that, the Reverend told me I could never be an animal.

A lot of what he had said resonated with me. He had inspired me to look at this thing from a different perspective. Of course I wanted to live. But the idea of people not believing in my innocence drove me crazy.

Latrice leaned in closer.

"Party Girl, if I wasn't guilty, I would've written a letter to everybody I could think of. Even though I did it and I know I did it, you better believe I'd be trying to get out of here."

She went back to her stitches.

I looked at her. "Latrice, you do believe me when I say I didn't do it, right? I swear to you, I had no idea Trey and Q had robbed that place."

"Girl, we know your ass ain't capable of killing a soul. I'm gonna tell you one thing, Party Girl, some of us, we deserve to be away from society. We're not animals, but we may have animal-like tendencies and those tendencies are a good judge of character. I knew you wasn't a killer from the first time I laid eyes on you!"

I wanted to laugh at that. "If it was so apparent to you, how come that damn jury couldn't see what you saw?" I joked.

"On a serious tip, juries would get it right a whole lot better if they were made up of true criminals. Hear me out, seriously. A thief knows a thief, a crook understands crookedness, and once you've killed, I'm pretty sure you can pinpoint another killer, too."

What she said made sense in an awkward kind of way.

"A jury of my peers don't consist of people who've never committed a crime before. Requiring that jurors have a clean record is already slanting this in favor of the justice system. If you've never acted up or out, then you can't relate to my lifestyle and what I've been through. You've seen those movies when the agencies turn to the same bad guy that used to terrorize them so they can learn inside secrets." Latrice shrugged. "The concept is the same." Before I could say anything she chimed in, "I know it sounds crazy, but it makes perfect sense to me."

"It really doesn't sound crazy at all," I said. "But one could argue that the criminal will always side with the accused, since they're able to imagine walking in their shoes."

Latrice laughed. "Well, I didn't say the system would be perfect, but what I am saying is the shit would be better than what we've got today." She stopped again. "As it is now, we get these lily white people who've never gotten as much as a jaywalking ticket, and they're supposed to be able to relate to those who stole because they couldn't eat. It doesn't make sense."

It made sense to me.

"I don't know what the answer is. But too many innocent people get caught up, and it seems like it's so easy for you to fall through the cracks."

We worked in silence for a bit longer. Then without looking up, she said, "Well, regardless of the system in place, I'm glad the good Reverend was able to talk some sense in to you. And I'm glad you're still here with us, after um, well, you know, don't give up, make 'em work for it, Party Girl; shit, make 'em work if they wanna take you!"

I laughed nervously at that. Then Latrice looked over and asked, "Your ol' man coming this weekend?"

Some things really never changed.

FORTY-THREE
ADENA

I was behind on everything. I was supposed to cancel a speaking engagement and forgot so the organization was pissed at me. Leadership at True Justice was being questioned on a consistent basis and I didn't know how to handle the inquiries.

Reporters were surprised that I wasn't as accessible as I once was and I was a mess. Everything I had worked for over the last five-and-a-half years seemed to come into question, and I no longer had the answers.

I heard the keys at the door, but that didn't even startle me. These days Michelle was my only true connection to the outside world. She backed in, carrying brown paper bags.

"You hear the news?" she asked from the door.

"What now?" Each day was like a step closer to my son's fate, and I was on the edge.

"Hope Donovan's appeals are working their way through the courts."

Michelle spoke like she had to handle me delicately or I might crack. Perhaps she saw something I couldn't see. I knew I was defeated.

I looked up.

"What happened?" My question was out of curiosity more than a need to know.

"The Reverend Al Sharpton met with her and talked her into fighting to prove her innocence."

"Isn't that interesting," I said.

"Did you stop watching TV?" Michelle asked.

"I can't stomach it anymore. It seems like there's not a single newscast that doesn't feature a story about Raakin and what happened. What I hate most is when they bring in the legal analysts who sit and try to predict what will happen."

"You know how the game is played," Michelle said.

And, I did. I was once a major player in the game, but because I knew, and I used to play, didn't mean I could handle it when the other team scored.

"How's Raakin?" Michelle asked.

She came over every other day. If she didn't bring food, she brought groceries and she always asked about Raakin.

"He's pretty much the same. He can't believe he killed two people. I wish there was a way for a jury to see the remorse he's feeling. This was an accident," I said.

Michelle looked at me, but didn't say anything. If she agreed or disagreed, her expression didn't offer up any clues.

"So what has Sharpton promised her?" I asked.

"I'm not sure, from what I saw, he visited her for something like four hours. When he was finished, there was a news conference to talk about details of the case."

"Did they say anything new?"

"He mentioned the innocence project. He also threw out questions about the confessions from the jailhouse snitch and one of the co-defendants."

I rose from the sofa. I had enough on my plate. I couldn't worry about her or that right now. My son needed my full and focused attention. This was no time to think about splitting my time and effort between Hope and Raakin. If ever it came down to it, Hope Donovan could go free if it meant sacrificing my son. It would be a long time before I started back on the crusade.

"Have you rested today?"

"I did after my noon prayer."

Michelle looked at me approvingly.

I went to the window and gazed outside. I wasn't looking at anything in particular. Thoughts were going through my mind about the worst-case scenario. I wasn't afraid to go public with my desire to not see my son suffer for a mistake. Everything in me believed he had panicked and had made a bad choice. If only he had called me for advice.

Until she spoke again, I'd forgotten she was there.

"What are we going to do?" Michelle asked softly.

I hated being handled. I hated that people now felt they had to measure their words against me. I didn't wake up one morning and decide I was against the death penalty. What I had experienced was a life-altering situation.

When the door to Raakin's old room opened, Michelle and I looked in its direction.

We watched as he walked out, cleared his throat, and entered the bathroom.

"How's he holding up?" she asked.

I had a feeling that wasn't what she wanted to discuss, but I was relieved for the diversion.

"Glad to be out of jail and back home. I insisted he come home instead of going back to that apartment. His roommates call to tell me about the media that's parked outside their place."

"You can expect that to go on for a while," Michelle said.

"It's too much for him to have to deal with."

A few moments later, we hushed as the bathroom door opened, he emerged, then disappeared again. I could sense his fear and I shared it. I didn't want my baby to die. There were so many others who had maliciously broken the law, taken the lives of innocent people, if they were spared; you knew more bloodshed was in their future. That wasn't the case with Raakin; as I thought these thoughts, images of Mona Clarke kept popping up in my mind.

"We continue to get stacks of media requests and they all ask the same question. It's been nearly a month now," Michelle said.

Had it been an entire month already? I suppose it had. I could remember during the spring when I used to think happy thoughts about the month of November. My suffering would be over. How had my nightmare become a double feature? I had to tell Michelle something. It wasn't fair to her or the staff and members of True Justice.

I looked at Michelle and forced a faint smile. She had supported me well over the years. I knew what I had to do because my two worlds could no longer co-exist.

"I will no longer support capital punishment. I will resign from True Justice and we can hold the news conference whenever it's convenient for you," I said.

"That's fine," she said. "I know Rusty is working behind the scenes to lower the charges. The moment it's confirmed that he's worked something out, we'll release a statement about our position in this case," Michelle said.

"You do what you have to."

FORTY-FOUR
BRENDON

My head hurt. I tossed a little, then turned onto my side, but the pain wouldn't go away. If I could, I'd stay in bed forever. I was sick of what my life had become.

"Daaad, hungry!" BJ yelled.

I took a pillow and covered my head. When did this get so damn complicated? I still hadn't heard back from Desmond and Jemar, but something told me neither one would have a problem helping out with Linda.

There was a knock at the door. But before I could raise my head, it opened and the kids stormed in.

"Dad, what's going on? This place is like all nasty and stuff! And we want some real food. Where's Chastity? When's she coming back?"

Breanna was obviously the spokesperson.

I looked up at the three of them, but I didn't know what to say. I didn't really want to say anything. I wondered where the hell Mona was.

"I'm gonna get up soon," I said, but I didn't mean it. I wanted them to leave me alone. I didn't wanna think about Chastity. I didn't wanna think about her or Stacy.

"Dad!" Breanna hissed.

When did she develop an attitude? When did sarcasm seep into her voice? That's when I realized how much Chastity had handled as far as the kids were concerned. It was more than the kids; the place was always clean and she cooked up a storm.

Without her, the difference was like night and day. But I didn't know what to do. I didn't know what Stacy and Chastity wanted from me, and I was tired of trying to figure it out.

"Daaad, are you gonna just lay there?" Breanna asked.

"I'll be up in a sec," I said.

Breanna sucked her teeth. I didn't have to look at her to know she was probably rolling her eyes, and standing with her arms crossed at her chest. She was like the others, waiting for me to do what she wanted.

I grunted a few times and pulled the cover over my head.

It didn't take long for them to leave and I was glad. I was about to go back to sleep until the phone rang.

Without looking up, I reached over and felt around for the cell phone on the nightstand.

"Yeah," I answered.

"Brendon, what's good, my man?" It was Desmond.

"Just tryin' to make it; that's all," I said.

"I hear some stress in your voice and it ain't the normal Hope stuff. What's going on?"

I yawned. "Man, that's probably the Patrón you hear, dawg."

"Oh, like that? Okay, then what's up? Got your message. What you need us to do?"

My head was still hurting, but now, I was feeling better. I still had the mess with Stacy and Chastity to deal with, but at least I knew my boys were willing to help with the most important issue at hand. Desmond agreed to meet later for a drink.

I finally pulled myself out of bed and made it to the kitchen. The kids sat at the table eating cereal. Breanna gave me a nasty look, but I pretended like I didn't see it.

Mona walked into the kitchen. She rubbed her eyes and yawned. "What's going on around here? Where's some food?"

Breanna picked up the cereal box and dropped it back down on the table.

"I ain't coo-coo for no damn Cocoa Puffs!" Mona said.

I opened the refrigerator door and tried to bury myself inside, but it wasn't big enough.

"Damn, it ain't shit in here," Mona cried.

I wanted her to stop before she made a bad situation worse. The kids were already on edge, the place was a mess, and we were short on food. Chastity used to cook, clean, and shop. I was realizing how much she did for us now that she was gone.

"Where the hell is Chastity anyway? Lemme call her behind! This place is a hot funky mess!"

Mona's question made me think back to the standoff with Stacy and Chastity. It's like I was standing right in the crossfire.

"Oh, lookey-lookey, what perfect timing," Stacy had said. She had tossed in an extra twist of her neck for me.

Chastity's expression had changed from pleasant to confusion in a flash. My ears had started burning and I'd started to sweat. I didn't want to be sandwiched between two furious women.

"What's going on?" Chastity had asked, looking between Stacy and me.

I'd looked at Stacy; she was the one who started this mess.

"I'm glad you asked," Stacy had said to Chastity. Her expression had been a mix between sarcasm and anger, I'd guessed.

"You see, I was trying to talk to Brendon about this little game he's playing with us. I talked to Trevor," Stacy had said.

Whatever impact she'd expected that comment to have must've been lost on us both. Both Chastity and I had looked as if we weren't sure what that was supposed to mean.

"What does you talking to Trevor have to do with anything?" Chastity had asked.

"Well, he told me everything!" Stacy had snapped. She had behaved like she was pissed.

Suddenly, Stacy's bottom lip had begun to quiver. She had shaken her head. "I trusted you, Chastity, I trusted you."

Chastity had looked at me with confusion all over her face. I had shrugged a shoulder. I didn't want to be on the front porch having this discussion with the two of them.

"What are you talking about?" Chastity had asked Stacy.

"I'm talking about the fact that you've been screwing Brendon all along. You had me confiding in you, making a straight fool of myself, when all you had to do was tell me about the two of you." Stacy had looked at me. "And to imagine, I got rid of everyone else for you; my husband, Betty Jean, Jackie, Tamera."

If Stacy would've turned and walked away at that point, I could've possibly recovered. But she had to keep running her mouth. At that moment, I couldn't remember why I'd gotten involved with her in the first place.

"Got rid of?" I'd asked, not really wanting to know.

Chastity's eyes had grown wide. I had noticed her step back a bit. "Um, does this have anything to do with that shrine you have for Brendon in your bedroom?"

Now it had been my turn to look bewildered.

Stacy's eyes had narrowed and her face had contorted into the most evil frown I had seen. "You bitch!" she had spat at Chastity.

I had stepped between the two. "What's she talking about, Stacy? What shrine?"

Instead of waiting for her to answer, I had jogged across the street.

Stacy had taken off after me. When she'd finally caught up with me, she'd jumped on my back.

"Stop, Brendon, stop!"

My legs had wobbled slightly under the weight of her body, but she couldn't hang on. I turned back to see her sitting on the ground. She was pissed, but she had never broken my stride as I'd stormed into her house like I owned it. By the time I'd found the room, I was mad and scared at the same time.

There were three tall candles: one blue, another black and the other white. Pictures of my face, upper torso, and lower body were taped to each jar.

"This bitch is crazy, for real," I had said as I surveyed all my shit. She had my old hairbrush I thought I had lost. There was an electric razor that disappeared from my bathroom, a pair of my lucky drawers, a T-shirt and some socks!

"What the hell?"

There was a metal ashtray covered in black soot. I saw hair mixed with ashes. I didn't know what the hell she'd been trying to do. But what really spooked me was when I'd opened the black shoebox and found miniature cloth dolls with pictures of Betty Jean, Tamera, and Jackie's faces pinned to the heads.

My heart was thumping. I was hella nervous. What kind of shit was Stacy into?

I quickly had blown out the candles, snatched my pictures off the jars and taken my shit back. I had done as much damage as I could to her shrine. After surveying the damage, I'd turned and gotten up outta there. By the time I'd made it back outside, she and Chastity had been in the middle of the street arguing.

A few neighbors had started coming outside. I was glad the girls hadn't come out yet.

When I'd walked over to where they stood, Stacy had tried to plead with me.

"Brendon, I can explain," she'd said, tugging at my arm.

I had yanked my arm from her reach.

"You need help," I'd said to Stacy. "Let's go!" I'd said to Chastity.

But as we had started back across the street, Stacy had yelled something that had stopped me cold. "Did you know he was basically screwing prostitutes?"

Chastity had stopped, too.

"You don't even know the risks he takes? And then for him to pit us against each other, what kind of dog is he? All of this while he's frontin' like he's so devoted to Hope."

I had looked at Chastity. I could see the hurt in her eyes.

"I don't screw prostitutes," I'd said to her.

"What do you call those tricks at the strip club?" Stacy had asked.

I had turned to her, struggling not to smack her ass. "How long have you been following me around?" I'd asked.

"What about all those times you promised we'd be together?" Stacy had asked right back.

"So, lemme guess, you were telling me what you thought I wanted to hear, so you could get what you wanted, but then you were probably doing the same with her." She had hissed and had motioned in Chastity's direction.

I couldn't tell how Chastity was taking the information Stacy was spewing. She couldn't be happy about what she was hearing.

Chastity had looked at me like she was completely disappointed, then she had turned and walked away.

"I don't blame you, girl. Trust and believe you'd be a fool to keep messin' with this loser! Lyin ass!" Stacy had screamed.

At that moment, I had wanted to kill her.

That was nearly a week ago and I hadn't heard from Chastity since.

Mona cursed and I came back to my sad reality: Chastity was out of my life.

FORTY-FIVE
CHASTITY

What was I thinking? How did I allow myself to get caught up in this mess? I felt bad about running out on the kids, but I needed a break. I needed to figure out what was going on. I hadn't heard from Trevor since that run-in with him and Felicia. I guess that meant they were back together, again. It was the story of my life, always the second runner-up, even when I was first.

For the last few days, I'd been thinking about things I could've or should've said in front of Stacy and Brendon. Mostly I was hurt. I wanted all of what she'd been saying to be a figment of her imagination or plain not true. How could I have read him so wrong for so long?

When he stood there and couldn't deny any of what she was saying, I felt like the biggest fool. Stacy may have been pissed about him leading her on, but she hadn't been cooking, cleaning, and basically doing whatever might make things easier for Brendon.

True enough, he never made any promises to me. He never implied we'd be together, but we shared so much, I thought the two of *us* were working toward something. Stacy claimed I was her confidante, but I was really his. We talked about Hope, how he felt about the execution, and how upset he was when she made the decision to give up without asking for his input. Stacy could've won an Academy Award for her performance that day, but she'd shed a light on so many things for me, I couldn't deal.

I couldn't believe she was actually trying to put a hex on him! So much of what she'd said still shook me to the core. Did she set fire to Tamera's beauty shop? How did she know about Jackie getting arrested and what had she done to chase Betty Jean away? To Stacy, all of these women were standing in her way, so she'd found a way to get rid of them.

I was suddenly glad she didn't see me as a threat.

"I trusted you, confided in you."

Stacy's words were meant more for shock than expressing any real feelings. I couldn't believe she was standing there trying to fight me over someone who wasn't rightfully hers or mine. Like it or not, Hope still had papers on him, and obviously, she still had his heart.

I'd been hiding out at the Motel 6 off of I-45. I thought I needed my own space, so I could think. The truth was, now with Felicia back in Trevor's life, and me out of Brendon's house, I was basically homeless.

After being alone for the past few days, I'd come to realize that my life was basically nothing without Brendon and the kids. As sad as that may sound, it was true.

Since I worked from home, I didn't have the luxury of making friends on the job. I couldn't go to any office parties, or happy hours, unless I went alone. And there wasn't any fun in being alone.

I looked at my cell phone when it rang, but didn't feel like dealing with Mona. She called twice, but didn't leave a message.

Knowing Mona, I was sure she had more than an earful for me, and I really wasn't in the mood. Besides, it wouldn't hurt her to have to wash a dish or fix a meal for her grandkids.

I wondered if Brendon was still home, but told myself it was none of my business if he was.

This time when the phone rang, I didn't ignore it. It was Breanna.

"Chastity, where are you?" she cried.

I closed my eyes and exhaled.

"I needed some time alone. I needed to think," I said. It wasn't a complete lie.

"When are you coming home? We totally don't wanna be here without you!" she whined.

"I need to clear my head."

"Well, come and get me; I don't wanna be here without you. Pllleeeeeeaaaase!"

How could I tell her I couldn't come because I felt hurt after learning her dad was screwing Stacy, all while he was making me feel like we had something special?

"Okay, if you won't come get me, you have to come back. I don't know what I'm gonna do without you."

"Breanna, be reasonable," I said.

"You have got to come back; we all miss you. Grandma was fussing about you not answering your phone, and Dad, ugh, he's such a mess without you!"

I heard her smacking gum. She was so dramatic, but I did miss her and her brothers. Each time I thought about going back, I couldn't stop thinking about Stacy sitting at that window of hers. Then I'd start thinking of the candles she was burning to get her hands on Brendon.

I should've known she was crazy. Who sits and watches some-one's house the way she watched Brendon's? Maybe she was some New Age witch or something. It was all really kind of creepy, but I didn't think anything of it before. Sometimes when I walked out to get the mail or even to the trash, I'd wave to her. You couldn't pay me to think Brendon really was messing with her. She seemed so unstable and so doggone needy. And she was always looking out that damn window.

"I'm so gonna die if you don't come back! It's totally unfair; first, my mom leaves me, now you! Come back," she whined. This time her voice was so high-pitched. "You know what, forget it! Maybe I should run away! Fine! Don't come back; stay away!" she yelled before hanging up the phone.

Even after I heard the click, I still couldn't believe Breanna had hung up on me. I looked around the shabby motel room and wondered if it was really worth it. I was taking a stand. I was sending a message to Brendon but at the expense of the kids?

I tried to call Breanna back but her phone went straight to voicemail.

"Shit!" Now I was panicked.

Mona! I dialed her number only to get the same thing; voicemail.

My heart started racing a bit. Should I call Brendon? What would I say? I didn't really want to talk to him, but what if Breanna made good on her promise and tried to run away? I should at least give him a heads-up.

With shaky fingers, I dialed his number. I had erased it from my contact list, but couldn't erase it from my brain. It rang twice.

What would he say to me?

A third ring.

Should I ignore everything that went down with us?

Ring number four.

Was *he* ignoring *my* calls? After that mess, he had the nerve to ignore *my* calls?

Ring number five.

FORTY-SIX
HOPE

I was not about to get the least bit excited. What would've been the point? The shit always sounded better than it actually was in reality. Every eye in the rec room was on me, but I didn't want them to think I was falling for the okey-doke!

As the news lady started explaining why DA Joel "Chuck" Conley was resigning, I sat there cool as a cucumber. Had he finally gotten caught? Was he ever gonna be called to the carpet, or would he be able to quietly resign, leaving the tons of innocent people he'd helped convict to rot in prison?

"Party Girl, ain't that that snake that handled your case?" Latrice asked.

"Yup, that's him," I said calmly.

We watched the screen as she carried on.

"...Conley is accused of withholding evidence, and at least one witness says the DA threatened to quote, take away his life with the stroke of a pen, end quote, if he didn't implicate another man."

She could've been talking about me; she could've been talking about my case.

"...now a review is underway of some of Conley's other cases, including one involving a Houston area woman who was convicted and condemned under Texas' controversial Law of Parties."

"Party Girl!" Latrice yelled. She jumped up and started cheering. "They talking about you! They talking about your case!"

"Sit down! Shit, we can't hear what they talking about!" Pauline yelled.

I sat there staring at the screen. Nothing was worth me getting all worked up about.

"Party Girl," Latrice squealed. You would've sworn the warden himself was coming to free Latrice. "You not excited? Oh God! Did you know about this?" She looked at me with wide eyes and a grin that stretched completely across her face.

"Quiet down in here!" C.O. Ramirez shouted. She sounded irritated.

I rolled my eyes. I wasn't about to allow myself to get excited, but damn, it wasn't like a melee was about to break out.

When Latrice finally settled down and they moved on to the next news story, I admitted what I knew. "Some reporter Jennifer something started asking questions. They were already investigating Conley after a former inmate filed a lawsuit against him. I think dude got out after they started looking into some of the scandalous stuff Conley has done."

"That's incredible! You'll finally get out this mug!" Latrice said.

She really was happy for me. I couldn't share her enthusiasm because I had prayed for so long. I tried to tell any and everyone who would listen, but no one wanted to hear my claims of innocence. I was another criminal on death row who was trying to avoid the needle.

"I'm not getting worked up yet; we don't know what's gonna happen," I said.

Latrice looked at me and frowned. "This is your time, I don't give a damn what they say; this is your time. You gettin' out this cage." Her finger pointed to the floor to emphasize her words. She was so adamant; I wished it were her decision to make.

Later, alone in my dark cell, I briefly let myself run away with the idea. What if someone got to Trey? What if he recanted his story, and what if they found out that Conley had lied about my fingerprints being on that gun? What if *he* admitted that there was no gunpowder residue on my hands?

I lay there for hours staring up in the darkness. Would I be able to hold my children again? Brendon? How would we adjust? What would Adena have to say? She'd been really quiet lately. I was sure she was up to her ears with her son's own case. I would love to tell her to be careful what you pray for.

She'd prayed to Allah for years for the death penalty, and looks like she may finally get it, after all. I smirked at that thought, then felt bad for thinking it.

The next day Conley was all over the news again. He was the hot topic everywhere and I was struggling to hold on to my sanity.

At work, it was all Latrice wanted to talk about. "You not gonna forget about us, are you? What you gonna do first?"

I finally stopped.

"Latrice, I ain't heard nothing from nobody, so I'm not hanging my hat on any of this shit we keep hearing."

That made her stop working, too. She looked over at me. "Listen, you ain't got to get excited; you ain't even gotta say anything about all the foolishness they say this man has been doing; we're excited for you!"

She looked down at what she was sewing, straightened it out, then looked back at me.

"I understand you not wanting to get too excited 'cause you're scared you'll get disappointed, but don't take it away from *us*, okay?"

"Okay," I said.

"So we got a deal then," she said.

"We got a deal."

I went back to my work and tried not to think about what it would mean if they did finally hold Conley accountable for the stuff he'd been doing.

Later, in the rec room, it was like déjà vu all over again. This time one of the TV stations was doing an in-depth investigative piece about DA Conley.

"...Defense attorneys are lining up. They are asking for reviews of their cases. Several discussed complaints they filed against DA Conley and their surprise when he was never disciplined."

I glanced up to see an attorney being interviewed.

"He was known nationally for his incompetency, official misconduct, alcoholism, and racism had a personal vendetta with me. I stood by help-lessly and watched as he did everything in his power, both legally and illegally, to convict my client," the attorney said.

"Illegally? What do you mean?"

"If the evidence wasn't there, it would suddenly appear; that's how he operated and everyone around him was aware. It wasn't a secret, but he still he was allowed to oppress the poor with no regard for the law he was sworn to uphold. It's a disgrace and the Justice Department needs to step in."

The Justice Department?

I didn't have to look at her to know Latrice was excited.

The question for me was, did I feel like taking a chance? Did I dare get my hopes up at all?

FORTY-SEVEN
ADENA

"Y ou don't get to decide; it is what it is! Why should your son get special treatment? You was out there demanding a capital charge with this case, but now that we know it's your boy, you got the nerve to wanna change the rules, huh?"

I was trying my best to ignore her. I understood her anger, I really did, but what did she want me to do? And how the hell did she find me at the grocery store, of all places?

Here I was minding my own business on the pasta aisle, or trying to, but she wouldn't let up. There was the finger pointing, the neck twisting and all the shouting.

"What do you say now that your old best pal, Conley, is under investigation? What did you say about my daughter?"

When I realized she would stand there and scream for as long as I stood still, I wheeled my cart up the aisle and tried my best to get away from her. But she caught up with me.

She got up in my face and lit into me again. She snapped her fingers dramatically. "Oh yeah, I remember, why should *she* be given any special treatment simply because she spawned children who were of no concern to her when she committed this crime? Isn't that what you said, Adena?"

I wasn't about to play into whatever she had going on. It wasn't enough that she'd come here to confront me, but a camera crew was capturing every moment of the one-sided argument. It was ironic, but she was taking lessons from my own playbook. She disgusted me.

Mona reminded me of those reality show people. The moment they saw the camera, they ramped it up. How tacky.

"I'm not going to have this talk with you here," I said sternly.

"Oh, nothing to talk about now, right? You have nothing to say about the way you tried to talk the DA into taking the death penalty off the table?"

"I did what any mother would've done," I said. I was so mad at myself. I needed to let her have the floor to herself. She was loud, obnoxious, and borderline belligerent. Spittle gathered at the corners of her mouth, and it looked like she was really working overtime to tell me off. By the time security showed up, and I don't know what took them so long, I simply walked out.

I left the cart of groceries, stormed out of there, and rushed to my car. Because security started asking questions, Mona and her crew were detained. That gave me a head start; I was able to make it to my car without the drama.

I was so frazzled and upset. At the door, I fumbled with the keys, but finally made it in. When I took off and prepared to leave the parking lot, I saw Mona and the camera crew standing there and prayed they wouldn't follow me.

Not wanting to take any chances, I drove around for a good thirty minutes before I dared to go home. I was sure Mona could find my address if she really wanted it, but I was grateful she didn't decide to show up at my front door. Poor Raakin, oh, what would become of him? I didn't want him to pay the ultimate price because of what I had done.

I needed to find a way to make this right. I needed to get Mona off of our case and hoped she'd ease up long enough for us to try and work something out.

The change had come almost immediately. The hate mail came by the bundle and seemed nonstop. Accusations of being a hypocrite were never-ending and my former media darling status was now a thing of the past.

I was so afraid for my son. I wanted to go and tell everyone the difference between his case and that of someone who was malicious, but I knew no one would understand.

Pushing for the death penalty had become a passion for me. I was fueled by such revenge that I was completely blinded by what I thought would make me whole again. I believed the moment Hope took her last breath, I would experience some form of relief or sense of justice.

But now lately, when I woke late at night in a cold sweat, all I could think of were the days when I'd nursed Raakin from my breasts. He would try to fill his little belly, then cold deathly hands would yank him from me.

When I arrived, I snatched a note from the front door. Michelle had been here. I had been driving around for nearly thirty minutes, but still I looked over my shoulder and around the parking lot.

I rushed inside and tried to pull myself together. I didn't want Raakin to hear me crying. He'd get completely upset and I'd have to figure out how to calm him down.

We needed food, but I didn't feel safe going out; I wasn't sure when Mona and the camera crew would pop up again. I didn't like living like this.

By the time I'd settled down and remembered Michelle's note from the door, I was emotionally exhausted.

"Wine, I need wine." My nerves were shot. I put the note down and walked to the kitchen. I grabbed a glass from the cabinet and pulled the bottle of Merlot from the refrigerator.

I poured a glass and stood there to down it before I closed the door. Once I swallowed the first glass, I poured a second. I took that one back to the living room with me.

Before I sat back down, I looked toward the hall. I didn't hear anything coming from Raakin's room. I walked over and eased my ear up to his door.

Quiet.

I turned to walk away, but decided to look in on him and make sure he was okay. I knocked on the door gently and opened it. When I looked in, he was sleeping with the covers up to his chin. He looked so peaceful. I stood for a moment, telling myself I had to do whatever it took to keep him safe.

Once I eased the door closed, I went back to the sofa and picked up Michelle's note. With the wineglass in one hand, I flipped the note open and took a sip from my glass.

As my eyes took in the words, I spat out the wine I'd just inhaled.

"What the…"

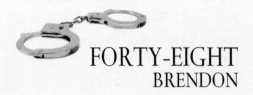

FORTY-EIGHT
BRENDON

I took off from work. I used a personal day because I wanted to meet with lawyers from the Defender Services. Before I visited Hope and got her all worked up, I wanted to make sure I had my facts straight.

Carrie came out to talk to me after I'd been waiting for nearly twenty minutes. "Hey, Brendon, good to see you. Come on back," she said after we shook hands.

I followed her back to a conference room where files and stacks of papers sat on a large table.

"I'm so excited," she said. She smiled and took a seat near the table. Carrie's eyes followed mine to the stacks and stacks of papers and files. "This is nearly six years of your wife's case. We've been going through everything with a fine-tooth comb, looking for anything we can use."

"What's got you so excited then?"

"Conley, Conley!" she screamed.

I felt my eyes widening. I'd heard about all the drama surrounding him. But except for mentioning Hope's name on the news, they never really said anything about looking into her case.

"That's good and all, but what does all this mean for Hope?"

"Here, take a seat." She motioned toward a chair next to hers.

I sat. I sighed. I needed good news. I didn't wanna come off like I wasn't happy, but I needed her to tell me exactly what this meant; like was Hope coming home?

"If there are enough cases to imply that Conley routinely fudged the rules, coerced confessions, and basically threatened people to get the evidence he wanted, we can use that to get a new trial," she said. Her eyes were bright and she smiled even when she was talking.

"A new trial?" I asked.

"Yes, if we can get a new trial…"

I cut her off. "Carrie. Hope doesn't need a new trial. People hate her, thanks to Adena and all of the bad press we've had over the years. A new trial won't do us any good."

Carrie was shaking her head before I finished what I was saying.

"We've gotta start somewhere. If we can get a new trial and get the death penalty off the table, we can try to push for parole if a jury still convicts."

I felt my scalp burning. Parole?

"Parole? She'd still be in prison," I said almost to myself.

"One step at a time. We've gotta make sure we dot our I's…"

I cut her off again. "But she didn't do it! She's innocent! Don't tell me; doesn't matter, right?" I felt defeated all over again.

"That's not what I'm saying. What I'm trying to tell you is, we have to play by the rules. We go for a new trial, we work toward an acquittal, but worst-case scenario is we end up with a lighter sentence and parole." She nodded slightly. "It's a whole helluva' lot better than death row."

What she was saying made sense, but I wasn't prepared for this. I thought news of this educated thug and all he'd been doing meant Hope would be sent home; she'd be free. All charges would be dropped and we'd be able to sue the state for tossing her in the slammer in the first damn place.

Hadn't we been through enough? I didn't want a new trial. I wanted a "get out of jail" card now!

"It's probably not what you wanted to hear, but you've gotta trust me when I say this is the right path to take. Once we create doubt, let that jury know she's already lost six years of her life, there's no way she'd get the death penalty again. We're working to try and find Linda, and I was hoping you'd given some thought to our last conversation."

It took a few seconds for what she said to sink in. The best I could hope for was a new trial.

I sighed, swallowed back my disappointment, and told her what was going on. "My friends and I found Linda. My buddy is working on talking to her, but we weren't sure how to approach her, so he did what he does best."

Carrie's eyebrow went up. "What's that?"

"He's real smooth with the ladies, like a real Casanova."

She looked skeptical, but she didn't know Kemar like I knew him. "Oh, and how's that working with her?"

I shrugged. "They have a date this weekend."

Carrie looked surprised. I wasn't; some women are desperate. Linda was single and like most women who were, she was tired of being alone. I needed to keep an eye on Kemar, though; things could get out of hand if he didn't have any boundaries.

"Well, we have someone working on Trey. Right now, he's not sure what we want to talk about. I think he's enjoying time away from the other inmates and the special attention."

"What if he won't recant?"

"That's what makes this news about Conley so good. If enough defense attorneys demand a review of their old cases, we can hold off until the new trial to deal with Trey. Remember we started in on him before we knew an investigation was under way with Conley. And let's not forget we're still going through Jennifer's information."

It was a lot of information to take in, and it wasn't the immediate answers I wanted, but I figured the possibility of parole was better than a death sentence, even on a bad day.

My meeting with Carrie wrapped up with promises to check back in a few days. I was encouraged—not as excited as I was trying not to be earlier—but I was encouraged.

As I rode the elevator down, I started thinking about the call from Chastity.

"Hello?"

"Brendon, I don't mean to disturb you. I'm calling because I just had a conversation with Breanna that didn't end well and I was worried about her."

"She was storming out when she bumped into me, and she was crying. I talked to her, but I'm glad you called," I said.

"So she's okay?"

"Yeah, she is. I talked to her, but she didn't really say much back to me. I knew she was upset. She's upstairs in her room now."

"Oh well, good. I wanted to make sure she wasn't gonna do anything stupid."

"What set her off?" I asked.

"She wanted me to come back, got upset when I told her I needed some space. She started telling me how much she misses me and if I didn't want to come back, would I come and get her. Then things went downhill from there."

"She was right," I said.

"About what?"

"We all miss you. It's not the same around here without you. Why don't you come back so we can talk this thing out?"

I heard her exhale.

The elevator doors opened and I headed to the parking lot. Now that I knew Hope wasn't coming home next month, it helped me decide what I needed to do about Chastity and Stacy.

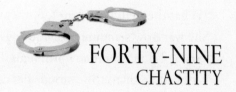

FORTY-NINE
CHASTITY

I t was like I suspected. The moment I stepped out of my car, I could feel Stacy's eyes on me like a hawk. She didn't even try to duck behind her drapes. As a matter of fact, when she noticed me getting out of the car, she came into full view. I didn't speak when I saw her. We made eye contact, and I noticed her throwing her hands onto her hips, but she didn't shy away from looking at me and I really didn't give a damn.

Actually, I took my time walking to the back of my car, opening the trunk, and grabbing my bags out. If she wondered why I was there, seeing my bags confirmed I was coming back home, and back to claim what would soon be mine.

Before I got to the front door, it swung open and Brendon smiled at me. At that instant, all I could think was, he's forgiven.

He came out and met me halfway up the walkway. The look in his eyes told me everything he didn't say and the feeling was mutual.

"How many more bags?" he asked as he took the one I was struggling with.

"Three more," I said.

He nodded. "You go inside and relax for a bit. We got a lot to talk about."

I turned and noticed Stacy was no longer in the window. I didn't know if she'd seen enough, or if she'd missed the exchange between us altogether.

As I walked up the walkway and was about to enter the house, I heard her.

"What the hell, Brendon?"

She was now standing near my bags at the trunk of my car.

"Stacy, I don't want any problems," he said calmly.

I looked at them. She stood, hands on her hips, as Brendon reached for the bags. When he tried to move, she stepped in front of him.

"I wanna talk about this and I wanna talk now," she hissed.

Brendon looked in my direction. I was frozen where I stood; I wanted to see how he was gonna handle her this time.

"Well, lemme get these bags in the house, then you can come on in, 'cause I need to talk to you and Chastity anyway," he said.

You could've knocked me down with a feather. Did he invite her in so the *three* of us could talk? What happened to everything he said to me on the phone? Could he have had a change of heart that fast? The moment he turned to come into the house, she was right on his heels. When she didn't say a word to me, I knew what kind of meeting this would be.

Holding my cool, I walked in, looked around, and found a spot to take a seat on the sofa. Stacy walked in and followed him to the hallway, then stopped. It was like she was trying to avoid being alone with me, and that was fine.

When Brendon walked back out, she was right there to greet him. "I can't believe she's back here, Brendon."

"Uh, she's right here, so you don't have to talk about me like I'm not," I said with much attitude.

She glanced at me long enough to roll her eyes in my direction. What had I done to her? Brendon walked completely into the living room. He stood near the window and I suddenly felt like he was trying to avoid being close to either one of us.

"This is long overdue," he began.

Stacy was still leaning up against the wall near the hallway. Suddenly, she couldn't stand to be in my presence? Brendon cleared his throat and seemed a bit nervous as he started to speak.

"I wanted to talk to both of you, so there wouldn't be any confusion behind what I'm planning to do. I wanna say thanks for all you've done while Hope's been away." He looked at me. "Especially you, Chastity; I don't wanna think about how we would've made it this far if it wasn't for you."

He looked down and my heart took a nosedive. Was he about to reveal some devastating news? Is that why he'd asked me back here?

"I'm planning to move," he said.

I frowned. Move? Had I been gone that long?

"This house holds a lot of bad memories and pain, and it's time the kids and I start in a new location. We've refinanced and are upside down like everyone else, but instead of a house, we're moving into an apartment community. It's what's best and it'll help us make an easier transition into the new life I want for us."

"When the hell did you decide this?" Stacy snarled. Her neck twisted as she asked the question.

"Hold up a sec, Stacy."

"No, you hold up a sec," she mocked.

"Can you let him finish?" I snapped in her direction.

She finally shut her mouth and stood there with her arms crossed at her chest. I didn't understand how I had become her nemesis when I hadn't done anything wrong.

"I've made a decision about my future and well, I wanted to tell you both what I'm gonna do. Stacy, you want a replacement husband; that's not me, and it's not gonna be me. I already have a wife."

Stacy's expression changed. Her twisted frown was even more contorted now. She looked like she was ready to pounce.

"You knew what you were doing all along," she snarled.

"I was probably wrong for not being as strong as I should've been. But you should take some blame here, too. You kept persisting; you wouldn't take no for an answer..."

"So that's how we playin' this one?" Stacy started walking up on Brendon and I wasn't sure what she was about to do.

"Um, Stacy, let it go," I said.

She whipped around and shot me a look that chilled me to the bone.

"You didn't win," she said.

I jumped up. "It's not a contest. I'm not sure what you think is going on, but nobody is competing here but you!"

"You think I'ma' let the two of you ride off into the sunset and live happily ever after? After all I've done to be with you? I've given up my friends, my husband and now, I'm supposed to sit here and agree to whatever arrangement you've come up with? Is that what you thought?"

I realized, there was no reasoning with her. She looked at me like she wanted to spit on me. Thank God she turned back to Brendon.

"I gave up my marriage for you! You may not have *said* what was going to happen, but we're both grown. You knew when I put my husband out, it was because I expected things to move forward with us! Now you're gonna try and play me like this was all in my imagination?"

Brendon shook his head, saying no. He said to Stacy, "I wanna see what the future holds for me and Chastity."

"I'll bet you didn't tell her, huh?" She had a cynical smile on her face. "You wanna take the high road now, tell your beloved sister-in-law here how we were messing around before Hope ever even went to prison!"

My mouth dropped and so did my heart.

I didn't know how much more I could take!

FIFTY
HOPE

"**D**amn, a new trial! I need to get out of here! I want away from this place. People hate me. You really think I'm gonna earn my freedom with a new jury? Umph! I'm innocent, didn't do anything!" I felt sick all over again. I started rubbing my temples, hoping to calm myself down a bit.

This is the exact reason I didn't want to start getting all excited. I knew something would happen to slap me back down again. I figured damn well the minute I started daydreaming about being home, someone was gonna come in and pull the freakin' rug right from under me! And that's exactly what was going on now.

With everything that had been said about DA Conley, with all of the protests surrounding the Law of Parties, I knew I'd be getting out sooner instead of later! Just the other day, this TV show had a rundown of all the inmates who'd been caught up behind this law! I was shocked to learn that I wasn't the only one; sitting right there about to die for some mess I didn't even do! And they're telling me the best they could do is try to get me a new trial?

"Hear us out," the lawyer from the Defender Services said. "We're saying if we wait for the Conley mess to boil over, our chances of getting a new trial are good. That's the one thing we know for sure."

I wasn't sure why she thought I'd misunderstood, or wasn't clear about what she'd said the first damn time!

"I heard what *you* said. But what I'm saying *is*, I don't want another trial. That was a nightmare for my family. Nothing good came from that."

They listened as I talked, but I felt like they weren't really feeling me. I want out, I want to go home, and I'm tired of being here.

"We can't make you any promises, and we don't want to because we have no idea where this thing is going. But we can tell you, you'd probably get a new trial before you'd get released."

I sighed. I was disgusted, but mostly with myself, because I knew better. When Latrice and Pauline were jumping up and down like the President himself had come down to the Mountain View unit to pardon me in person, I was skeptic.

Then, when Latrice started asking why I wasn't at least a little bit excited, I gave her the easy answer; I wasn't sure what was going to happen. But late at night, when I was alone in my cell, I started to allow myself to get caught up in the mess.

Day after day, there were stories about DA Conley and none of them were good. When Brendon had started talking about what *might* happen, I had allowed myself to try and see what he must've been seeing.

Before I knew what was happening, I started looking at the calendar and wondering if maybe I'd be home by Thanksgiving, Christmas, or at the worst-case scenario, New Year's Eve.

"You guys do what you feel is best," I said, defeated. The bottom line is, they were trying to help me out. I didn't want a new trial but if that's the best they thought they could do, I needed to get myself ready mentally.

Several days later, I was in deep depression mode. I started feeling like I was reliving the very same day over and over again. I was thinking that I had already lost everything. Then, I started wondering if I should've given in to the pressure. I hadn't heard from Reverend Sharpton since he'd left. It wasn't like I expected him to move mountains for me, but hearing the lawyers say a new trial was their trump card, well, that seemed like such a long shot.

I found myself wanting to be alone. I quit my job, so that meant I was holed up in my cell for what felt like the entire day. When the guards came in to check for contraband, or whatever the hell they were looking for, I didn't offer any resistance. I sat outside, hands cuffed, until they finished doing what they needed to do.

All of my fight was gone once again. Nearly a month after the lawyers had left, I felt like my life wasn't worth living anymore. I couldn't go back and stop the appeals a second time, but I didn't want to stay in my cage. It felt like it was closing in even more.

"Maybe I need to take my power back," I said aloud.

I shook the thoughts from my head. What would my kids think if they found out I was thinking about suicide again?

Who gave a damn what anyone thought at that point? I tried not to think about that option. Brendon would probably be too through with me. Lord knows, I'd taken him through enough!

Imagine my surprise when, during mail call, a letter nearly took my breath away. I looked at the envelope twice to make sure I wasn't imagining things. In all the years I'd been behind bars, I could count the number of letters I'd received from Mona on one hand. Brendon wasn't a big writer, but he'd sent more than a few. But that's about it. Not a single friend of mine had ever sent me a letter, so stunned couldn't describe how I felt when I saw the letter addressed by Stacy.

I was more than a little excited. I had heard bits and pieces about her over the years, but she'd never written me a letter.

As I sat in my cell, I ripped the envelope open and prepared to reconnect with one of the best friends I'd had before my life took a turn for the worst.

"What the hell..."

My breath caught in my throat. As I read the words on this letter, I wanted to cry. Why would she send me something like this?

The more I read, the more horrified and pissed off I became.

FIFTY-ONE
ADENA

As I stood at the podium, I struggled to fight back tears. They'd been threatening to push through since I'd made the decision to face the press. Now they were burning at the corners of my eyes, but I was determined. The decision to face the press was more of a shove by the note Michelle had left for me.

In it she talked about the embarrassment I was causing to True Justice, she talked about how the board had decided it was time I disassociate myself. I read her words, and surprisingly, I wasn't as angry as I thought I would be. I had come a long way.

Most people wanted to focus on *how* I'd arrived, but I say they should judge the person I was today, not who I used to be. As I stood looking out at the cameras all focused on me, I took in a deep breath, blew it out, then started to read my speech.

"I want to thank all of you for coming. As most of you know, I've been reluctant to speak about this as I feel it is a private family matter. But, because many of you have kindly pointed out to me that I've been an outspoken advocate for capital punishment because of my longstanding belief that capital punishment deters crime, I thought it only fair that I speak to you all about my change of heart."

Possible tears were still threatening, but I was holding them back. When I glanced up from my notes, I saw people leaning closer to each other to talk and others taking notes. I glanced back down and was glad I found my place.

"My personal connection to this unfortunate accident has given me an entirely new perspective and outlook." I looked farther down on the paper and cleared my throat. I wanted this to be over. "I've been in prayer since my son was identified as the alleged driver involved in this horrific accident. Since then, in addition to prayer, I've reflected on all things related to capital punishment. My change of heart has shown me that, as human beings, we will all make mistakes. And while some mistakes are so grave and seem unforgivable, oftentimes, those are the kinds that require our true understanding. And to those who might call me a hypocrite, please know, that I'm a mother before I'm an activist. And while I don't condone crime on any level, I do believe that when we look at those who commit crime, we should not look at a mere snapshot, but an entire picture to try and determine the most effective form of punishment."

"So does this mean you are no longer in favor of the death penalty?" a reporter yelled in my direction. I hadn't expected to last as long as I had before that question.

I wanted to finish my statement before answering, but I was aware, where there was one question, there was bound to be another.

"You've been a staunch supporter of the death penalty, not only for killers, but you've been leading the push for Hope Donovan's execution. How do you feel about her, now that you've had a change of heart?"

I expected this one, too, but before I could refocus my thoughts, another question was thrown at me.

"Are you now anti-death penalty because your son could face a capital sentence?" someone else yelled before I could think about responding to the previous question.

Suddenly, I decided to abandon the speech. I had done this long enough. I looked in the direction the last question seemed to come from and said, "Yes. This experience has opened my eyes in ways I've never had to consider before. I don't want my son to die, if in fact he's found guilty and condemned." I swallowed back tears, but I was determined to get through this. "My feelings..."

"Yeah, tell us all about *your* feelings, you hypocrite!"

I didn't need to look up to see who had cut me off. I recognized Mona's voice.

When our eyes finally met, I was at a loss for words. She had every reason to be angry with me. I had mounted a successful campaign against her daughter for years.

"Now that it's *your* child's life on the line, you've suddenly had a change of heart?" She smirked, and crossed her arms at her chest. "Isn't that convenient!" she hissed.

The reporters looked back and forth between us like they were watching the French Open. They expected a showdown that would get nasty in front of the cameras, but I wasn't about to play into it. Mona's features were twisted, she was bitter, and the anger in her eyes was evident. She hated me with a passion, and I didn't blame her. How could I?

"Mona, I was going to call you," I said. I meant it, but at the time, I realized I should've waited until we were out of the camera's view.

"I don't want you to call me. Over the years, you've said everything you wanted to say to me."

"But I was wrong," I admitted.

It was so quiet, you could hear a cricket piss. I repeated myself.

"I was wrong. I was so very wrong, completely overcome by my quest for revenge. I hope that one day you'll be able, willing, to forgive me. I had no idea; from one mother to another, I pray to Allah that you will have mercy," I cried.

The reporters fired questions at such a rapid speed, I turned and walked away. The tears I'd been fighting to contain flowed like water from a broken dam. I did nothing to stop them as I rushed to my waiting car.

FIFTY-TWO
BRENDON

Stacy had been sitting in front of her large picture window throwing daggers for half the day. I could see the hate from way over here, but we kept working. I told the guys to ignore her. I didn't know what she was over there thinking about doing or trying to do, but I wasn't about to get caught up again. We kept it moving, and she kept watching.

When Stacy tried to lie about when we had hooked up, I was glad Chastity didn't fall for it.

I wasn't proud of some of the things I had done. I'd be the first to admit it, but I'd received my share of payback, karma, or whatever else you want to call it. I wasn't sure what was going to become of me, Chastity, or our family. We all knew that Hope was probably going to be in prison for the rest of her life. And we'd pretty much decided to move on. I needed to live like I had a future, not like my wife might one day walk up off of Texas' death row.

As the weeks flew by, it looked more and more like Hope would be able to get a new trial. But the lawyers we talked to all said the outcome would more than likely be life in prison.

It was still so crazy. They acted like life in prison was a good deal, and maybe it was. Sure, it was better than the death penalty, but it was still *life* in prison, *life* away from family and friends.

"I think we got everything," Kemar said.

I looked around the empty living room one more time, determined to be able to leave everything that had happened there in the past.

"Yeah, I think we're good," I said.

The place was empty, this was moving day for us and I was eager to go. Kemar rushed back out to the U-Haul truck.

Desmond and Kemar had helped me pack up and move to the new place. I was hoping they'd still have energy to help unload the truck once we got to the new place.

This place was full of bad memories and I was ready to close the door and this chapter of my life. I looked around one last time. As I was about to close and lock the door, Kemar came running back up the walkway, holding his cell phone in his hand.

"Dawg, she said yes! She said yes! She's gonna do it!"

He nearly tripped making his way up the three steps that lead to the front door.

"Who? What? What are you talking about?"

"Linda. She says she'll sign something and tell what happened!" he yelled. "You know, to get Hope out!"

I couldn't believe what I was hearing. All of the despair and depression I was feeling started to vanish. I felt myself getting excited, but I wanted to make sure I understood exactly what he was saying. He'd been working on Linda for a while now. Desmond and I had teased him, saying he must've lost his touch because we thought the girl was just that *bad!* Most women couldn't resist Kemar, no matter how much they tried. Linda seemed to be holding out like a champ defending his belt.

"She's willing to talk about what Conley said: how he told her if she could remember Hope saying anything while they were in county, he'd make things easier for her; she'd cop to a lesser crime in exchange for her testimony."

He was more excited than I had seen him in a long time.

"Slow up, slow up," I said.

"Dude, she's willing to tell it all. She didn't even remember who Hope was at first; said she couldn't pick her picture out or anything."

I stood still for a while, taking in everything he was telling me. "Why is she doing this now?"

Kemar looked at me like he was stunned and confused. "'Cause she wants to make me happy, why else?"

By now Desmond was standing near the door.

We started laughing at his answer. But Kemar was serious as cardiac arrest.

"Www-what?" he asked, looking at us.

"So, she's now ready to tell the world how she lied on a woman she'd never met, couldn't remember laying eyes on, and just 'cause she wants to keep you happy?" I asked.

"I don't think you understand the power I'm packing," Kemar bragged.

We started laughing again.

"But all joking aside, dude, she remembered Hope because she said for a long time, she couldn't sleep at night, knowing how she'd lied on her. Says she left the state for a couple of years when she got off probation just to get away from the stories about her."

"Crazy, huh?" I asked.

"Yeah, but she says she's ready to talk. And I think she'll be believable. When I heard her, I could see how she'd done this 'cause she felt like she didn't really have another option."

I leaned up against the side of the door. Hope's jailhouse snitch was prepared to admit she'd lied. I sighed hard.

"Dude, I thought you'd be ecstatic; whassup?" Kemar asked. He looked worried.

He and Desmond looked at me like they didn't know what to think or what to say.

I started to wonder, what difference would it really make? Hope was never getting out, and now, what would Chastity say? Once again, I was in the middle of a mess. Regardless, I told myself, I knew what I had to do.

"This is good, Brah," Kemar said, slapping me on the back. "This is good, man."

Wanting to believe him, I smiled faintly. I kept telling myself my life, my future was with Chastity, not rotting away in prison with Hope. When she refused to talk to me about why she tried to kill herself, that told me she had already given up. I had come to realize it didn't matter who recanted; Hope's destiny had already been determined, but me, I still had a chance.

FIFTY-THREE
CHASTITY

Brendon had something on his mind and although I wasn't sure what it was, I was not about to press him about it. I knew for sure when he was ready, he'd come and talk to me. Until then, I went about our new life.

We'd just finished breakfast, the kids were gone, and Brendon was on his way out. Once they cleared out, that was my cue to start working.

"You good?" he asked.

I was a little confused, but I didn't want to let on to him that I suspected he was the one with the problem. I didn't want to stress Brendon. In our short time together, we'd already been through a lot.

"I'm good, go on. Get off to work before you're late," I said.

He reached down to kiss my lips. I closed my eyes and opened them quickly. I felt like some 1950s housewife as I stood in the doorway and watched him take off. I waved as he smiled. We were in a good place.

I was happy, I felt loved and wanted. I was so glad we had moved away from Stacy's street. Now I didn't have to worry about being watched from her large picture window. I walked back inside and closed the door.

As I got ready to start my own work day, the phone rang. I started to ignore it altogether, but decided to answer. Lately, we'd been getting a bunch of crank calls. I, of course, thought it was Stacy's crazy behind, but didn't say anything to Brendon about my suspicions. I couldn't believe she was practicing or trying to practice voodoo. Just when you think you know somebody.

The funny thing about our new arrangement, Stacy still had to come by because she had to drop McKenzie off or pick her up. The girls were still best friends and we decided to not let on about what had gone down with the three of us. We decided the kids had been through enough.

To make things easier, I tried to stay out of sight if and when Stacy was dropping off or picking up. I didn't need the drama.

"Hello?" I answered.

When I didn't hear anything or anyone, I started to hang up.

"Hello?" I said into the phone again.

The faint voice was so soft I nearly missed it.

"So you finally get the last laugh, huh?" she said.

"Excuse me?"

"I know," she said.

My heart crashed into my ribcage. My ears suddenly began to sear with heat. I didn't need to talk to her.

"Hope, I don't wanna have this conversation with you," I said.

"I couldn't believe it. I read the letter, over and over and over again, but I still couldn't believe it."

"What do you want from me?" She was not about to get the best of me. She could try to play the victim if she wanted, but she'd be having that conversation alone.

"You *had* to have my husband? Wasn't enough that you took over my family, my place in Mona's heart? You've always wanted to be me." She chuckled.

I was really trying to keep it together. I didn't want to say anything to make this conversation any more uncomfortable than it already was, but she was pushing me.

"How could you do this to me, Chastity? You mean to tell me

there was no other man walking around out there? You had to take your sister's husband, while she's fighting for her life on death row?"

"Save the bullshit, Hope!" I screamed.

Silence.

"Yes, save the bullshit! You didn't want Brendon when you were running around hopping in and out of any bed you could slide into. Don't try to act like you two had the perfect marriage, and I don't know what letter you're talking about, but at this point, I really don't care!"

She didn't know I knew, but the same people she considered friends wasted no time spreading her secrets.

"Then you tell Stacy to break the news to me because you couldn't? Not woman enough, huh? I don't understand; why didn't you keep sneaking around with him? Did I really need to know?"

"Stacy?" I said. But then, why was I not surprised?

"Yes, *Stacy*. She was kind enough to write me a detailed letter explaining how you pounced on my husband the second the gavel fell. She even told me about Betty Jean and the baby. She runs off thinking what? That running would change the fact that my husband may have fathered her child? I could swallow their betrayal, but you?" She sucked her teeth. "Not sure why I'm surprised. I always knew you were a pathetic bitch, but honestly, I never thought you were this pathetic," Hope said.

"Oh, I'm pathetic? I'm pathetic, Hope?" I didn't want to go off on her, but I wasn't about to sit and take her insults much longer.

"Yes, you are! You are because the least you could've done was wait until the state put me out of my misery. But you know what, Chastity? I guess this is your way of paying me back for all the years you had to live in my shadow, right?"

"*Me* live in *your* shadow? No, darling, it was you who wanted so desperately to be like me, so much so, you had to have everything you *thought* I wanted."

I'd hated my own sister for years. But when I needed to, I'd stepped up and done the right thing. I hadn't planned to fall for Brendon, and I damn sure hadn't expected him to fall for me, but we were together now.

"Yeah, I fucked Trevor! There, I said it. Back then, I tried to tell your simple behind he was nothing but garbage, but you wouldn't listen to me..."

"Since he was such garbage, Hope, what does that make you that you had to have him because you knew he was mine? You're really sad, Hope. You've always been and you always will be!"

I could tell she was trying to keep her voice down, which let me know she wasn't supposed to be on the phone. I didn't wish any more bad on her, but thoughts of calling that prison and telling them about her illegal cell phone was flashing through my mind. She just didn't know.

"Hope, don't call here anymore, seriously. Brendon has moved on, we've moved on, and we really don't need the past trying to creep back up on us. Besides, it's bad enough we have to deal with Stacy. I'll bet when she wrote that letter, she didn't tell you that she and your husband had been messing around before you even went to prison! Oh, but wait, you were busy doing your own thing anyway, right?" I chuckled. "I guess they're right when they say payback's a mutha, huh!"

Before she could respond, I hung up the phone, then when I confirmed she was gone, I left the receiver off of the hook and started my work day. I thought about driving over to Stacy's job and whupping her ass. But I decided she'd really done me a favor because Hope's last thought in life would probably be of me taking her place in the ultimate way.

"Oh well," I said as I walked into the room that doubled as my home office. "Payback really is a mutha!"

FIFTY-FOUR
HOPE

Weeks after my return from the infirmary, Stacy's letter was still fresh on my mind. She'd told me in great detail about the love triangle involving her, Brendon, and Chastity.

She also had told me about Brendon and Betty Jean. Had he fathered a child with her? According to Stacy's letter, that's what had chased Betty Jean away for good. She said no one had heard from her since the blow-up with Brendon that had happened in my front yard. I didn't know what to believe anymore.

Now, when I looked into Brendon's eyes, I wondered about his real motives. It took some time to accept his visits again. He didn't give up, but I needed some time. He still dropped an occasional letter or card, but did he really think I wouldn't find out about him and Chastity?

My own sister?

It was obvious she never told him about me calling her. This was his second visit and he was still carrying on like nothing had happened. He was going on about Linda, the jailhouse snitch, who'd helped Conley put the final nail in my coffin.

Since that phone call with Chastity, nearly a month ago now, I'd decided she and Brendon must not be as close as she'd tried to pretend they were. Knowing her wannabe ass, she could be making it all up. I decided I'd wait for Brendon to say something to me about it one way or another. What was the point of questioning him about Stacy, Chastity, or even Betty Jean? I wasn't exactly in a position to do anything about it anyway.

"What else have you been doing, 'sides working with Kemar to get this chick to recant her story?" I asked.

We were near the end of our visit and most of what he talked about while he was there was about how this Linda was ready to make things right.

"I'm hyped about Linda; that's all. It seems like I'm all over the place, but we're so close." He used his thumb and index finger to indicate how close we were. I wasn't amused.

He looked at me and his eyes were bright and happy, but I knew he was thinking that the best we could hope for was a new trail.

"Has Carrie been here yet?" he asked.

Brendon had a nervous habit. He'd bounce from topic to topic, unable to focus when he was hiding something. I knew him and I knew how he operated.

During this visit, he'd talked about Adena's press conference, told me about the kids, talked about Mona high-tailing it out of town with some new man for a few weeks, and Linda. None of his conversation had centered around him and what he had been doing.

What he didn't realize was that he was already telling me so much. I sighed as I listened to him talk about Carrie taking Linda somewhere to have her statement recorded and blah, blah.

"Did you just roll your eyes?" He seemed bewildered. "Damn, Hope!"

I didn't realize he'd noticed. It's not that I wasn't interested in what he was talking about, but I was tired. I wanted him to try and see my position in all of this, but he seemed unwilling to even try.

"You know, it pisses me off that we're all out here working, trying to come up with anything we can drum up to save your life and you seem so blasé about it! You act like I'm bothering you because I'm trying to figure a way out of this death sentence!" he yelled.

For once, I felt myself wondering when the C.O. was going to come and threaten to end the visit, or at least hush us. But nothing; it was like Brendon was invisible.

"This shit is crazy. Does the thought of living really repulse you that much?" he asked. The frown on his face was a mixture of anger and frustration.

"The thought of living in here?" I asked. Before he could respond, I snapped, "you know what repulses me even more?" Before he could answer, I jumped in. "The idea that you would be screwing my own sister, but sitting up here acting like the devoted husband who cares about whether I live or die. Imagine that! I guess you finally decided to take my advice and go on with your life. You think I wanna be stuck up in here thinking about you and my own damn sister? Stop wasting your time coming up here; go on with your life, Brendon."

He'd better be glad I couldn't reach out and touch his *simple* behind!

He sighed hard. For a moment, he sat there looking at me. I wasn't sure what was running through his mind, but it couldn't be anything good.

Chastity and I were nothing like normal sisters, but still.

Finally, our visit was over. I swallowed back tears, and jumped up to assume the position. The C.O. was right there and for a change, I was glad.

As far as I was concerned, Brendon, Chastity, Stacy, and Betty Jean could go straight to hell. I didn't care what happened next.

By the time Tuesday rolled around, I was emotionally drained.

Thoughts of Chastity and Brendon stayed on my mind all weekend long. Suddenly, I hated Brendon for coming to visit. Since I was no longer working, the days dragged on like a broken-down snail with no sense of direction.

All I could do was sit in my personal little hellhole and listen to the voices going on and on in my head.

"Donovan!"

I jumped up at the sound of my name. When I wiped drool from the side of my face, I realized I'd fallen off to sleep.

"Attorney visit!" the C.O. shouted.

I stumbled to my feet. I wondered how long I'd been asleep, then stretched and got ready for my visit. For a second, I thought about staying right where I was. I didn't need to be fed any more bullshit. Brendon was under the impression that Carrie or someone from the Defender Services would be visiting soon. I wasn't even excited. What were they going to tell me; that I'd won a new trial?

As I waited to be cuffed, I thought back to the last visit with Carrie. I shook my head and did as I was told. I followed the C.O. to the visiting area and tried not to look bored. No one understood my position. It was more like they didn't care, but whatever.

Massive smiles greeted me as I walked into the visiting room. I wasn't sure what the hell they were so excited about, but I figured I'd sit there, listen and go through the motions.

"We have such great news, Hope; we could barely sleep last night," Carrie said. She could hardly sit still. She was fidgety like she didn't know what to do with the nervous energy running through her veins.

"I had to literally stop her from driving up here after we talked to the judge in chambers yesterday evening," the lead attorney said.

I smirked and lifted a brow.

Carrie placed her hands palms down on the table and leaned forward. She took a deep breath, then began to talk. "Hope, I don't think you understand what's going on here."

I blinked a few times and looked between the two of them. Did they want me to do a jig because people finally found out what I'd been saying about DA Conley for years? Did they want me to jump up and down because I *might* get a new trial after all I'd already been through?

"Hope. You. Are. Going. Home!"

My heart crashed into my chest. I tried to force my brain to process what she'd just said, then I pinched myself. If this was a dream, it would be the cruelest of them all.

Two sets of eyes stared back at me.

Silence hung in the air.

Suddenly, the room was too cold. Then it was too small. My mouth felt like it was stuffed with cotton. I looked around; I fidgeted with my hands and swallowed nothing in my dry throat. My scalp felt like someone had lit a match to it, then my ears began to burn. It was burning up.

"I'm going..."

It wasn't until tears started streaming down Carrie's cheeks that I realized my pulse was racing uncontrollably. I felt like I couldn't breathe.

They started nodding.

I was lost and confused. And I didn't dare allow myself to believe what they were trying to tell me.

FIFTY-FIVE
ADENA

I 'll never forget where I was when I got the news that Hope Donovan was being released from prison. I was standing in the kitchen, pulling yogurt from my refrigerator. I nearly dropped the container as I listened to the news spewing from the small TV monitor mounted beneath my cabinets.

"We now bring you breaking news. A woman who spent more than six years in prison for the murder of a convenience store owner, and another man, was released from prison after another former inmate, Jerome Singletary, filed a civil lawsuit against former Harris County District Attorney Joel 'Chuck' Conley, the current DA's office, and the city. Hope Donovan was released after her attorneys filed a brief charging 'blatantly illegal investigative tactics' were used by the Harris County prosecutors to secure her 2005 conviction."

I stood with my mouth wide open as I saw video of Hope surrounded by reporters, Mona, and a few other people. She was walking out of the court building in downtown Houston.

I rushed to the phone and dialed Michelle. We were still friends, despite being on opposite sides of the fence now. I tried to multi-task as I listened to her phone ringing and the anchorwoman on TV.

"Hope Donovan, now thirty-five years old, was released from prison yesterday after prosecutors said they were abandoning efforts to retry her for the murder of the convenience store owner, Raakin Binnaz Senior,

and a store clerk, Mustafa Muhammad, who were fatally shot in 2005 during a robbery attempt in rural Harris County.

"Mrs. Donovan's conviction was vacated last week when information surfaced that one of the witnesses had recanted prior to the original trial; but Mrs. Donovan's trial attorney was never notified. That witness has since come forward to tell a twisted tale of lies, deceit, and threats leveled against her by the former prosecutor who won a death sentence against Mrs. Donovan.

"Donovan is one of four prisoners released in the light of revelations that former DA Conley took a 'by any means necessary' attitude toward securing convictions. A string of defense attorneys are demanding criminal charges against Conley himself, but no word yet on whether that will happen. Some two hundred-fifty other criminal cases are now under scrutiny. We'll have more on Hope Donovan's release in our later newscasts."

"Hi, Adena, I thought about you when I heard the news," Michelle said as she answered the phone.

"Was I completely blinded by my thirst for revenge?" I asked. "She's innocent?" I murmured.

"You did the best you could. It was nothing personal," Michelle said.

Listening as Michelle told me that I only did what anyone in my shoes would've done, I realized how obsessed I was with making sure Hope paid for something she *didn't* do. I felt disgusted with myself.

"It *was* personal, Michelle, because I made it personal," I said.

Michelle didn't seem too sympathetic. It was almost as if I bored her now that we no longer shared our passion for capital punishment.

"Listen, we're organizing a rally and I need to get some last-minute details finalized," she said. "Really, Adena, I wouldn't worry about Hope; for every one true innocent person on death row, there are three who are there because they really are guilty."

That wasn't the point. But it was obvious she didn't care what I had to say. Lately, Michelle seemed to not want to entertain conversation with me unless she needed information about one of her cases.

I hung up with Michelle and thought about Hope and Mona. They both tried to tell me she wasn't guilty. I wouldn't listen; I didn't want to listen. I wanted her to pay with her life because I thought her death would bring me peace. I thought it would mean closure for me. Now I was haunted by the thought that the state of Texas could have executed an innocent person, one that I was all but pushing to the death chamber.

"She didn't do it," I said. Suddenly, I was desperate to listen to the rest of the story.

When I heard the gunshot, I screamed and ran toward the door.

FIFTY-SIX
BRENDON

My head was spinning out of control. I was sitting across from Hope on Mona's sofa. This wasn't the kind of reunion I had in mind all those years of thinking about her getting out.

We were in a standoff and even though I understood why, a part of me wanted her to try and forgive. She was out! She was home! How did I not know? It was now obvious to me that I had fallen way off as far as she was concerned. We were sitting there, not saying a word. Mona walked by and went into the kitchen and my mind started to drift.

Hope had been locked up and away for nearly six years and now she wasn't. Last I knew, Carrie and the attorneys were working on trying to get her a new trial, but when I got word that she was already out, I didn't know what to do. That was three days ago. I was at work, in the middle of my route, when dispatch called and told me they were sending a driver to relieve me.

"Relieve me?" I asked, dumbfounded. I looked at the handheld radio like it must've malfunctioned. The only time you were pulled from your route was in an emergency. I remained under the radar at work. I did what I was supposed to, and kept my nose clean. Other people were relieved, not me.

"Yes, the supervisor needs you to come back to the barn as soon as possible."

I was hot. All kinds of thoughts ran throughout my mind. I hadn't done anything wrong so it couldn't be that. I didn't need any bad news, but I couldn't imagine why they were calling me in.

As luck would have it, traffic was already building at 2:30 in the afternoon as I tried to make my way back to the barn. Highway 59 going south felt like it was 5:30 instead of 2:30. By the time I made it to the West Park Toll Road, it eased up a bit, but I still wasn't going as fast as I wanted. It seemed like my thoughts became crazier the longer it took for me to maneuver my way through traffic.

By the time I made it back to the Metro Bus barn, I was sick. I wasn't even in the door a good five minutes before my supervisor called me into his office.

"What's the matter, Donovan? You don't carry your cell phone with you?" he asked, irritated.

Johnson was a short and stocky man. He wore lifters to give himself a few extra inches. Most of the other drivers didn't care too much for him, but he was cool with me.

"I usually do, but forgot it at the house today. Why, what's up?"

He waited for me to sit down, then he walked to the other side of his desk, sat down and started banging on his keyboard.

"You haven't heard, huh?"

"Heard what?"

He blew out a breath and shook his head a bit. "Donovan, your wife, she was released from prison today," he said.

I didn't know what to say.

"She was www-what?" I looked at him like he was crazy.

"Man, go home; just clock out and we'll see you in a couple of days," he said. "I already got someone to handle your route; use PTO."

He looked at me like I was a dumb ass and that's how I felt.

After all this time, I couldn't wrap my mind around the possibility that Hope was now free. Why hadn't someone called me? How did the entire city of Houston know and I didn't?

As I walked out of Johnson's office and stumbled to the back to remove my things from the locker, people were patting me on the back.

"Congrats, man!"

"Wow, I know you're excited outta this world!"

I really thought and felt like I was dreaming. We were trying for a new trial. That's what the Defender Services attorneys said we should shoot for. It would be our best chance, considering all the crap that was coming out about Conley.

I adjusted my body behind the wheel of my car. I took a deep breath and cranked it up. Being without my cell phone meant I was cut off from the rest of the world, but I never expected anything like this.

But as good as the news was, it suddenly hit me like a bulldozer; my world was jacked up. Hope was home? As I cruised the streets of our neighborhood, I started to slow down. What in the world was I going to do now? What about the kids? What about Chastity? I didn't think Hope was gonna get out; none of us did. They told me we'd get another trial. They said if we were lucky, we'd do better this time and she'd get life in prison. They never even mentioned parole, and now she's out?

Sweat started forming on my forehead. It was already racing down the middle of my back and I felt an anxiety attack coming on. I needed to call Chastity. Mona no longer stayed with us, but I had to find out why she hadn't said anything. That's when I remembered I didn't have my cell phone.

All was quiet when I pulled up outside of the house. I took a deep breath and walked up to the door. I unlocked it and walked inside. I heard Chastity talking on the phone. So, I crept up behind her and eased my hands onto her shoulders. She touched one hand and I suddenly felt the boulder that was lodged in my throat grow even bigger.

She was clueless, too.

The second Chastity got off of the phone, she turned, looked at me and said, "Your wife is over at Mona's. Why didn't you tell me she was getting out?"

"I didn't know," I said. Chastity shot me one of those *puhleease* looks. I shook my head. "I swear, last time I talked with the lawyers, they were saying we could probably get a new trial. Nobody said anything about her getting out."

"You expect me to believe you had no idea she was getting out?" Sarcasm dripped from each word. Chastity was mad at me, but I was telling the truth.

"I didn't even know where she was until you just now told me. I left my cell here, on the charger. I didn't know until my supervisor told me," I said.

"Well, she's at Mona's," Chastity said.

I wasn't sure what to do or say. I stood there.

"Don't act like you don't wanna go over there," Chastity said. She seemed sad and pissed at the same time.

"Y'all don' created a fine mess!" Mona said from the kitchen. Her voice brought me back to the standoff with Hope. She sat on Mona's sofa, right across from me, but had never felt farther away than at that moment. "It ain't none of my business, but for sake of them kids, y'all need to fix this and y'all need to fix it fast!" Mona said as she walked out of the kitchen.

"You and Chastity living together," Hope said.

We'd had this talk when she was in prison. Maybe she needed to say it aloud but I didn't need to hear it. The way she'd said it told me she was done with me.

Did it matter that no one thought she'd ever be a free woman again? It didn't seem like it did.

FIFTY-SEVEN
CHASTITY

All of my life was spent living in Hope's shadow. Even after her ass was locked up, on death row for six years, here I sat, still playing second fiddle. I wanted to be a fly on the wall when Brendon and Hope laid eyes on each other again. She knew what was up, she knew he was mine now, but I was sure that wouldn't stop her; it never did before.

The whole time he was around that corner, I was a nervous wreck.

It had been a few weeks now and I had to admit, every day when Brendon came home, it was a surprise to me. I had nightmares about waking up and finding him gone with a note on the pillow.

I remember how scared and alone I'd felt when he'd gone over there for the first time.

Maybe I should've gone with him? I didn't need to be present for the reunion. I could tell he was hurt that Mona and the attorneys basically had left him out of the loop, but I was glad they had. It was nothing but Hope being her usual evil self, but I didn't comment about it.

I didn't feel one way or another about her being out. I guess I wouldn't want someone sitting on death row for something they didn't do, but knowing Hope the way I did, I wasn't so sure she *hadn't* done it.

As she sat over there with Mona, I was still taking care of her kids. The boys stayed with their dad and me. She hadn't come around the corner yet, and I was hoping she stayed away.

When the front door opened, I breathed a sigh of relief. I wondered when that would go away. It was still hard to believe Hope's husband was now mine.

"Hey, babe," Brendon said as he greeted me. We had a lot to talk about, but I wasn't ready yet. "It's kinda quiet in here," he said, looking around.

"Yeah, the kids are over at Mona's," I said.

"Everybody?"

"They were going somewhere," I said. "I think to buy a Christmas tree or something."

There was a lost look on his face. Our time had come, regardless of whether I was ready.

"We should talk, huh?" I said, casually.

Brendon blew out a breath. He stared at me and I couldn't read his expression.

"Yeah, it's probably a good idea if we do."

It was déjà vu all over again. Even though we were the only people in the house, I felt like I was back at that uncomfortable place when it was Stacy, him, and me. But this time, I had a feeling that when it was all said and done, I'd be on the losing end of this odd triangle.

FIFTY-EIGHT
HOPE

N early six years of my life were gone. The state of Texas had stolen them from me. I thought about other people who had been robbed by the state. Anthony Graves had spent eighteen years on death row for a crime he didn't commit. Clarence Bradley was another man who'd spent years on death row before being freed. I had been gone for six years, but still everything was different now.

In six years, so much had changed. My husband was now living with my sister. My kids were happy to see me, but I was now a stranger to them, and all of my old friends were gone. I'd have to start all over again.

In the weeks I'd been home, I was living with Mona and her boyfriend in their two-bedroom apartment, and I had been struggling.

I still got up before the break of dawn. No matter how much I tried, I couldn't go back to sleep. Then when I ate, I'd eat a little food. Mostly, I kept to myself, staying locked up in my room. I had no idea how hard it would be to fit back in and this was only around the house. I didn't even want to think about having to venture out into the world.

My family was a mess; the boys stayed with Brendon and Chastity, but Breanna stayed with me. She was older so she understood better than the younger two. We spent hours hugged up, with her shadowing me everywhere I went. It was as if she feared leaving me would somehow put me back in prison.

She finally moved away from me when Stacy's daughter, McKenzie, came over. After they left for the mall, Mona eased her head into the room.

"Girl, whatchu' doing locked all up in this room?" Mona asked. I didn't close the door completely after coming back from the bathroom.

I didn't want to be an inconvenience. Her boyfriend was a truck driver, so he was on the road for long stretches, but when he was off, he stayed close to home. Mona said it was cool, but I didn't want to overstay my welcome.

"C'mon out here, I'm fixing myself a drink," she said. Mona motioned me over to the kitchen table.

I pulled myself up and followed her over to the kitchen.

"I sure am glad you home," she said. "I don't know what's gonna happen—this mess with you and your sister—but I'm glad you out and back at home!" Mona smiled while she poured vodka into her glass.

I kept wondering if this wasn't too early to be drinking, but I didn't dare say a word. Mona moved around, fixing her drink like we were at happy hour.

"You want something?" she stopped to ask me.

"Mona, I don't drink," I reminded her.

"Oh, chile!" she sang. "Don't worry, I'ma' drink enough for the both of us." She added something else to her drink. She stopped and looked at me like she wasn't sure whether to believe me, then she started laughing.

"Umph, umph, umph! Six long years," she said.

I watched her as she stirred her drink, sipped it, then she added more vodka.

"I'm so glad you home," she repeated. Mona and I were always close. So I could imagine she'd missed our bond while I was away.

"It's weird. Chastity and Brendon; I still can't really wrap my mind around it. How long did you know what was going on with them?" I asked, unsure of what else to discuss with her.

Mona sat at the table across from me and held her glass between both hands. She behaved like it was coffee instead of a cocktail.

"For a minute there, that hoochie Stacy from across the street was trying to slide in. See, they thought I didn't know what was going on, but I saw them carrying on the way they did. I thought there might've been something between him and Stacy, but suddenly, I look up and Chastity don' eased her way in."

Mona sipped her drink again, swallowed, then smacked her lips.

"I didn't think it was a good idea for Chastity to slip in the way she did. I understood her stepping up to take care of the kids, but she got too into it. Next thing I know, she and Brendon are acting strangely when they in the same room together. I told myself it was nothing; you know that Trevor is a fool," Mona said.

"Trevor? He still around?"

"Yeah, he moved back to the neighborhood; lives off Cullen and Odem."

"And he didn't trip off Brendon and Chastity?"

"Oh, he was cuttin' up for a minute, would show up at the house. He kept a cool head, but you know with him; you never know what you'd get, so it always made me uncomfortable. But when Felicia popped up with their two kids, he calmed down real fast. Once she came back, Trevor started acting like he had a little bit of sense. But honey, before Felicia came back, I thought for sure nothing was gonna go down with Chastity and Brendon. We all know Trevor is two cans short of a six-pack." She giggled.

"So you think she and Brendon just started seeing each other?"

Mona took a gulp of her drink.

"Chile, I saw where this thing was going before it went there. They were bound to wind up in bed. There he was, all alone, with these kids, then Chastity eased on in, cooking, cleaning. It was just a matter of time," Mona said.

I was relieved when there was a knock at the door. I wondered why she didn't do more to discourage my sister from sleeping with my husband, but then I told myself I had no right. Both Brendon and Chastity were adults; if they wanted to hook up, even a force of nature couldn't keep them apart. I swallowed my anger and regret as I watched Mona walk to the door.

"Oh, that must be Carrie," she said over her shoulder.

I was happy to see Carrie as she walked into the small apartment.

"Hope, how's it going?" she asked.

I knew better than to tell the truth. I smiled and said, "I'm trying to get used to it."

"It's gonna take some time, but don't worry; you'll be fine."

Mona escorted Carrie over to the kitchen table.

"I'm hoping the press has given you a break," she said as she pulled folders from her bag.

"It was rough the first few days, but they've moved on to the next breaking news story," I joked.

"Yeah, it happens like that." Carrie began looking through her things as if she was trying to take inventory of what she had.

"I wanted to tell you more about the case that led to your freedom. I also wanted to tell you that the fight isn't over. We want the state of Texas to compensate you for the years you spent locked up for a crime you didn't commit."

"Compensation?" Mona asked like she had a dog in this fight.

Carrie turned to Mona. "Yes, the state is supposed to give her up to eighty-thousand dollars for each year she was incarcerated."

"Whew! That's more than a quarter of a million bucks!" Mona said with a short whistle.

Carrie nodded.

"You know what my baby could do with that kind of money?"

I sat there listening as the two talked about what the state owed me, like I wasn't there.

"But…" Carrie put up a warning finger. "Don't think for a second that the state is going to willingly come up with that kind of money," she warned.

"Another fight?" I asked.

Both heads snapped in my direction.

The expression on their faces told me that I'd better get ready because neither was about to let the state get off without paying up.

FIFTY-NINE
ADENA

ecause of my faith I understood that death was a departure from the life of this world, but not a person's existence. I wanted my son to still be of this world. But now, all I could do was pray for Allah's mercy to be with the departed, in hopes that he may find peace and happiness in the life to come.

Days after burying my son, I couldn't stop thinking about those last moments of his life. How desperate and alone must he have been to think *that* was his only option? I felt like a complete loser for not seeing the signs. Upon finding his body inside of his bedroom, I uttered the declaration of faith for him. "I bear witness that there is no god but Allah."

I remained calm, fell to my knees and immediately prayed over my son's body. Using trembling hands, I closed his eyes and found a clean sheet to cover his body. I moved quickly, knowing I had mere days to prepare him for burial.

My mind didn't want to accept the fact that I was once again burying a man I loved. The next day, as members of the Muslim community washed Raakin's body with clean and scented water, I could barely maintain my strength. His body was wrapped in the kafan and was prepared for burial the next day.

My religious beliefs prevented me from accompanying my son's body to the gravesite. Only men were allowed there. My goodbyes were said during the funeral prayers. During the mourning period, which lasted for the next three days, my home was open to visitors.

Once mourning was over, I replaced my jewelry and sat wondering what would become of my life. I already felt incredibly alone. It wasn't because the stream of visitors had stopped. I had a chance to think of all I had lost in my personal quest for capital punishment.

I was a relentless crusader always speaking out in support of an eye for an eye. Was this Allah's way of punishing me? I had lost so much? I thought of the years I spent pushing for Hope's execution. Various ways of keeping her story in the media invaded my dreams. And oftentimes, I'd daydreamed about seeing her body strapped to the gurney. It wasn't until Raakin was identified as the hit-and-run driver did I consider something other than capital punishment for those who kill. Sure, I was a hypocrite; I simply didn't want to lose my child.

A knock at my front door pulled me from my thoughts. I wasn't expecting company, so at first I wondered if I'd imagined the sound. At the next round of knocking, I rose from my seat to get the door. When I pulled it open, I nearly fell off of my feet.

"I brought these for you," Mona said and shoved a large bouquet of colorful flowers into my arms. "I didn't know we couldn't put flowers graveside because of your religion."

I nodded, but my eyes immediately looked around searching for the TV cameras, and reporters. There were none. Did she come to me out of the kindness of her heart?

I was speechless. I had accepted the flowers because they were shoved into my arms. But I was touched by the gesture.

"I was so sad to hear about your son's suicide. My heart aches for you. I can't imagine birthing a child, then burying him."

At that moment, I felt so moved by her presence. Mona had every reason to hate me for the way I had hated her child. She had every reason to darken my doorstep with the press in tow, as I had done hers in the past.

But there she stood, woman-to-woman, face-to-face, offering me her very best.

"You don't have to invite me in. I wanted to offer condolences from my family to yours," she said.

Before I could find my voice, she turned to leave.

"Mona, wait!" I called after her.

She stopped, then turned back and looked at me. "Do you have to rush off? Don't you have a moment to spare? Do you drink coffee?"

"Not unless it's spiked with vodka or Hennessy," she said.

At that response, we both began to laugh. It was the first time I had laughed in days. She'd never know how much her visit meant to me.

"Uh, I can't really come in. Someone's in the car," she said.

I peered over her shoulder and noticed Hope sitting in the passenger seat. I fought to swallow back the tears that wanted to gush from my eyes.

"Please, Mona, I'd be honored if you *and* your daughter would come inside," I said.

She looked at me like she was unsure of what to say or do next. I pleaded to her with my eyes. I didn't know what I would say to Hope, but something in my heart told me a face-to-face visit was long overdue.

It seemed like she gave it some thought, then she raised a finger and said, "Let me see what she says."

I waited with baited breath as I watched her go back to her car. She walked around to the passenger side and leaned down to talk to Hope. There was no way I could hear what she said. But a few seconds later, I noticed Hope turn and look in my direction.

A few seconds later, she was unbuckling her seat belt and getting out of the car. Mona charged up my walkway like a woman on a mission. Hope was right behind her. Suddenly, I became nervous and wondered if I had made a mistake.

As they approached, I could see Mona's eyes misting. She walked up and they stopped at my doorstep.

"Adena Binnaz, it's my pleasure to introduce you to my daughter, Hope Donovan."

I didn't know whether I should shake her hand or wait and follow her lead. Mona stepped to the side and Hope fell into my embrace.

"I have dreamed of this moment for so many years," she said in a whispered sob.

I did nothing to stop the tears that fell from my eyes.

"I'm so sorry," I cried. "I'm sorry."

Once inside we dove into a long overdue conversation. And I began with a confession. "My quest for the death penalty was out of a desire for revenge. I believed in my heart of hearts that you were guilty. But I now know, I was so sadly mistaken."

Hope said, "Nothing is worse than sitting on Death Row for a crime you didn't do. My issue with capital punishment is there are too many cases where you can't know for sure whether someone is truly guilty."

"I wish they'd do away with it, period. For as long as we have man in charge of this, there's gonna be wrongful convictions, and innocent people being executed," Mona added.

"Allah has taught me in a way that no mother should ever experience." I instinctively reached over and grabbed Mona's hand. "I was so lost back then. I pray one day you both will find it in your hearts to forgive my ignorance."

For the next two hours, we talked, cried, laughed, and realized despite our differences, we were more alike than we could've ever imagined.

SIXTY
BRENDON

I felt like an imposter. My kids talked about Hope, some of the things she said and did, and I listened but tried not to appear interested. I wasn't mad at Hope. I had done the best I could to hold it all together while she was gone. I wasn't proud of my relationship with Chastity, but I never took the time to think about what it would mean if Hope found out. Hope was on death row, and she wasn't coming home, not even on a good day. Then *bam*! Suddenly, she was out and back in our lives like magic.

I was supposed to be around the corner having dinner with her, Mona, and the kids, but I couldn't bring myself to show my face over there. Instead, I drove to Sam's Boat in Missouri City and waited for Kemar and Desmond to show up at the bar. I was on my second beer by the time they strolled in together.

"Whassup?" Kemar asked. "Drowning your problems?"

"I'm trying, dawg, I'm trying."

We exchanged greetings, and pounds before they grabbed bar-stools.

The bar was crowded and busy, just what I needed to keep my mind off of the problems at home.

"How's it going?" Desmond asked.

I sighed and shook my head. Instead of answering his question, I took a long swig of my beer. When I realized both sets of eyes were still on me, I knew it wasn't a rhetorical question. I didn't really want to talk. I wanted to sit and think. I needed a solution that would leave all parties involved happy.

"It's a damn mess;" I admitted, "don't know how shit got so out of control."

For once, my friends didn't have any jokes. The somber looks on their faces told me they understood the mess I had created.

"What's Chastity saying?" Desmond asked.

It wasn't too long ago that they couldn't get me to admit something was really going on between Chastity and me. But when they came to help us move, they both told me they'd suspected all along.

Back then, I was still the hero. I was still the stand-up guy who had waited for years on Hope's release. I had been keeping secrets for so long, I started believing them myself. The truth was, I wasn't the hero everyone thought I was. Most of what I did, I had done out of guilt. I'm not saying I wouldn't have helped Hope; she was my wife. But what I am saying is, when I thought of all the wrong I had done, it fueled me to work that much harder for Hope. Who knew one day we'd come face to face again? It seemed damn near impossible.

"Is Stacy still tripping?" Kemar asked.

"I can only handle one problem at a time," I admitted with the shake of my head. I didn't want to think about Stacy and how pissed she was at Chastity and me.

"Since the last incident, I try to stay clear of her. 'Sides, between Hope and Chastity, I've got enough to deal with."

When the waitress came over for drink orders, we stopped talking. They ordered their beers and I wondered what the hell I was going to do.

As if he was reading my mind, Desmond asked, "So what are you gonna do? How you gonna fix this?"

"I really don't know. Every time I leave the house, Chastity looks nervous. Then when I come back home, she looks surprised. I tried to talk to her the other day and she burst out crying." I threw my hand up. "Hell, I donno' what to do."

"Damn, dawg, I don't envy you at all!" Kemar said.

"Who told Hope?"

"Shit! I'm not sure; I thought it was Mona. Nowadays, she looks at me like she could kill me with her bare hands," I said.

"Yeah, Mona don't take no shit! I'm surprised she ain't castrated your ass by now," Kemar said. "You don' had *both* of her daughters? Dude!"

"I'm glad she ain't trippin' like *that*," I said.

We all chuckled.

"What happened when she started crying?" Desmond asked.

"I forgot all about what I was gonna tell her and we wound up in bed," I admitted.

"That's not all that much of a bad thing," Kemar said.

"Which one do you want?"

I thought for a long moment. That was a very good question.

"The lawyers said the best we could get with Hope was a new trial. Nobody said anything about her getting out. I'm glad she's out, but it caught me—all of us—off-guard."

"Well, whatchu gonna do?" Kemar asked.

"I donno', that's the problem. I was trying to explain to Chastity that I didn't know Hope was coming home. And I guess I wanted her to say, since you didn't know, maybe you should go to her and see if it'll work."

Kemar and Desmond looked at me like I was crazy. It sounded crazy and it wasn't realistic, but that's what I was hoping. The minute she'd started with all the waterworks, I'd thrown in the towel. I was down for the count.

Drinking with my boys didn't solve a single one of my problems, but it did allow me to forget the shit that was now my life. I couldn't sit there and get sloppy drunk, but for the first time in a long while, I had no desire to go home. By the time Kemar looked at a text message and decided he had better plans, I was still in the exact same place.

I was no closer to solving my problems, no closer to deciding which sister would be better for me, and certainly no closer to determining what, if anything, I should do about the fact that Hope and I were still married.

"I'm probably about to call it a night, too," Desmond said.

"Okay, cool."

"You gonna be okay getting to the house?"

"Yeah, I'm straight," I said, standing up to prove the four beers hadn't fazed me at all.

"You all right, dawg?" Desmond asked. "You stumbled a bit," he joked.

"I'm good, man! I'm good," I said. He knew damn well I didn't stumble. I didn't want them to go, but I couldn't hide out all night in the crowd. I needed to go back to the house and try again to talk to Chastity.

I wasn't surprised when I pulled up to a dark house. I figured Chastity must've gone to bed early. When I unlocked the door and stepped inside, I was stunned by what I saw.

SIXTY-ONE
CHASTITY

I felt like I had no choice but to do what I did. Deep down inside, I knew if I left it up to Brendon, things would get worse before they got better. He didn't even realize he was being tested when I suggested he go to Mona's for dinner with Hope and the kids the day before Christmas Eve. *It was only a test!*

Everything in me wanted him to decide to stay home with me. But he didn't.

"You coming, Daddy?" Blake asked. His kids were super-excited and I was glad for them. I loved them; I wanted them to be happy with their mother.

But when Brendon turned and looked at me like he needed my permission, I smiled and said, "Go on!" I shooed him toward the front door with a wave of my hands.

When I noticed the twinkle in his eyes, my heart shattered into a million pieces. It was so wild, the way he and the kids bounced out of the front door. I actually stood there for a little while, thinking, *He's gonna come back in and say something.* But he never did. *It was only a test!*

"Really, Brendon, really?"

Hope getting out had completely blindsided him, but that told me we had a problem. It also told me that if he had a choice, he wouldn't choose me. I didn't want Brendon to feel obligated to be with me. Sure, I had taken care of him and the kids, but I didn't help him to get inside his bed.

What happened with us really simply happened. I thought it was fate; I thought it was real. When he chose me over Stacy, I really thought we had something. I didn't realize he was settling because Hope was not coming home. Thinking about it made me so mad.

I didn't have lots of money, but I did have enough to find a place of my own. I rented an apartment and opted to move in right away. I was alone.

As I sat looking at the empty walls, I wondered what I would do next. Trevor was gone; back to Felicia. And Brendon didn't know it yet, but he was gone, too; back to Hope. Hope wasn't supposed to be here. She was supposed to be dead. She was the one who had wanted to die, she was the one who had given up, so why did she get to come back home and pick up right where she left off? I had worked hard to keep her family intact; I had given up on my own relationship to give her kids stability. I was used to it; all my life I had done the heavy lifting so she could slide in and reap the benefits of my hard work. It didn't seem fair. But I had learned long ago that life wasn't fair.

If I was strong, when the phone rang, I would've allowed it to go straight to voicemail, but I was weak. By the second ring, I pressed the talk button and answered his call.

"Chastity, where are you?" Brendon asked. He was breathing hard and heavy. It touched me to know I had pulled some emotions from him. But they had come too late.

"I left. I've moved out. I didn't want to wait around for you to leave me, so I did what I wasn't about to wait for you to do."

He didn't say anything.

I wasn't about to cry over the inevitable. I'd get over him like I had gotten over everyone else. If Hope hadn't been released, we may have had a future together. I wasn't expecting her to ever come home, but if I felt like Brendon was really over her, I would've fought for him. I knew from day one that I was taking a chance with him.

"You just up and leave like that?" He sounded hurt.

"I wanted to make it easy for you," I said. It was lame, but I already knew how Hope operated. She may have been gone for six years, but the minute she got back on her feet, she'd come and take Brendon back. "You think I didn't notice the way you'd stare off into space, like you got so much on your mind? How do you think that made me feel? I'm tired of wondering if that's where you really want to be."

"Where's all this coming from, Chas?"

"I'm trying to tell you!" I yelled. "I don't feel like waiting around until you make up your mind. Go back to your wife. You don't have to worry about me. Go back; put your family back together."

"After all we went through together?" he asked.

"But that was *before* we knew Hope was coming home; that's *before* she popped up one day. I don't wanna argue about this. Go to her, beg her to take you back or whatever. I'm done!"

"I can't believe this shit," he said.

I didn't regret moving. I wasn't about to join in on the big happy family reunion. I hated Hope and I didn't plan to be around her—especially on Christmas.

The kids had already left, so it was only natural he'd be right behind them. I didn't understand why he was making this so difficult.

"You've done so much for us," he said.

He wasn't making sense. Was he trying to stay with me to pay me back for the years I spent taking care of them? Oh, God! The longer I stayed on the phone, the more he was hurting my feelings. When he'd chosen me over Stacy, I'd thought it might have been because he cared about me and saw a future for us. I didn't realize he was trying to pay me back for what I had done for him and the kids.

"So you not coming back?"

"Brendon, go back to your wife," I said.

The conversation was exhausting. The more he talked, the more he was pissing me off.

SIXTY-TWO
HOPE

I hated that I had to be interested in this. I wanted to be out and free. I didn't want to think about the courts and Conley. I was ready to move on with my life.

"Did you hear what she just said?" Mona asked.

I wanted to tell her, *Of course I heard; I'm sitting right here next to you.* But I nodded instead. Carrie was telling us about the lawsuit and Linda, and how what she ultimately said that led to me getting out.

"When the DA's office was talking about a retrial, Linda said that when she refused to cooperate in the original investigation, Conley threatened to send her back to jail. All of this is stated in the 106-page lawsuit filed by Jerome Singletary a few weeks ago."

"Who all is he suing?" Mona wanted to know.

Carrie looked down at her notes. "The suit names the city and nine investigators; prosecutors, including Mr. Conley; and the current DA as defendants."

Mona was chewing on crushed ice. It worked my nerves, but what could I say.

"We ain't heard nothing from Conley yet?" she asked.

"Oh yes, he did release a statement through a spokesperson."

I rolled my eyes as Carrie started to read.

"Mr. Conley is not guilty of any misconduct; he plans to defend himself and his exemplary record vigorously."

Mona laughed. "We should sue that bastard, too," she said.

I held my hand up. "We're not suing anyone, Mona. I'm not in the mood. I want this to be over!"

Mona's neck snapped back and she looked at me with a twisted frown.

"We gon' do whatever it takes to keep you out of jail and to make sure you get what's coming to you. If that means we sue somebody, then dammit, that's what we gonna do!"

"I wanted to tell you about this lawsuit and the role Conley plays in it." I was glad because that killed the brewing argument between Mona and me. "The lawsuit includes fifty-six appeals court decisions from the two decades in which Mr. Conley had been district attorney. Under his watch Harris County prosecutors were found to have improperly withheld evidence potentially favorable to the defense, or misled the court. No disciplinary action was taken against prosecutors involved in those cases. The lawsuit claims that the 'deliberate indifference' by Mr. Conley created an 'anything goes' atmosphere that contributed to Mr. Singletary's wrongful conviction. Much of the lawsuit concerns Mr. Conley's conduct during the investigation and trial. The lawsuit claims that as the prosecution's case began to 'evaporate' in 2000—with three witnesses either recanting, refusing to cooperate or fleeing the area in violation of probation—Mr. Conley employed illegal tactics to coerce the witnesses into giving false statements and testimony."

"It's the same shit he did to me," I said.

Carrie nodded. "After you were freed, the list of alleged misconduct contains a new charge that three notarized or sworn affirmations and affidavits purportedly signed by Mr. Conley appear to have been forged."

I didn't understand how this man was allowed to get away with so much for so long. Every time I heard about him on the news or from Carrie, it made my stomach feel like it was twisted into knots.

"What are we gonna do? Why is all of this information important to me?" I needed to know.

Carrie eased back in her chair and put the pen down. I braced myself for bad news.

"We need to convince a judge that you need an actual innocence declaration, otherwise, you won't be eligible for compensation."

"What?" Mona yelled.

I rolled my eyes. It was always something. The state robbed me of six years of my life and now I had to jump through hoops to get what was owed to me? I was pissed, but not surprised.

"Actual innocence?" Mona balked. "What the hell is that supposed to mean? They let her out, didn't they? If that doesn't say she's actually innocent, then I don't know what does."

"Well, because Hope was released on her own recognizance, there was no declaration of actual innocence. At the time, we weren't sure whether the DA's office was going to seek a retrial. Remember we wanted a new trial, but in light of all that's come out about Conley, Linda's story of being coerced, we saw the opportunity to get her out and worry about a retrial later. With mounting evidence of misconduct, they've since decided against a retrial. So now, we simply need to make it official that Hope is actually innocent."

Hearing those words made the hairs on the back of my neck stand up. I had gone to prison for a crime I didn't commit. I had gone to death row because a law in Texas said I was guilty by association. What Conley had done was illegal, but the law that allowed him to put me on trial was still very legal and still on the books.

"What about the Law of Parties?" I asked Carrie.

"One battle at a time; let's legally clear your name, get your compensation, then we can tackle the legislature about that law."

"That sounds like a plan," I said.

"That's my baby! That's what I'm talking about!" Mona chimed in. She did a couple of fist pumps into the air and settled back down to listen to Carrie. I knew Mona and all she needed to hear was that there was money at stake. If the state of Texas knew like I did, they'd gladly cough up that money.

"It won't be easy," Carrie said, "but if you're up for it, we can start with this declaration, then focus our energy toward your compensation."

I had nothing to lose and since I had been out of prison, I finally realized, I had everything in the world to live for.

EPILOGUE

Six months after being home, my life was slowly beginning to take shape. Carrie helped me get a job at a law firm and I was planning to go to school to be a paralegal.

Carrie was right; getting that innocence declaration was going to be an uphill battle. And we were still waist deep in the struggle. I started to think this was all a big conspiracy between the justice system in Texas and state lawmakers. First, I had to fight them for my freedom; now I was having to fight them for compensation.

The Law of Parties is still on the books, and people are still being convicted and condemned through it. When I talk to the kids, I tell them now more than ever that you really need to know the company you keep. I also visit schools and talk about my experience on Texas' Death Row. In addition to that, once a month I take a trip up to the Mountain View unit to visit Pauline and Latrice.

I believe everything happens for a reason. I'm not sure yet why I spent six years of my life behind bars, but I'm so happy to be alive and living freely. Brendon and I divorced shortly after I got out, but we're still partners in raising the kids.

One day I bumped into Stacy in the grocery store and she seemed so nervous, she scurried off in the opposite direction. I got a kick out of tracking her down in the frozen food section where I told her it was okay.

"Once you've faced death, you find a way to not sweat the small stuff," I said.

She stood in the middle of the aisle with her mouth hanging open.

I couldn't tell if she was shivering from the refrigeration or out of fear. But I let her know I had no hard feelings toward her or Chastity. I still haven't seen Chastity. One day I saw Trevor at the gas station and he told me that he really loved her. But when Felicia walked out of the store, he quickly changed the subject and started telling me how good it was to see me back out on the streets again.

Adena and I met up at various anti-death penalty rallies, and it was good to see her putting her energy toward life instead of death.

The kids and I were all cooped up in Mona's apartment and it felt good being with all of them. I was happy that Mona's boyfriend was back out on the road, and even more pleased that this time, she'd gone with him.

READER'S DISCUSSION GUIDE

1. Where do you stand on the Death Penalty?

2. Are you aware that several states that use the death penalty have a law similar to Texas' Law of Parties?

3. What do you think about the Law of Parties?

4. What did you think about Hope's reluctance to let go of the people from her past?

5. What would you have done in Hope's case?

6. Which character did you connect or identify with?

7. How did you feel when Hope decided to throw in the towel?

8. How did you feel about Hope and Chastity's relationship?

9. What were your thoughts about Brendon and what he had been doing while his wife was in prison?

10. How long would you wait if your spouse was sent to prison?

11. What did you think of Adena and her thirst for revenge?

12. Did Hope's story change your views on the death penalty in any way?

ABOUT THE AUTHOR

Pat Tucker is the author of eight novels and a participant in three anthologies. She is a radio news director in Houston, Texas, and co-host of the *Cover to Cover* show with *Essence* bestselling author ReShonda Tate Billingsley.

DADDY *By* DEFAULT

By Pat Tucker
AVAILABLE FROM STREBOR BOOKS

ROXANNE

Goosebumps rose on my arms and legs. The hairs that stood up on the back of my neck were nothing compared to the chill that touched me to the core. Even at twenty-nine years old I still wasn't comfortable being in hospitals. I never liked the cold and impersonal feel you got while in there. You always knew bad news was hot on your heels, and this time was no exception. I watched my husband pace the area inside the small exam room as we waited for the doctor to come back. I sat at the very edge of the table with my legs dangling.

"You okay?" he asked again, for the umpteenth time.

I simply nodded. My voice had left long ago. I wasn't all right, but his was a rhetorical question. I laced my fingers together and placed my hands in my lap.

"What's taking so damn long?" I muttered nearly to myself. I cringed at the thought of what was to come.

Parker sighed. His broad shoulders slumped. His smooth, chocolate-colored skin seemed to lack its normal glow. I could see the stress etched into his features. Bags had formed beneath his hooded bedroom eyes; his pink lips looked pinched. Parker was in need, but how could I comfort him when I needed comforting myself? I wanted to curl myself into a ball and holler until I woke from this nightmare.

By the time the doctor came back into the room, I had already braced myself for the worst. He was a tall and thick man, of Asian descent; although I couldn't pinpoint which ethnic group. The sad look in his slanted eyes gave him away before he even spoke. Although I was prepared for his diagnosis, the actual words made my pulse slow.

"Mister and Missus Redman, there's really no easy way to say this," he began, and cleared his throat.

Parker came and stood next to me. He grabbed my hand, but I barely gave it to him. I started swallowing back tears and fought against the bile churning in the pit of my belly.

"...so our estimation is the baby died at ten weeks," I heard him say.

Despite his attempt to handle me, us, gently, his words were still as lethal as a machete that sliced through my chest and punctured my heart. How could my baby have died and I not even know it? I shivered at the thought of what was to come next. We'd been down this road before, but despite that, nothing prepared us for this, for the heartbreak that followed.

"...a D and C," the doctor was saying now, but I kept hearing the heartbreaking words that had once again changed our lives.

...the baby died at ten weeks.

My head hung low, and I couldn't even attempt to suppress my sobs, which grew louder. Last time, we didn't make it out of the first trimester either.

"It's gonna be okay; we'll make it through this," Parker assured me. He stopped short of saying, "just like before." His voice was soft, soothing, but not enough to ease my pain. I felt Parker's massive hand rubbing my back as I buried my face into his chest and cried uncontrollably. I felt myself gasping for air as I sat, completely overwhelmed by emotions.

"I, um, if you guys don't have any questions..." the doctor mumbled.

Parker continued to rub, as my shoulders convulsed.

"Why don't I give you some time alone? I'll leave a prescription at the nurses' station." The doctor took a few steps, then stopped at the door and turned back to us.

"If you all have any questions, anything at all..." the doctor's voice trailed off.

I felt Parker move; he must've nodded his response, because I didn't hear anything else. Then I heard the door open and close.

The last time Parker cried like that was the last time we went through this. I couldn't wrap my mind around why, or even how, we were going through this again. What a way to spend a Friday evening. For us, summer was off to a horrible start.

"Let's go home," he mumbled, sniffling back his own tears. He scooped his arm around me and we headed out of the exam room. We stopped long enough to pick up the prescription. The doctor left, then we headed out.

I don't even remember being led out of the emergency room and into the parking lot. I stood by, watching, as Parker gave his keys to a parking attendant. I was in a fog as he helped me into the car and fastened my seat belt.

"We're gonna make it through this," he assured me again as he threw the truck into gear and took off.

"Again," I emphasized, seething. Tears pushed their way through and I started crying all over again. What had we done to deserve this, *again*? I didn't understand.

Friday night traffic was a bit light and I was glad, figuring we'd make it home quickly. After we'd been on the road a while, I said, "I know you're gonna get tired of this, Park. I know how badly you want kids—just as badly as I do. We've been married for three years now and this is our third mis…" I couldn't bring myself to finish.

He reached over and touched my hand; I couldn't stop trembling. This wasn't fair to him; I saw how he watched his friends and their sons, and even his best friend, James, with his daughter. I noticed the longing his eyes couldn't hide and I felt awful. It wasn't his fault that I couldn't carry a pregnancy through full-term. Why should he have to suffer, too?

"Hey! We're in this together," he said, squeezing my hand.

I wanted desperately to believe him, his words, but in my heart of hearts, I realized that with each failed pregnancy, I was losing a small piece of him.

"What now?" he blurted. That's when I looked at him and noticed his narrowed eyes focused on the rear view mirror.

"Great!" he snarled as he steered the truck over to the right shoulder of Highway 59.

I turned my head to see the red and blue strobe lights announcing the police cruiser that was pulling us over. My cell phone rang. The caller ID showed Serena Carson, my closest friend. I figured there'd be time to call her later, so I let voicemail answer.

Once at a complete stop, Parker put the truck in park, turned down the radio, and turned off the ignition. We sat for a long moment and I wondered what was taking the officer so long. Parker's eyes remained locked on the rearview mirror. His jaw tightened, and I tried to be patient.

"What's he doin'?" I asked, frowning. I wasn't in the mood for this. I needed to be home.

Parker shook his head. "Ain't no tellin'. Running the plates, I'm sure," he said, half lifting a shoulder. He seemed frustrated, too.

"Great! I'm ready to get home and we're sitting here like some common criminals," I sulked. "What did you even do?" I asked as other vehicles zoomed past us.

"I guess I musta been speeding or something, but it's gonna be fine." Parker tried to reassure me as he reached for my hand again.

I turned my head. Now the officer was stepping out of the cruiser and heading for Parker's side of the truck.

"I'll make it quick; take my ticket and get you home," he promised. He took my hand to his lips and kissed it softly.

"Driver's license, registration and proof of insurance, please," the officer said sternly, the moment Parker lowered the window.

"What's the problem, Officer?" Parker asked as he reached for his wallet and the insurance and registration papers I had already pulled out of the glove box.

"Do you know how fast you were going back there?" the officer asked as he took the papers and license from Parker's hand.

"It doesn't matter; I'll just take the ticket so we can go. We've had a very stressful evening. My wife's tired and we're ready to get home," Parker explained.

"That doesn't give you the right to break the law. I'll be right back," the officer said firmly, before he spun on his heels and made his way back to his cruiser.

✪ ✪ ✪

It felt like an eternity had passed, sitting there, under scrutiny. I wanted this to be over so I could go home and mourn our loss in peace.

Parker must've been reading my mind because it seemed like he also started getting restless, shifting in his seat and checking the rear view mirror every so often.

"What's takin' so damn long?" I wondered aloud. When I turned, I saw the officer looking at our car, then talking into his radio. My stomach began to twist into knots.

Parker shrugged his shoulders and sighed. He glanced into the rear view mirror again, then reached for me.

"I'm sorry 'bout this, babe," he said sincerely.

We didn't have to wait long for the second biggest shock of the evening.

The officer walked back to the vehicle and said, "Mr. Parker, I'm gonna need you to step out of the vehicle, and keep your hands where I can see 'em."

"Huh?" Parker sat with a bewildered expression on his face.

"Sir, I'm gonna need you to step out of the vehicle, and keep your hands where I can see 'em," the officer repeated his request slowly.

When I noticed his hand on his taser, my heart thudded loudly in my ear. I didn't want an incident; we'd already been through enough.

"What's going on?" I lowered my head, trying to see the officer through the driver's side window.

"Ma'am, please be quiet," the officer said.

Parker hadn't moved. He sat with a dumbfounded expression on his face.

"Ah, Officer, I thought I was getting a ticket for speeding. I told you my wife and I…"

"Sir, I'm not gonna ask again. I need you to slowly get out of the vehicle, and keep your hands where I can see 'em!" This time he spoke with such firmness, ice raced through my veins. What was this about? Parker shook his head as if he couldn't comprehend.

I was thunderstruck. I didn't understand what was going on either.

"Honey, I'ma just do what he's asking. Ain't no need to get upset. I'll get out, talk to him and we'll be on our way real soon."

I nodded, agreeing with his decision, but something didn't feel right. Why would all of this be necessary for a doggone speeding ticket? It simply wasn't adding up.

Parker eased out of the truck slowly, as the officer stood back. They made their way to the hood of the truck.

"Is your name Parker Delewis Redman?" I heard the officer ask.

"Ah, yes; what's this about?" Parker asked.

"Does your wife have a current driver's license?"

"Of course!" Parker said.

"Mr. Redman, you're under arrest. I'm gonna need you to turn around and put your hands on top of your head."

"Under arrest? What'd I do?"

By now, I had opened the door and stepped out of the truck, but I stayed on my side of the vehicle.

"Officer, what's going on?" I asked.

"Ma'am, I need you to get back in the vehicle. Mr. Redman, you are under arrest for delinquent child support. Look, I don't want to do this, but I'm only doing my job," the officer finally admitted.

For the first time since he'd pulled us over, I started calming down. This was definitely a mistake, but I needed to understand what was going on.

"Child, what? Oh, you definitely got the wrong man. That's got to be a serious mistake," Parker said, as he was being handcuffed.

"Sir, I have a warrant for your arrest. Records show you owe more than forty-five thousand dollars in back child support payments."

Parker's eyebrows bunched together and we both shook our heads at the foolishness. Here we were, trying to deal with yet another miscarriage, and now he was being arrested for being delinquent on child support payments? If it wasn't so serious, I'd laugh at the sick irony.

"Officer, I swear, this is some kind of misunderstanding. You're making a huge mistake. I don't have any damn kids! Ask my wife. I may have been speeding, but it was only 'cause we just found out she had another miscarriage. We don't have any kids," Parker said, trying to reason.

What he said made my heart sink. Yes, it was *another* miscarriage, but did he have to say it like *that*? However, it seemed to give the officer pause, because he slowed and looked over at me.

"He's telling the truth. We've been married for three years; no children, I promise you that," I confirmed softly. Again, I started to cry.

The officer's face softened a bit, his green eyes showing sadness. Then he cleared his throat and said, "Well, if this is a mistake, we'll clear it all up down at the station, but for now, I have to take you in." He'd turned his attention back to Parker.

"For not paying child support?" Parker asked as if he was trying to get clarification.

"That's right. Again, I'm just doing my job. If this is really a mistake, you're gonna have to clear it up with the judge." The officer looked at me. "But to avoid having the vehicle towed, Ma'am, you can drive it home," he tossed my way like it was some sort of consolation prize.

My head was spinning as I stood on the side of Highway 59 watching helplessly as my husband was being hauled off to jail.

This was an absolute mistake because there's no way in hell Parker has a child.